Unconditional

Tanya Eavenson

UNCONDITIONAL
Copyright © 2013 & 2018 by TANYA EAVENSON
New Edition: ISBN 978-1-945981-00-5
Cover Art Designed by AM Designs Studios
Library of Congress Control Number: 2018903290

All scriptures are taken from the King James Version of the Bible.

Published by All Roads Publishing

Praise for Unconditional

"*Unconditional* is a powerfully-gripping story of deep heartache laced with fears, yet even through the sorrow, Tanya Eavenson reminds us that nothing can separate us from God's love."
~ *Alice J. Wisler, author of "Still Life in Shadows" and other novel*

"Not your typical amnesia story, *Unconditional* tells a tale of loss, betrayal, and forgiveness. Eavenson drags her characters through the fire, then reveals God's power through their broken lives. The writing is stellar; the emotion, raw and palpable; the cast, impeccably crafted. This author is one to be watched!"
~ *April W Gardner, award-winning author*

"*Unconditional* explores the struggles that married couples sometimes experience, and the decisions they must make after going through difficult circumstances. A powerful story of hope and healing."
~ *Laura V. Hilton, Healing Love (Whitaker House)*

"Unconditional is a beautiful story of God's never-ending love. Throughout its pages, Tanya Eavenson evokes a myriad of emotions in her readers, from deep despair to heartfelt praise. The characters gripped my heart, showing me the reality of man's sin but also the depth of God's grace. Unconditional is a well-written, heart-stirring novel written by a talented new author."
~ Jennifer Slattery, multi-published author

This book is dedicated to Shelley, Krista, Angela, Dana, Amy, and Kelli for the love and support you've shown me.

To my wonderful prayer and critique partners, Mary and Jennifer, this novel wouldn't have happened without you.

To my husband, Chuck, who has loved me unconditionally.

This story is dedicated to the Lord.

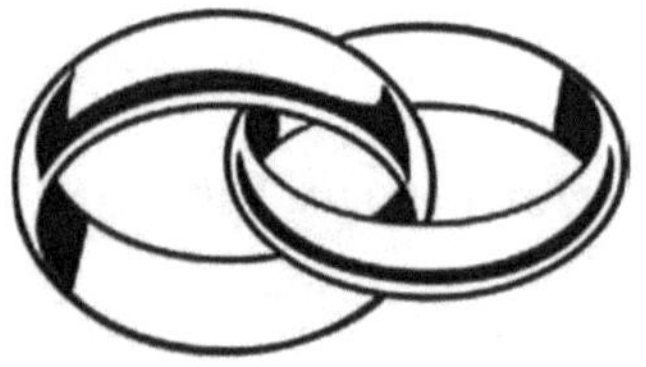

Prologue

"Please, Elizabeth … I can't lose you." Chris Roberts gently kissed his wife's hand. He focused on her bandaged head and breathing tube, looking for any sign she heard his pleas, felt his touch. Nothing.

"Your daughter needs you. I need you." His voice faded into the quietness of the room. He wiped his cheek with the back of his hand and tried to force his mind clear. The image of his pregnant wife slipping from the church steps still haunted him. He should have been closer, should have caught her.

The doctor and nurse came into the room, but he barely acknowledged them as they checked his wife's vitals and changed her bandage. There was nothing more they could do.

"Mr. Roberts," the doctor spoke from Elizabeth's bedside. "There's been no change, but the wound to her head is healing nicely."

"It's been two weeks. Will she ever come out of this coma?"

"I don't know. All we can do is wait and pray. But I thought you should know about your daughter."

Chris met his gaze. "Katherine. Is she all right?"

The doctor's eyes softened. "Her breathing is still our main concern since her lungs weren't fully developed, but she is doing better than we expected. What I'm trying to say is she's thriving and should be able to go home within the week."

Chris tried to smile but failed. Katherine had survived the terrible incident, but what about Elizabeth? He turned back to his wife and squeezed her hand. "Did you hear the doctor? Katherine's doing well. We can go home soon, but you have to wake up." He bowed his head and fought against his tears. The door clicking closed behind him echoed in the room.

The days passed in slow motion—the next day, and the next—all blending together into one long vigil, one long prayer that never seemed to go farther than the ceiling. Where was God? Was he even listening?

Doubts preyed on Chris as he entered Elizabeth's room and found his brother standing at Elizabeth's bed. Phillip's eyes were closed, head bowed. He held Elizabeth's limp hands in his. He spoke in soft whispers, and though Chris couldn't make out his words, his brother's expression suggested he was pleading to God in prayer.

What good would it do? Another week had passed, and still his wife lay unconscious. Three weeks, and Elizabeth's condition hadn't changed. The window to her recovery was quickly closing. He'd never in his life felt so helpless.

After several minutes, Chris touched his brother's shoulder. "Phillip."

Phillip whirled to face him. "She squeezed my hand. It was soft, but I felt it. I think she's waking up."

Chris went to Elizabeth's side and searched her features, her eyes, as he'd done many times before for any sign she'd come back to him. A vise tightened around his heart. False hope, yet again.

He fought the desire to sink into a chair and sob, but instead collected her hands within his. A small moan escaped her lips.

Chris's breath caught. "Oh, Elizabeth. I'm here. Look at me."

"I'll get the doctor!" Phillip rushed from the room.

Chris touched her forehead where the bandage had once been and smoothed down her hair. "Open your eyes." He ached for her touch, for her smile, for her love. "Sweetheart, I'm here. I love you."

Slowly, surely, Elizabeth's eyes fluttered open. Tears filled his own eyes.

The doctor burst into the room with a nurse on his heels. Even while they examined Elizabeth, he refused to leave her side. She squinted and blinked twice. A frown touched her brow as she gazed around the room, then at him.

He smiled down at her, joy filling his heart. His wife was alive. "Katherine's home. We've been waiting for you."

Elizabeth licked her lips, her gaze never leaving his. "I'm sorry..." she paused. "Who is Katherine? Who are you?"

Chapter One

Elizabeth turned the page of the photo album, searching through a sea of faces for anyone who could spark a memory. Her third album. She slammed it closed in frustration and leaned back in her sister's dining room chair.

Her sister, Samantha, covered her hand. "Give yourself time. Several memories have come back to you. You remember being pregnant. You remember Katherine."

The sound of Katherine's name caused Elizabeth to glance at her sleeping child. Her tiny cheek rested against a thin pink blanket. "I can't imagine my life without her."

"Then you understand how Chris and I feel about you." Samantha grinned and opened another album then pointed. "Do you notice anything similar?"

Elizabeth sat up and glanced at the photo of their parents. "You look like mom, and I resemble neither."

"Look closer." She pointed to Mom's mouth. A small freckle.

Elizabeth touched the top of her lip with the tips of her fingers. She had a freckle and so did Katherine, in the same spot.

"Yes, you're connected, visibly and invisibly through DNA, but also through God. And though you can't see the cords that bind you together, it doesn't mean they don't exist. We have a bond with our parents that brings us together. But also like Phillip and I, you and Chris have a bond of marriage that also brings you together. We are all part of you. We are family no matter if you remember us or not. We love you and will stay by your side."

Elizabeth quickly wiped the moisture from her cheek.

Her sister frowned. "Oh, Lizzy, what's the matter? You're crying."

She shook her head. "I don't know. I wish I could explain. My thoughts are such a blur. I feel so lost."

"Chris and I will help you."

"But how can you when I don't know who I am? I feel like an imposter living someone else's life. And Chris…" How could she explain her feelings for her husband when she didn't understand them herself? She wanted to look at his handsome face, to feel his hand within hers, to have him near, but when he was, he wanted more than she could give. "…I don't think he loves Katherine."

Her sister's face seemed to study hers. "Why would you think he doesn't?"

"He never wants to hold her or care for her like I do."

"Of course he does. I'm sure his new job has been keeping him busy. It's not like working with us at the bookstore where he can come and go as he pleases. How is it going anyway? Is he enjoying his new position?"

She shrugged. "I'm not sure. He doesn't talk much about it, not like the first few weeks he was there."

"And you haven't asked?"

"I've been so busy caring for Katherine that when he comes home, I'm tired and forget."

Samantha chuckled and pointed to her mug. "Since our girls are the same age, I understand. Second cup of coffee today. Thankfully Phillip took Juwonya to visit Linda and Henry." Her sister searched her face once again.

"Stop doing that." Elizabeth leaned back in her chair and glanced away.

"What?"

"Trying to read me."

"Okay, I'll ask what's on your mind from now on. Have you and Chris had any time to yourselves since you've been home?"

Her stomach churned at the thought of being alone with Chris. Heat rose to her face. She lifted her water glass and took a sip, hoping her sister hadn't noticed. She shook her head. "No."

"It's time you did. I'll talk with Phillip when he gets back. Perhaps you both could go to the beach." She tilted her head. "Did you know you love the beach, ever since you were a child?"

"That might explain why I've felt drawn to go lately."

Samantha grabbed her mug and rose from her chair. "Just you wait. I'm sure everything will come back to you soon enough." The front door opened, and Samantha smiled. "Look who's home." She met Phillip and Juwonya, their adopted daughter, and kissed them both.

Elizabeth couldn't help but notice the way her brother-in-law held her sister close or how their smiles reflected one another's or how Juwonya slightly kicked her legs as if she was excited to be home as well.

A vibration came from Katherine's diaper bag. She reached over the chair, grabbed the bag, and pulled out her cell. *Chris.* "Hello."

"Hey, are you still at your sister's?"

"Yes, but I'm about to leave."

"Do you want to have lunch? Maybe Samantha will watch Katherine for us?"

She glanced at the happy couple. Samantha did say she'd speak with Phillip about watching Katherine tomorrow. If it worked out, perhaps Elizabeth could surprise her husband. She turned her gaze away. She wanted the love she witnessed between Phillip and her sister. She wanted to love Chris that way. "Katherine's been out most of the morning. I should probably get her home."

There was a long pause, and Elizabeth glanced at her cell to see if the call had ended. It hadn't. "Chris, will you meet me at the house?"

He cleared his throat. "I think I'll just pick something up."

Elizabeth's shoulders slumped. "All right. I'll see you tonight." Chris hung up, and her heart fell. She dropped the cell into the diaper bag. "I think we'll be going."

Phillip's smile dimmed. "Please don't leave on our account."

"I planned on leaving an hour ago anyway. Time seemed to fly while I studied old family pictures." She gave him a reassuring smile.

Phillip leaned down and kissed her forehead. "Our home has always been your home. In case you've forgotten."

She smiled into the kindest eyes she'd ever known. "Thank you. If I ever forget, I'm sure the two of you will remind me."

"You got that right." Samantha gently lifted Katherine's sleeping form from the play yard and set her in the car seat, buckling her in. "I don't think we have plans for tomorrow, but I'll call you later on so you can let Chris know."

"Maybe I'll surprise him."

Her sister's face beamed. "What do you have in mind?"

Elizabeth's stomach fluttered at the thought of spending time with Chris. Could she do this, initiate romance with a man she barely remembered? She had already disappointed him on more than one occasion since she'd been released from the hospital. Would she disappoint him again? God knew she was trying. Tomorrow she'd try harder.

"Chris proposed to you at the beach."

Elizabeth felt a jolt in her spirit. She giggled. "Maybe I'll make my own offer."

Samantha's smile widened, and her eyes flickered with an emotion she couldn't name. She linked her arm through hers, and they walked toward the door. "Now we're talking."

Chris turned his leather chair around and glanced out of his office window, oblivious to what was in front of him except for his wife's constant rejection. He closed his eyes and exhaled a long breath. He needed Elizabeth, he always had, and she had always wanted him in return, but no longer. She didn't need anyone but Katherine.

After Elizabeth's accident, the fear she'd never wake up nearly killed him, but it was nothing like what he endured now, watching her push him away day in and day out.

Moisture filled his eyes, and a tear slid down his face. He wiped his cheek with the back of his hand and opened his eyes. Allison, his coworker, knelt before him. "Allison." He sat up quickly in his chair. "What are you doing here?"

"I came to see if you wanted lunch, but it seems you need more than food." She smiled, her expression open, friendly, compassionate even. "A friend perhaps?"

Allison wasn't the type of friend he needed. She was an exotic beauty who could have any man, yet she pursued him. He'd spent the last two months since he started working at the architect firm pushing her advances away, and it was becoming more difficult, even now as her low-cut blouse drew his eyes.

He swallowed and forced his gaze to meet her dark brown eyes that a man could drown in. Big mistake. He shook his head, weary.

"Allison, I'm in no mood for this today."

"I can tell. You've been crying." She reached up and cupped his cheek. The tips of her fingers rested against his jaw line, and he shuddered.

Chris knew what he needed to do, but he didn't have the strength. He closed his eyes and took comfort from her touch. Why wouldn't Elizabeth love him?

Elizabeth checked on Katherine before heading back to her room to prepare for her afternoon with Chris. She was surprised to find he'd already left for the office when she awoke, since he climbed into bed well after midnight. She thought he had the day off, but it worked to her advantage.

Her sister had called last night and told her everything was all set; they'd watch Katherine, and Phillip would cook Chris's favorite meal. All Elizabeth had to do was pick up the food when she dropped Katherine off at their house. They'd enjoy their time together at the beach, then spend the rest of the evening at a condo Samantha insisted they'd been to before.

She dialed Chris's number, and after several rings the voice mail answered. "Chris, call me. I thought we might have lunch together. If you're free of course." She hung up and stuffed her cell in the front pocket of her jeans. Her stomach fluttered as she rummaged through her closet and lifted a cute sleeveless brown and turquoise dress from its hanger. Although it was October, the short length would work well for walking along the beach.

After dressing, Elizabeth tended to Katherine, packed her diaper bag, and headed to her sister's. Once in their driveway, the phone rang, and her heart raced. She answered. "Chris. Where are you?"

"At the office, why?"

"Want to have lunch?" She couldn't keep her excitement from her voice.

"Why? What's going on? You seem…happy."

Is that the way she seemed? She almost laughed. Yes, for the first time since she could remember. "I miss you."

When he didn't respond, she repeated the words. "I miss you, Chris. Will you have lunch with me today? I made—"

"I can't. Maybe next week we can plan something. How does that sound?"

Her heart pounded, and tears pricked her eyes. Today she was going to propose, making a commitment to love and trust him even if her memories and feelings were scattered, giving herself to him.

"Okay," she whispered into the phone, her heart aching, "next week."

Chapter Two

Maybe it was a noise. Maybe mother's intuition, but whatever it was, Elizabeth awoke and pushed herself up from the bed. Her gaze swept the dark bedroom and fixed on the hall nightlight. Her hand grazed over her husband's shoulder when a thought gripped her. *Katherine.* The baby monitor stood silent on the dresser. Darkness shrouded the red and green lights that indicated movement.

Her chest tightened. She hurled the covers away and leapt to the floor. Panic made her clumsy as she rushed to her daughter's room. She lunged over the crib. No sound. No movement. Not even a stirring of air from her tiny nostrils.

"Katherine!" Elizabeth snatched her daughter from the mattress. The infant drew a heavy breath as her eyes flung wide open.

Lord, what's happening?

Elizabeth's bare feet pounded the cold tile as she ran back to her husband. "Chris, wake up! Katherine quit breathing again!"

Chris sat up, rubbed his eyes, and scowled. "What is it?"

"We need to take Katherine to the hospital. She stopped breathing."

He studied their child. "She seems to be breathing now. Are you sure?"

"Of course, I'm sure."

"She's fine." Chris fell back against the pillow.

"Please—"

"We don't have the money to take her to the hospital when there's nothing wrong with her."

"But there is. She stopped breathing."

He sat back up. "You've been worried about her since before she was born. You're all worked up because she hasn't rolled over yet. The doctor said that's normal for being early."

She's called a preemie. She glared into his eyes. "If you were home more often you'd know she's not fine."

"I'm home, Elizabeth, and she's fine."

Heat flushed her cheeks as tears filled her eyes. "I'm scared. Can't you see that? I need you to pray for our daughter. I need you to hold me and tell me everything will be all right."

"Look, she's sleeping." His voice softened as his hand ran down her thigh. "Come to bed."

"How can you care so little? I'm worried about our baby."

Chris's hand dropped to the sheets. "Shut the door when you leave." He turned away from her.

Elizabeth stood for a moment, unable to speak. With their baby in her arms, she slowly closed the door behind her and sank her teeth into her lip to keep from crying. If tears came, it would be for her daughter, not for the stranger in her bed.

The nightlight's faint glow lit the hallway as Elizabeth slipped back into Katherine's room. She laid her sleeping child in her crib. Her knees buckled, and tears streamed down her cheeks.

"God, please…"

Elizabeth grabbed Katherine's bag from the breakfast bar and glanced out the window at the bright sunshine. The mid-January temperatures for South Florida remained in the seventies. A beautiful day to visit her sister, but thoughts from last night latched onto Elizabeth's mind from the moment she awoke until now. Nothing she'd done could erase the uneasiness over Chris's behavior, her daughter's health, or the constant oppression of *what ifs*.

Something seemed to be on Chris's mind as he paced from the kitchen to the front foyer with his hands in his pockets, head down. He stopped abruptly when she entered the living room. "Are you ready?" he snapped.

She drew back. What had she done to cause this kind of reaction from Chris? At times he spoke of their past, their marriage with love radiating through his voice. But then there were times like now when there wasn't a hint of affection. "Almost. Will you carry Katherine?"

Without looking at her, Chris linked his arm through the handle of the infant carrier that held their five-month-old daughter, and Elizabeth followed him to the car. With a single motion, he snapped the car seat and Katherine into place.

He barely waited for her to climb into the car before backing out of the driveway and driving down the street. He didn't say a word—not about Katherine, not about last night, or any other night.

How long would they sit in silence? Would he speak to her? The questions nagged at her, but as she neared her sister's home, she couldn't stand the quietness. It was killing her. "What's going on, Chris? You're never home."

"I have a job, Elizabeth."

"You had a job."

"It was nice when I worked at the bookstore with you and Samantha, but we weren't making it. I told you that. Now I have a job that requires my time. It's helping us get out of the hole we're in."

It was because of her the "hole" even existed. She never meant to fall from the church steps or accumulate such hospital bills, never meant to forget who she was or her life, yet she was the cause of their rocky marriage.

Chris sat a bit taller in the driver's seat and placed both hands on the steering wheel. "Not only that. At work, clients, the bosses—they're impressed with the blueprints I've drawn up for the new office complex. They have faith in me. I can go places, and this job will take me there."

He smiled.

"I had no idea." Her husband had always provided for his family, even putting his career on hold to help out at the bookstore when the doctor put her on bed rest with Katherine. So she was told. She still couldn't remember many things after her accident.

Elizabeth looked over at her husband. "I know you're working hard for us."

His smile vanished. The maddening silence returned.

A few minutes later, Chris pulled into her sister's driveway. She watched as he hurried from the car, carrying their daughter in her car seat toward the house. Elizabeth followed with the diaper bag and portable swing.

Samantha greeted them at the door with a grin. "Come on in, you two." But her sister's gaze trailed Chris as he passed.

Elizabeth forced a smile and suppressed her unsettled thoughts as she set everything onto the living room floor. She wrapped her arms around her sister, needing her strength. Surely Phillip and Sam could make the distance between her and Chris disappear and ease her worry over Katherine. They had to. She was at a loss at what to do, how to make things right. She sensed Chris walk past her to the front door, and it closed with a bang.

"Are you all right?" Sam pulled her back at arm's length. She glanced over Elizabeth's shoulder. "Where's Chris going?"

Elizabeth turned in time to see what her sister must have seen, the back of the car pulling out of the driveway. *Please, don't go.* She rushed outside to catch him, but he'd already driven down the street. He'd never intended to stay but hadn't bothered to tell her. She gathered strength she didn't feel and forced herself to re-enter the house.

Phillip bounced their daughter in his arms as she cooed. "Look who's here, Juwonya. It's Aunt Beth. She and Mommy are going to pick out some books for their store while you and I go to Grandma's." He glanced around. "Where's Chris?"

A knot grew in Elizabeth's throat as she kissed her niece on the forehead. How could she answer his question about his brother when she didn't know herself? "Hey there, JuJu. You're growing so fast, and pretty, too."

"She is." Phillip beamed with pride, his brown hair tousled as if he'd been rolling on the floor with Juwonya only moments ago.

"And so is Katherine." Sam knelt over the car seat and made cooing noises like Phillip had done. "Just you wait. Before you know it…" Sam gasped, hurrying to unfasten Katherine's straps.

A cold sweat washed over Elizabeth. "Please, no. Not again."

Phillip rushed to the play yard and set Juwonya down. "Samantha, lay her down! I need to start CPR."

Sam lifted Katherine from the car seat, and she gasped a large breath. "Wait! She's breathing." Sam handed the baby to her husband.

Phillip took Katherine and watched her breaths grow stronger. "I don't like this. She looks too pale. You need to take her to the hospital. Better yet, I'll call an ambulance."

Elizabeth reached for her daughter and cradled her against her chest.

"And I'll call Chris for you." Sam rushed toward the kitchen.

Time seemed to freeze while Elizabeth stood in the middle of their living room, her daughter's baby-fine hair against her cheek as tears filled her eyes. Her pulse throbbed in her ears, blocking out Sam's words.

Phillip motioned for her after several minutes, but it was if she were caught in quicksand. She couldn't move. Couldn't speak. "Elizabeth, the ambulance is here. We need to put her back in the car seat so they can take her to the hospital."

"Yes, this way." Sam directed the paramedics into the room and pointed to Katherine. "She stopped breathing. She's almost six months."

"Ma'am." One paramedic reached for Katherine, while the other commented on the bluish tint around her lips.

Elizabeth didn't resist when he took Katherine from her arms, though everything within her screamed to hold on tight. The pace quickened—Katherine, in her car seat, strapped to the gurney.

Mechanically, Elizabeth climbed into the ambulance. The doors slammed, and the siren took up a wailing cry. A paramedic placed a mask over her daughter's face and began checking her vitals.

"Which hospital are you taking us to?" Elizabeth fought back her tears. The taste of salt seeped into her mouth.

"Miami Children's."

Elizabeth cradled her daughter in her arms, inhaling the delicate lavender fragrance that rose from Katherine's skin. She turned toward the shadow that stretched into the room.

Sam stood in the doorway. "Did you hear anything while I was gone?"

Elizabeth's gaze followed her sister, stopping next to the rocking chair. She wiped a tear from her cheek. "No."

"I wasn't able to reach Phillip or Chris. I can't imagine what's taking them so long to get here. How's she doing?"

"She's breathing."

"Oh, Sis—"

A deep voice sliced through their soft whispers. "I'm sorry to interrupt. Do you mind if I turn on the light?"

Elizabeth's head shot up. A doctor stood in the doorway, silhouetted by the hallway lights.

Sam placed a palm on her shoulder. "Yes, that would be fine."

Light filled the room, and the doctor gave Elizabeth an odd look before his gaze jerked away. Perhaps it was because she hadn't stood or said a word to him, but what could she say that would make her daughter well?

"I'm Dr. Moore. Would you mind placing her in the crib so I can examine her?" He pointed with one hand while he removed a stethoscope from his pocket with the other. With the same fluid motion, his long strides reached the crib before Elizabeth had a chance to process his request.

Elizabeth considered the sleeping child cradled in her arms. All she wanted to do was close her eyes like Katherine, and maybe when she awoke, the events from the last twenty-four hours would turn out to be only a terrible nightmare. But it wasn't a dream. The doctor was waiting.

Sam reached for Katherine. "I can take her to the crib."

"No, it's all right. I've got her." Elizabeth stood and approached the metal-framed crib. Her heart rebelled as she laid Katherine against the sheet. The doctor inserted the stethoscope into his ears and leaned over her daughter.

"Mrs. Roberts, a nurse will be in shortly to apply patches along her chest and one on her toe."

"Do you know what's wrong with her?"

The doctor didn't answer. She waited while he examined Katherine, but after a few more seconds passed, her eyes bored into him. "Doctor—" She glanced at the name badge that hung from his white coat. "Dr. Moore."

He turned and stuffed his stethoscope back into his pocket. "I believe she has apnea, but we'll need to run a few tests."

Wasn't that a sleeping disorder? It took a moment before her focus met the doctor's gaze, his dark eyes bore into her. "When will you know?"

"I'll have more of an idea once we start monitoring her heart and oxygen levels."

"Hopefully my husband will be here soon." She lowered her head as she felt Sam's arm encircle her waist.

"He will, Elizabeth," Sam reassured.

"Dr. Moore, this is my sister, Samantha. You can disclose any information to her. Her name is listed on the paperwork I filled out earlier."

"The nurse should be here shortly." He nodded then slipped from the room.

Elizabeth pulled away from her sister and wrapped her arms around her middle. "Where are they, Sam? Where is Chris?"

"He's right here." Phillip came into the room, Chris behind him.

Elizabeth hurried to Chris and buried her face in his shirt. Her heart was so heavy she could barely breathe. "I'm so glad you're here."

Chris's arms came around her in a loose hug. "How is she?"

"I don't know." Elizabeth inhaled his spiced aftershave as she reluctantly moved from the warmth of his arms. Her tears left marks on his shirt. She slid her hand across one of the moist spots, where a button was undone. Chris buttoned his shirt.

"What took you guys so long to get here?" Sam's hardened tone drew Elizabeth's attention from her sister to Chris, the anger and hurt from last night resurfacing.

Phillip stepped forward. "When I couldn't reach Chris on his cell, I went to his office and waited until he returned."

"Where were you?" Suspicions gnawed at Elizabeth's gut. Like a flash of lightning, she remembered the cigarette she'd found in Chris's car two weeks ago, stamped with mauve lipstick.

Chris's face paled. "I had a dinner engagement. I turned off my cell for the meeting, but if I had known Katherine was ill, I'd—"

Elizabeth's hands fell to her sides. "You did know. I told you Katherine had stopped breathing twice before. You claimed it was all in my head."

Was it sadness, regret, she witnessed in Chris's eyes? He walked to Katherine's side and ran a finger along her face. Drawn to comfort him, she moved toward the crib, but when she reached him, he turned away.

A nurse breezed into the room. "Mrs. Roberts, my name is Brooke. I've come to put some patches on this sweet little thing." She placed her hand on Katherine. "Dr. Moore has ordered several tests for tomorrow, but in the meantime, we're going to monitor her through the night."

"What are you monitoring?" Chris asked.

"Her breathing, heart rate, and oxygen levels. Now, Dad, if you don't mind giving me some room to work, it shouldn't take me too long."

The nurse placed white circular patches on Katherine's chest, then strapped a glowing cord on her toe. Wires dangled everywhere.

"I won't be able to hold her," Elizabeth moaned. Chris's fingers intertwined with hers.

"Being at a children's hospital, Mrs. Roberts, we cater to children and their parents. This crib she's lying in will hold both you and her. Actually, it's not unusual for moms to sleep in there with their babies. Besides, those patches aren't going anywhere, so you are free to hold her at any time." After applying the last patch, the nurse stepped back. "All finished. I'll be by later, but don't hesitate to call if you need anything."

"Thank you." Phillip kissed Sam on her forehead. "Does anyone need anything before I go?"

Elizabeth leaned over the crib and stroked Katherine's hair. "Sam, go home with your husband. There's nothing you can do, and Chris is here now so I'll be fine."

"Are you sure?"

"Yes." Elizabeth hugged her sister in a tight embrace. "If I didn't have you, I wouldn't know what to do." She meant it. Over the six months since her fall, her sister had been her strength, encouraging her to remember and not to give up on the things she didn't understand or feel, like her marriage to Chris. And bit by bit, small memories were coming back; her feelings for her husband was one of them. Yet, she never dreamed her life would be like this, standing in a hospital while her daughter struggled for each breath and her husband seemed to enjoy a life without her.

"Well, little sis, that's something you don't need to worry about."

Phillip took Sam's hand. "Before we go, I want us to pray." Chris hesitated then moved into the circle as they began. "Lord, we come humbly before You because Katherine is struggling to breathe. Please be with her little body, Lord, and heal her. Be with Chris and Elizabeth through this time. Amen."

Sam kissed Elizabeth's cheek. "If you need me, call. All right?"

"I will." After they left, Elizabeth struggled to find words, anything to hold a conversation with her husband. At times, it seemed they were strangers, but she needed him. "Will you hold me?"

Chris ambled over and wrapped his arms around her. Sobs racked Elizabeth's body as she tried to catch her breath.

Tears that were not her own trailed down her face as Chris clung to her.

"I love you, Chris. I love you so much."

Chris drew back. "I'm sorry, Elizabeth. I'm so sorry."

She searched his tear-streaked face and red eyes, and fear clenched her stomach. "What is it?"

"I have to go." He wiped his face with the back of his hand.

"I need you." She reached out and gripped his arm. "Don't leave me. Not now."

Chris pulled away from her. "I can't stay or I'll lose you." He darted to the door.

Lose me? "Chris, wait!" Elizabeth called after him, but he disappeared down the hospital corridor.

As she reentered Katherine's room, Elizabeth dragged her heart through the door. Her mind screamed from the taste of fear, while anger toward Chris trickled into her veins like ice water. If Chris didn't want her, so be it. As long as she had Katherine, she could live through anything.

Chris ran through the parking lot, passing cars of every color and size—including his own. He pushed himself harder, faster, desperate to escape his broken promises and what he'd done. Nothing would ever be the same, and the blame landed on him.

God. He almost laughed as he ran. How long had it been since he'd thought of Him?

Sweat trickled down his back. "I can't lose her. If she ever knew … I can't allow that to happen. Not ever." Chris slowed his steps and glanced around at the unfamiliar neighborhood. A bank-owned sign on a white post leaned sideways in the middle of the yard a few feet away. He surveyed the empty driveway and the lock box attached to the front door.

Mustering the will to move, Chris stumbled his last exhausted steps onto the fragmented driveway and fell heavily against the concrete. His elbow gashed open, but he ignored the pain.

Resting his arms over his knees, his mind sorted through memories of Elizabeth.

He missed her whispered "I love yous," or the way she nuzzled alongside him. Her touch used to set him afire, but that uncontrollable blaze he'd never wanted quenched had gone out. His companion, his helpmate, had disappeared.

A picture materialized in his mind, betraying what he truly wanted. Images from earlier in the afternoon proved too enticing, and he allowed them to carve into his heart.

His phone vibrated. Lost in the moment, Chris shoved his hand into his pocket and pulled out his phone and answered.

"Chris?"

"Who's this?"

"Hmm…," a sultry voice murmured on the other end. "I never thought you'd forget me so soon."

He cleared his throat. "This isn't a good time, Allison."

"I wanted to make sure you were all right. Thought you would have called after you got back to the office."

"I … Katherine's in the hospital."

"Oh, Chris. Is she all right?" Allison's provocative tone, turned serious, rattled him.

He shouldn't have told her about Katherine, or anything for that matter. With every word she spoke, regrets mounted, like steel bars closing around him.

"I'm coming. Where are you?"

"No!" He jumped to his feet. "You can't! Elizabeth will find out. She can never find out about—"

"Us, you mean?"

"There is no us, Allison."

"You need someone. You've needed someone for months, and I filled that void. I want to be there for you again. Tell me where to meet, and I'll be there."

Chris wrestled with an answer. Being desired, cared for, filled a need in his life. Allison made him feel all those things and more. But right now, he was more concerned about Elizabeth finding out. "You tell me."

"Since you don't want me at the hospital, how about the office?"

"Fine," he snapped, ending the call. Chris didn't care to be forced into anything, but he couldn't think of any other way for this to work out. He'd tell her what happened was a mistake. She knew he didn't love her.

He slipped the phone back into his pocket, took a quick look around, and headed toward the hospital. The massive building stared down on him as conviction ate at his core. A photo sitting on the mantel at home flashed in his mind—Elizabeth holding their precious daughter, kissing her cheek. Tears filled his eyes. He'd framed that picture himself.

Determined to protect his life from shattering around him, Chris knew what he needed to do. Hopefully Allison wouldn't stand in his way.

Chapter Three

Pushing back the blanket, Elizabeth sat up from the hospital couch, her eyes felt grainy and sore. She glanced at her watch, thankful it was finally morning, and rolled her head from side to side. It should have loosened the knots or at least helped with the crick in her neck, but the pounding in her head intensified. The citrus and ammonia smell from the hall flooded her nostrils and nauseated her.

With a yawn, she stood and stretched her stiff legs, glancing at her watch.

"Mrs. Roberts?" The cracked door swung open, and Dr. Moore entered, his chiseled face solemn.

She tiptoed to the crib as Dr. Moore took out his stethoscope, lifted Katherine's shirt, and listened.

"How are you this morning?" He didn't look at her as he spoke, but kept his gaze on Katherine.

Elizabeth regarded him. Was that genuine concern she heard? The doctor's trained eyes and hands moved along Katherine's chest. Her little girl squirmed under his touch but continued to sleep.

"We'll take care of her." He continued his examination.

She'd tried to convince herself last night that everything would be all right, but something in her wouldn't agree. She'd heard about mothers who could sense things when it came to their children, even though others couldn't. Chris had dismissed it, dismissed her. From this moment on, she would do what *she* thought was best.

"Mrs. Roberts." The doctor pulled the stethoscope from his ears and faced her.

She gave herself a mental shake and nodded. "Yes?"

"Katherine had a rough night, as you are well aware. We will continue to monitor her until they take her for the tests. They should come for her in a few minutes."

Thirty minutes later, Elizabeth struggled to keep her eyes open as she waited for Katherine to return. The waiting drew itself out, and she drifted to sleep.

Elizabeth.

A voice in her subconscious called to her. Warmth invaded her dream, touching her hand. Something about the voice comforted her, yet the more she heard it, the farther away it moved. "Katherine!" Elizabeth jumped to her feet.

"She's all right," the same voice whispered back, the warmth she felt on her hand gone. "I didn't mean to startle you. You must have fallen asleep waiting for Katherine."

"Dr. Moore? I'm sorry. I didn't hear you come in." She glanced at a nurse hovering over Katherine's bed, reattaching the wires to the monitors. "How is she?" She moved to her daughter's side. "What did you find out?"

Dr. Moore approached the crib. "I won't know anything for sure until I get the results back."

Katherine's eyes fluttered in her sleep. Elizabeth reached in and tucked a blanket around her. A smile tugged on her daughter's lips as she dreamed. "When will that be?"

"Tonight or tomorrow. Her oxygen levels are lower than I'd like them to be. We also turned up the volume on her monitor, so try not to be alarmed when you hear it sound. Do you have any questions?"

Tears welled up in her eyes. Everything seemed surreal—Chris not being there and her daughter fighting to breathe. She wasn't strong enough to stop the train of emotions. "I'm so scared. I don't know if I can do this alone."

"God will help you."

The certainty in his voice acted like a balm over the newly formed scars and puncture wounds in her heart. God would indeed help her. She'd always believed, but fear of the unknown captured her mind.

"In the meantime, I'll have the nurse bring you something to eat." Dr. Moore left, and within a few minutes, a nurse walked in with a brown tray filled with sandwiches, chocolate pudding, and fruit.

Later that night, loneliness threatened to smother her. Elizabeth paced Katherine's stark white room, hating the confinement. With the monitors going off, constant interruptions for temperature checks, and worst of all, waiting for the test results, her nerves were about rubbed raw. She squeezed her eyes closed. "If only You would answer my prayer." Shivers coursed through her.

Dr. Moore's voice cut through her thoughts. "I've looked at Katherine's chart throughout the day, and everything is the same." He advanced into the room. "I haven't received the results for her tests, and I thought you would like to know before I left for the night."

Elizabeth smeared her tears against her cheek. The doctor lingered near the wall. Perhaps to avoid her? She hadn't showered in two days, and the film on her teeth told her that wasn't the only thing she'd neglected. Her sister had brought her a change of clothes and other essentials, insisting a shower would make her feel better. Right now the only thing Elizabeth cared about lay in a hospital bed.

"You're shaking." His long strides ate up the distance between them. "Are you cold?"

"I think it's my nerves."

"Believe me." He tilted his head, eyes piercing into hers. "We're hopeful."

Elizabeth couldn't answer. When she remained silent, he turned and left.

She pulled her purse from the cabinet next to the sink and dug out her cell. Should she call Chris? He hadn't come by or even called. Why? She pressed his number, then quickly jammed her finger on the end call button and turned the phone off. Her finger lingered as a stout woman entered.

"Here you go, sweetie. These blankets should keep you nice and warm." The nurse laid them on the chair.

"How did you know I needed them?"

"Dr. Moore told us to bring them to you."

Elizabeth nodded her thank-you. *Where was Chris?*

The next morning, Elizabeth came out of the bathroom, rubbing her hair with the towel her sister had brought. Dr. Moore entered. Heat rushed to her cheeks, and her gaze fell to the floor. She must look horrendous, but at least she was clean.

"Well, I see you're up early this morning. I didn't know if I should wake you or come by later."

She combed her fingers through her long blonde hair. "I'm awake. My sister just left. Katherine had another rough night. Did you get the results back?"

"I did. Reflux is causing Katherine's apnea. I've noticed at times that around her lips she looks a bit purple or blue, and that concerns me more than anything. I need to make sure she's getting enough oxygen before she goes home."

"When do you think that will be?"

"I'm unable to say, but when she does, she'll need to wear a monitor at all times."

How could she have let this happen? "This is entirely my fault." She clamped her mouth shut, wanting to propel her towel across the room.

A puzzled expression crossed his strong features, wrinkling his brow. "What is?"

Elizabeth realized she'd spoken out loud, the truth pressing against her chest. "The reason Katherine is here." She turned around, unable to face him. She hadn't shared her feelings with her sister, or even Chris for that matter, but now she exposed herself to a perfect stranger.

"You're upset. Please sit." Dr. Moore came to her side with eyes that pleaded for her to do as he asked. She tucked her arms around herself, walked toward the chair, and sat. He stood across from her in silence, emotions she couldn't name spanning his features.

"When I was pregnant with Katherine, I had a wedding to attend. It was the same day the doctor released me from bed rest. I went to the wedding and, while I was leaving, I lost my balance on the steps. I hit my head pretty hard, hard enough to send me into a coma." She looked up at him. "I have very few memories of the accident or my past, but I'm convinced that if I hadn't fallen, Katherine wouldn't have been born so early and wouldn't be here now with all these wires."

His eyes softened. "It wasn't your fault. Things happen that are out of our control."

"They didn't expect me to survive. It shocked everyone when I came out of the coma six months ago." Elizabeth's breath caught. She wasn't the same after her accident, even if there were no lasting physical effects. She was affected, and so were her daughter and husband—a husband she'd almost forgotten.

"I attended to Katherine," he finally said. "I cared for her then, in the NICU, and now. I guess you can say I've been her doctor since the beginning. She's grown beautifully."

A smile jerked her lips. Was it gratitude from saving her daughter or the possibility he could save her again? It didn't matter. For the first time, Elizabeth felt a sense of hope. Her baby girl might be fine after all.

A monitor sounded from a room as Chris walked down the hospital corridor. Uncertainty plagued him. He needed to see his family and find out about Katherine's condition. Staying away was no longer an option. Nothing could justify him not being there for Elizabeth during this time, but maybe she'd forgive him as long as she never found out about Allison.

As he approached the nurses' station, Dr. Moore entered his daughter's room. Did he dare enter? How would Elizabeth react to finally seeing him? His pulse raced, and self-preservation battled with his emotions. He waited outside the door, listening.

How could she think it was her fault? She fell down the stairs at church because of me. The moments before that tragedy replayed in his mind. If only he hadn't reached out to shake someone's hand. The screams jolted him, and by the time he turned, Elizabeth had fallen out of reach.

"Six months ago?" He repeated her words. It seemed like years. His body thumped against the wall as he ran his fingers through his hair. From the moment they wheeled her out of surgery until she awoke from her coma, he'd prayed by her bedside. He never left.

Chris balled his hands into fists and stared at the ground. But he did leave her after all. He didn't deserve her. He had known it the first moment she walked through the door that Sunday morning, but when the other men in church took notice, he'd grown envious. He'd pursued her relentlessly, even when she didn't reciprocate his attention. At first he thought she was playing hard to get, but as he got to know her, her true beauty hypnotized him. From that point on, their friendship turned into something he would never forget. He fell totally and completely in love.

Tears blurred his vision. *God, please.* The thought shook him for a second time. A nurse walked by, eyeing him. He turned and hurried down the hospital corridor to his car.

Lately, he couldn't stop running—first from the pain, now from God and his conscience. Guilt stopped him cold.

He dropped to his knees and they cracked against the hard pavement. He lifted his face to the afternoon sun. "Oh, Lord! What have I done?"

Chapter Four

The ornate clock in Chris's office ticked. If he couldn't pull something together in less than twenty minutes, this up-and-coming architect would lose the account. He prided himself on being quick on his feet, and when companies initiated impromptu meetings, he'd always been in control. But not today. He was coming unglued. He'd failed as a husband and a father, and now he was failing his company.

"Mr. Roberts." His secretary poked her head in the door. "Mr. Carlyle called. He'll be here in ten."

Great. Chris sighed and straightened his tie. "Thank you, Ms. Nelson."

Of all days, Carlyle picked today to be early. Chris stood, bumping the chair and sending it against the wall with a thump.

Through the window, a pair of Sandhill Cranes honked from the far end of the pond, strolling in his direction. Once he'd resembled those creatures—tall, loud, walking with a bit of a swagger, glad to be part of a flock. Not anymore.

"Am I interrupting?" Allison's voice startled him.

He turned as the office door clicked shut. Her sweet perfume reached him first.

"Yes." He spun back to the window. The alternating lights from the pond painted the fountain green, red, and blue as it shot mists of water into the air.

"A dollar for your thoughts."

"I thought it was a penny."

"Too cliché. Besides, I have rich taste."

He met her gaze. She did have expensive tastes, and he'd paid dearly.

She ran a finger along his arm. "How about dinner?"

"We already went over this."

"Oh Chris, you need me. Just admit it." Her hand slid from his shoulders to his waist. "I can make it all go away."

"You have the money." He shrugged off her caress and headed toward the door. His pulse quickened.

"I want more, but money seems to be all you're willing to give."

"And that's all you're going to get." Chris threw open the door and raced toward his consultation. If there was ever a time to be quick on his feet, it was now.

An hour later, Chris shook his head as he exited the meeting. They loved his idea of using double-paned thick glass with tropical fish swimming in the middle as a dividing wall for the children's area. Brilliant man! At least something went right today.

"Hey Chris! Word gets around." Joe waved from down the hall.

That's what I'm afraid of.

"What a way to lock them in. How about some lunch?"

"Thanks, Joe." He shot his friend a winning smile. "Need a rain check."

"Just say when."

Chris entered his office, grabbed his phone, and found his keys next to a letter. His insides churned at the sight of the flowing handwriting. Allison. He stuffed his keys in one pocket and the envelope in the other. He had to get out of here. There was only one place he needed to be, and if he didn't go now, he'd change his mind.

"Hi, Elizabeth."

Her head snapped up at the sound of her husband's voice. *Chris.* Suit pressed, tie straight, he walked in and stopped two feet in front of her, avoiding her gaze. "How are you holding up?"

How am I holding up? Are you kidding me? God … please, help me to hold my tongue. What pleasure it would bring me, Lord, to sin right now. I desire it more than anything. She gripped the blanket in her lap.

"How's Katherine?"

"It's been three days, Chris." Katherine's alarm sounded, and Elizabeth jumped from the chair. Chris hurried to the crib and picked Katherine up. Crossing the room, she hesitated touching them. She wanted nothing more than to hold her family in her arms. Instead, when she reached them, her hands and arms stiffened to her sides.

"I love her, Elizabeth … as much as I love you."

Those words that had once brought hope now stirred and tightened her stomach. Questions held back since she'd been at the hospital rushed like a tidal wave, knocking her back a few steps. The puzzle pieces she'd been avoiding came together. Anger stilled her breath as she recaptured her steps. She leaned close to Chris's ear. "Who is she?"

He pulled back. "What are you talking about? Who is who?"

"You tell me. Do you think I'm too stupid to figure things out?"

Chris laid Katherine back in the crib. "Elizabeth … I." He stepped toward her.

"Don't." She pushed his arms away. She feared she'd become sick and choked back the bitter taste of bile that rose in her throat. "I want you to leave."

"Please, Elizabeth."

"I don't want to hear it. I can't." She turned from him and from the lies.

Chris's hand gently touched her arm. "It was a mistake. She doesn't mean anything."

"Leave me—" She choked, tearing away and bracing herself against the crib, unable to breathe. Her stomach clenched.

His breath pressed against her cheek. "I can't. I won't let us go."

Chris's words, his closeness, launched her from the room. Angry tears flowed as she rounded the corner, slamming into Dr. Moore.

"Whoa, now!" He gripped her shoulders, steadying her. "I haven't seen you out of the room in the last three days. It's good to see…" He tipped his head, studying her with one hand to her back. "What's wrong?"

Her stomach rolled, and nausea bubbled up her throat. "I need to sit down. Not in the room."

He walked her down the hall, stopping in front of a door where a brass nameplate stared her in the face; Dr. Steven Moore, MD.

"Maybe we should go somewhere more—"

"No." She waited.

He swung the door open, and she entered. Black leather furniture lined two of the walls. Directly in front of her sat a single chair. Sweat beaded her brow. "Could you point me to the restroom?" Her world tilted.

"Are you all right?" His hand caught her elbow.

She wanted to close her eyes, but if she did, Chris would be there pleading. Elizabeth's throat bubbled once again. "Trash can."

He drew her to himself and quickly steered her, barely making it in time.

Her tears flowed. "I'm … sorry."

Supporting her with one hand, he reached behind him, then gave her several tissues. "There's nothing to be sorry for. You're obviously ill. I'll call a nurse to tend to you after I get you settled."

Taking the tissue from him, she didn't argue. At this point, all she wanted to do was sleep. "Check on Katherine."

"Katherine's fine. Right now, you're the one I'm concerned about." He helped her to the couch.

The leather crinkled as she sank into the cushions. "Please." She wiped her tears. "Check on my daughter. What happens if I'm not there and—?"

"She'll be fine, but I will check on her, *if* you promise you'll rest."

"I will," she whispered. Her eyes became heavy. She dreamed of two voices, one so close and the other, familiar.

The crunch of leather pulsated in Elizabeth's ear. Cold air blew against her face. When she sat up, the blanket that covered her slipped to her waist. As she scanned the dark room trying to remember where she was, Chris came to mind, and everything rushed back.

Elizabeth shot to her feet. She needed to see her daughter. Katherine gave her comfort. Once she held her little girl in her arms, any amount of pain would seem bearable.

She found the light switch and, in the sudden brightness, noticed an envelope lying on top of the desk with *Mrs. Roberts* scrawled across it. She picked it up, slipped out the letter, and began to read the masculine script.

After I left you and walked into Katherine's room, I found your husband crying. I prayed for wisdom. I brought him here to this room and watched as he knelt beside you. It's obvious he's a man torn inside, but I saw something else ... He loves you.

Dr. Steven Moore

She crumpled the letter into a ball, dumped it in the trash, and headed out the door. What an idiot she'd been, for who knew how long? And now Chris had the doctor fooled. A person's actions provided a true indication of the person's heart. Her own sister had taught her that. When Sam wasn't able to say those three little words she longed to hear, Elizabeth felt the sentiment in her sister's actions, a sentiment she couldn't feel from her own husband.

Rounding the corner, her heart fell as several nurses exited Katherine's room. Elizabeth ran to the nurses' station.

"What ... what happened?" She gripped the desk.

"Mrs. Roberts, we just spoke to your husband—"

"Well, I'm here, so speak to me."

The nurse shot a glance over her shoulder to a woman with a clipboard.

"Mrs. Roberts." The woman set the clipboard down and came around the desk. "Katherine's alarm sounded, and we just came from checking on her."

Elizabeth felt eyes piercing her from every side. "And?"

"We're monitoring her vitals."

"Is that it?" She fought to keep her tone under control. "That's what you've been doing for days. What aren't you telling me?" Her pulse raced, pounding against her eardrums. "I'm her mother."

"And I'm not the doctor. We called him, and he should be here in about..." She turned to look at the clock on the wall. "Five minutes or so."

"Dr. Moore. You called him from home?"

The nurse mumbled something, but Elizabeth's mind worked to wrap around what she wasn't saying. Something was terribly wrong. She hurried to Katherine's room, needing to see her daughter.

Chris met her near the door, holding Katherine. "She wasn't breathing, Elizabeth, but not like before ... they were getting ready to give her CPR."

She reached out. "Let me have her!"

Chris placed their daughter in her arms.

Elizabeth brushed her cheek against Katherine's. "I can't lose her. I won't survive." She rocked back and forth to keep Katherine awake. Her infant's limp body rested in her arms.

"Hey there, sweetheart. Mommy's going to hold you, okay?" She shifted Katherine to one hand, wiped her tears, and forced a smile. "I love you, my little girl."

"Chris, will you see if Dr. Moore is here yet?"

He peeked out the door, paused, and turned back around. "He's talking to the nurse. They're looking at a chart."

"I'm scared, Chris. Our daughter—" Chris's fingers slid under Katherine's body, touching Elizabeth's hand. She trembled.

"Mr. and Mrs. Roberts." Dr. Moore came in. "Please, if you wouldn't mind having a seat." Chris dashed for the couch, but Elizabeth didn't move, couldn't move. The doctor looked toward Chris, then gently took Elizabeth's elbow. "You are going to need to sit down." He guided her to the couch.

Chris's face blanched. "What's going on? What's wrong with her?"

"Katherine's apnea seems to be getting worse. We'll give her medication by mouth to stimulate the part of the brain that controls her breathing. This often reduces apnea spells."

"Why are you trying this now?" Elizabeth spoke through clenched teeth.

He cleared his throat. "I've noticed a trend, and it seems she has a mixture of obstructive and central apnea. It's happening whether she is awake or asleep. I pray the medicine will help."

"But?" Chris leaned forward as if begging for what the doctor failed to say.

"This is life-threatening."

Elizabeth held her daughter closer to her chest. "You can't let her die," she pleaded, walking over to the doctor and locking eyes with him. "You saved her before. You can save her again."

Dr. Moore held her gaze for a moment before running a finger along Katherine's cheek. His eyes widened. "Give her to me!"

Elizabeth felt the void in her arms before his stern words soaked in. Adrenaline coursed through her veins.

Nurses raced into the room. With quick movements, Dr. Moore began resuscitation. Elizabeth numbed as the alarms penetrated her ears. Chris reached for her, but she pushed him away. Her body grew cold, and she shivered uncontrollably.

No! She crumpled against the wall. Breath and life were snatched from her when the monitors finally stilled. A part of Elizabeth died, the only part that ever truly mattered. *Katherine.*

Chapter Five

The smell of fresh dirt and rain assaulted Elizabeth's senses as the wind blew in threatening clouds. Lines of white headstones stretched beneath the darkening sky. There was no sense of life except for the freshly placed flowers crowning the sites of families' loved ones. A green canopy swayed above her head, snapping in the wind, but it failed to distract her from the small black coffin in front of her.

"Elizabeth, you ready to go?" Chris grazed her arm.

"No, I'm not ready. I'll never be ready." She sank to her knees.

"We should go. It's starting to rain."

She hadn't noticed. Her head fell toward her chest. When she finally looked up, her sister knelt alongside her. Sam's clothes clung to her thin frame. "You're all wet."

"So are you." She pushed several strands of Elizabeth's hair behind her ear. "Are you ready to change out of these wet clothes?"

"If you help me. I can't do this on my own."

Sam helped her stand, then led her toward the cars. "You'll never be alone. God promises."

"Isn't it funny how I said that to you for years and now here you are, saying it to me?"

"True then, as it is now. Chris is waiting for you." She pointed.

Elizabeth veered slightly and headed for her sister's car. "I'm not going with Chris. I'm going with you." They approached the car, and Phillip opened the door, helping her inside without a word.

After they pulled up to their home, Phillip came around the car, opened her door, and held out his hand. Elizabeth bit back her tears, recalling only days ago she held Katherine in her arms, in their living room, struggling to breathe—but alive.

Sam followed close behind into the house. "Why don't you take a bath and then lie down? I'll bring you some clothes." The doorbell rang. Her sister met her gaze. "It's probably Chris."

"If it is, tell him I'm in the shower. I don't want to see him." Elizabeth climbed the stairs, hurried to the bathroom, and slammed the door against Chris's voice. She sat on the toilet lid, her head falling into her hands.

"Will you let me in, Elizabeth?" Chris pleaded from the hall. "I need to talk to you."

She stood. "No. Not now. I don't want to see you. I'm afraid of what I might say."

"Open up."

"Go away!" She turned the nozzle to full blast, the rushing water drowning out the sounds of her sobs, but not from within her heart.

Later that night, while everyone else slept, Elizabeth lay in bed. Alone. Alone in her thoughts and memories of Katherine. *Where can I go? I can't stay here.* Remembering Sam's garden, she uncurled from the fetal position, throwing the pillow from her chest to the floor.

She slipped from the room and headed out the patio doors. The night laid itself bare as her gown caught on a thorn from a rosebush she passed. Elizabeth stopped in front of a ceramic cross and stared. The glow from the moonlight reflected a shadow on the ground. Heaviness engulfed her. Pounding within her chest sounded a rhythm from her innermost being. Elizabeth had only one question for the Creator of that rhythm.

"Why?"

Chris rolled over in bed, grabbed his cell off the nightstand, and disabled his alarm. Another morning. Too bad he couldn't just sleep through this one. His head plopped back against the pillow as the phone rang. "Hello."

"I wanted to make sure you were up," a soft voice spoke on the other end.

Chris closed his eyes. "I'm a grown man, Allison. I can get up without you calling."

"I know, but with everything that has happened…"

And oh, how he wished he could erase everything that had happened. "You don't need to worry about me. I'm not coming in today. I have some things I need to take care of."

"Then I'm the lucky one who gets to tell you. They've officially set a date for the construction to begin. Your plans will literally be set in stone."

What did she want him to say? He'd planned to succeed, and he had, but it didn't matter anymore. He said nothing.

"I thought you'd be happy."

Happy? He lost his wife and his daughter. "What is there to be happy about? Now I can pay for my dead daughter's hospital bills. Thanks." Chris ended the call. He'd succeeded all right, allowing what mattered most to slip from his fingers.

He jumped out of bed, put on a pair of jeans and a burgundy polo, and then grabbed his keys off the bar in the kitchen. His plan didn't falter during the drive to the office, during the elevator ride to the fifth floor, nor as he wrote out his resignation. But once he saw Allison coming toward his office, he waivered, her smile drawing him.

"I didn't think you were coming in." She stopped next to him at his desk.

"I decided after talking with you, I would." He avoided her gaze and refocused on the paper in front of him.

"What do you have there?" She angled her head, touching his hand, and leaned over.

Chris's eyes trailed the length of her brown hair and rested on her low-cut blouse—a view no married man should see or, for that matter, explore. "My resignation."

Allison jerked upright. "You can't." She wrinkled her brow.

"I just did. I took this job for my family, but now I've lost them…" Chris rose from his chair and turned to walk away. It seemed ironic that, after the accident, he'd wanted more than Elizabeth could give him, and now she was all he wanted.

"What were you going to say?"

He stopped and faced her. "I wish I'd never taken this job." Her look of disdain didn't surprise him. The phrase "if only" ran through his mind night and day. He couldn't change the past—any of it—but if he didn't walk away now, the sin and lies would destroy him. That he knew.

"What will you do now?"

"Does it matter?"

"To me it does."

"It shouldn't have ever happened, Allison. And in case you think otherwise, you won't be getting another dime from me."

"So, this is goodbye then, just like that?" She snapped her fingers. "Well, don't worry, Chris. Your little secret is safe with me."

"God sees everything. Nothing is done in secret."

"Too bad you didn't think of that before." She reached for the door.

"Allison."

Without turning, she stopped.

"I hope you find someone who loves you more than I loved my wife."

She straightened her shoulders and walked out of his office.

Exhaustion pulled at Chris's limbs as he left his office for the last time and drove to his parents' house. He had finally done the right thing, but Allison was right; it was too late. Chris ambled to the front door and knocked.

The door swung open, and his mother greeted him with wide eyes.

His shoulders slumped. "Can I come in?"

"Of course." She ushered him inside the kitchen. "I called you yesterday, but I never heard from you. How are you? How is Elizabeth?"

"I know. I should have called." Something had been fried; the odor set his stomach growling as he passed through the eighties-style kitchen into the living room.

"Do you want something to eat? Your dad cooked veal parmesan for lunch."

"Not now." His halfhearted smile faltered as he sat. "I came because I need to ask you and Dad something. Where is he, anyway?" He glanced around.

"The deacons are golfing. Tell me how you're doing. How's Elizabeth?"

Chris stared at his hands. How could he possibly tell his mom how he'd behaved toward his wife, what he'd done? "Elizabeth moved out two days ago."

Her mouth gaped open. "What do you mean she moved out?"

He took a long breath. "There's nothing left in the house but memories. I can't live there, Mom. I can't. I'm here to see if I can move back home. I want to put the house up for sale."

"You can't do that." She shook her head, voice pleading. "What happens if Elizabeth wants to come back home and there's no home to go back to?"

How he wished it was true. "She won't."

"You can't give up. Your dad and I know all about losing a child and what it does to a marriage. But we made it, and so can the two of you. You have to rely on God for strength —"

"It's finished, Mom. When Dad gets home, talk it over with him and give me a call."

"Son, you know you're always welcome here. Let me pray with you before you leave."

"For what? What's done is done. All the prayers won't turn back the hands of time or change the mistakes I've made. What is that saying? You make your bed, and then you have to lie in it. I'm not only lying in it, I'm buried and suffocating." Chris stood. "Let me know soon what you both decide, because I plan to be out of the house in a few days."

"What did Elizabeth say about selling the house?"

"She doesn't know."

"Chris … I…"

"Bye." Chris kissed his mother on her cheek. He wanted her to hold him as she had when he was a child, but he was a man who made life-changing decisions. Growing up, she'd assured him that nothing he could do would separate him from God, but what about now? Did God still want him, even though he'd fallen so far?

Those questions followed Chris home but, in the driveway, his thoughts turned from his mistakes to Elizabeth. An image of her standing with Katherine played in his mind, the first week his wife came home from the hospital. Elizabeth was careful, too careful, carrying her from the backyard into the house. He'd become impatient and taken Katherine from her. Chris had seen the tears in her eyes, but he never thought to ask about them. Were they tears of joy or of something else?

He looked toward the house one more time. The ivy Elizabeth had planted climbed up one side of the brick home. He had bought the house as a wedding present, and now he didn't care if it burned to the ground. He would never step foot in it again.

Before marrying Chris, Elizabeth had lived above the bookstore. It should have seemed natural to be there, yet it wasn't. Not until she began clearing out the cobwebs and unpacking boxes did it begin to feel like home again. The hardest part was seeing photos of Chris from their last Christmas together. She tossed them away. A small leather Bible caught her eye. Her dad had given it to her before she moved out of her childhood home. She swiped it off an end table, and it opened to Ephesians 5: *"Get rid of all bitterness, rage and anger, brawling and slander, along with every form of malice. Be kind and compassionate to one another, forgiving each other, just as in Christ God forgave you."*

How? He lied. He didn't love me. She rose, slamming her Bible against the table's edge. It tumbled to the floor. At the sound of a knock, she shuffled to the door. Elizabeth stepped back at the sight of her brother-in-law.

"Phillip, what brings you by? Come in." She closed the door and motioned him to take the loveseat across from her.

He sat, looked around the living room, then back at her. "Your sister sent me."

She smiled. Her sister was persistent when she wanted something. "Well, in that case, I don't have much choice, do I?"

"How are you?" He held her gaze.

She sighed. She knew this was coming. "I'm broken. I have a failed marriage, and if it wasn't for my memories of Katherine, I'd have no proof I was ever loved. Is that what you wanted to know? Wanted to hear?" She hung her head, heat flooding her cheeks.

"I'm sorry. Is there anything I can do?"

She let out a hysterical laugh. "I wish there was something I could do, but as you can see..." She swiped her hands through the air. "...there's nothing."

"Your sister and I would like you to stay with us. I know our home isn't what you're used to living in, but it's bigger than this apartment."

"All I want to do is sleep. I don't care where that is as long as I'm alone, so no. But thank you for the offer."

"It's not good for you to be alone."

Scripture, huh, well ... "Phillip, am I really ever alone?"

"You know the answer to that, but I fear that if you don't cling to God during this time, you could cling to something else. Your sister and I can help, be a comfort —"

"There's nothing to cling to any more. Everything is gone."

"That's not true. What about Chris?"

A picture, now torn into hundreds of pieces, came to mind—Chris holding her close by the Christmas tree. Her jaw clenched. The next words spilled from her mouth. "What about him? Has he called or stopped by? I'll answer that. No! He has his own life. He made that crystal clear while I was in the hospital with Katherine." She bit her tongue, walked to the door, opened it for Phillip, and then headed toward her room. The door closed as she fell on her bed.

Throughout the rest of the evening, the white walls caved in, reminding her of the hospital, of Katherine, and of death. The prison she now lived in held her mind captive. "I've got to get out of here." She changed into the first thing she grabbed out of her suitcase and headed out the door.

Chapter Six

Steven thanked the waiter for the menu and scanned the restaurant. Lydia should've already been here. Her office was within walking distance.

"Que quiere usted tomar?"

"Tea will be fine." Steven laid the menu on the table and glanced at his watch. He inhaled. The garlic aroma of Cuban food filled his lungs. He hadn't felt much like eating in the last several weeks, no doubt prompting Lydia to suggest dinner at his favorite restaurant. He loved being in this place—the atmosphere of Havana, the rhythm of the maracas, the language—but it also brought back memories of his deceased wife. He picked up his glass and, for the first time since God had rescued him from himself, he wished the drink in his hand tasted stronger than iced tea.

"Were you waiting long?"

Startled, Steven set the glass down and stood. "No, not long at all." He pulled out Lydia's chair. "How was your day?"

She plopped into the seat and smoothed down a few strands of dark, wayward hair. "Long. A hazard of working in the helping profession."

Steven experienced it as well. Even now, Elizabeth's crystal blue eyes rushed to the forefront of his mind, pleading with him to save her child.

He shoved the image aside.

"Steven, what is it?" Lydia searched his eyes.

"I'm not myself right now."

"I'm worried about you. You can't sleep. You're not eating. I'm not the only one that's noticed. People at work —"

He laughed. "With the patients you have, I'm the topic of discussion?"

"It's not funny. They've noticed you've lost weight."

"Well, then, let's eat. Are you ready to order?" He took a sip of tea.

Lydia opened her menu but didn't look at it. "Are you still dreaming of Elizabeth?"

He choked and coughed out, "I'm fine. Everything … is fine." He placed his glass back on the table.

She glared. "I take that as a yes."

"This isn't the place or time, Lydia. And in case you've forgotten, I'm not your client anymore. We're friends. Maybe it's a mistake to share things with you."

"Have you thought about seeing someone else for counseling?"

He stiffened and lifted the menu. "What would you like to order?"

She tore it from his grip. "What you went through was traumatic," she whispered. "I held you after Katherine's death. You cried, remember? She wasn't even your child."

How could he forget? Holding Katherine's limp body in his arms had forced memories and the pain from his own son's death to the forefront of his mind. He'd cried then, wanting his child and wife back.

Steven leaned forward. "Why are you doing this?" He returned her whisper. "What possible reason could you have? I told you how I almost died when I lost my family, and how everything with Katherine brought back those memories." He sat back in his chair.

Lydia's gaze darted around the room, finally settling on him. "I guess I'm jealous."

"You've lost me, Lydia. Jealous of what?"

"I spent hours listening to your devotion for your wife. I've never known anyone to love someone that way. What do you want me to say? Maybe if we'd met under different circumstances…"

Steven stared out the window. Could Lydia have feelings for him? As he thought of the last few years, it made sense. Was he so blind he couldn't see her affection?

A steady stream of cars lined the road. Across the street, men and women flowed in and out of a club. One woman caught his eye. *Lord, please no! Let my eyes deceive me.*

Elizabeth giggled at her lack of balance. She'd dropped her purse several steps back, but with her broken heel, her lopsidedness turned her world upside down. Her purse was a casualty she'd deal with later.

Her hand throbbed as she ran it along the building to direct her path. Maybe the shards of pain were from the glass she'd broken inside the club. She continued against the rough wall.

A man with a black shirt, jingling his keys, approached. "Do you need some help? You have blood on your dress."

Elizabeth tried to look down, but the world swirled around. With her head spinning, she nodded in response. She shuddered when he touched her hair.

"I'm a lucky man." He placed a hand on her back. "Let me escort you to my car. It's right over there." He pushed her around the corner.

"I dropped my bag." Her speech slurred as she unsuccessfully extended her arm to point. She wanted to go back, but the man urged her forward. She stumbled.

"Get up!" Hot breath blew in her face as steel hands lifted her off the ground. He steadied her, gripping her close to him. "You're beautiful."

She kneed him in the groin, and curses rang out as she tried to push him away, succeeding only in flinging her own body in the opposite direction. Her head slammed against a wall. Fear broke through the fog as lips that tasted like ash stifled her pleas for help. Strong hands groped her. She thrashed her fists against his back, but nails dug into her shoulder and ripped into her flesh. He caught her wrists, holding them above her head. She screamed.

"Elizabeth!"

A familiar voice mingled with the sounds around her. The man loosened his hold. She tried to escape but fell to the pavement. Loud cursing erupted. Her head throbbed. The man's body thudded on the ground next to her, but he jumped up and scurried away.

"Let me help you." A hand touched her bare shoulder.

"No!" She crumpled into a ball on the ground.

"Elizabeth, I won't hurt you." A gentle arm encircled her, helping her to stand. "Are you all right?"

"I want to go home," she begged.

A feminine voice joined his. "I'll get the car."

He shrugged off his jacket and wrapped it around her shoulders. A soft masculine scent cloaked her. "Do you think you can walk?"

Elizabeth couldn't see his face while he held her upright, but that voice ... "Dr. Moore?"

"Yes," he whispered close to her ear.

Tears streamed down her cheeks, each step an act of will. Her body trembled uncontrollably.

"I have her purse," the female spoke. "Let me take over while you punch her address into the GPS." The woman came into focus as she gently steered Elizabeth into the front seat. Her short brown hair tucked behind her ears fell into her face as she strapped the seatbelt in place. A sugar sweet fragrance invaded Elizabeth's senses. Her stomach churned. Discovering her purse in her lap, she clenched it close to use if she became sick.

"Will you be all right to walk to your car?"

"I will. Call me." Lydia slammed the car door.

Elizabeth touched her temple.

"How are you feeling?" Dr. Moore's voice was gentle, even to her own ears.

"My head."

"Does your husband know where you are? You don't seem like someone who would go to a club, or drink for that matter."

"He doesn't care. He left me." Elizabeth looked out the window and watched the buildings race by. "I don't feel so well."

Once the car stopped, Steven checked his GPS and got out. He swung the passenger door open and helped her out. "Where are your keys?"

She leaned along the frame of the car and handed him her purse. Katherine's picture swung freely from the key chain. Tears filled her eyes.

"Lean on me. I have you."

"I don't care if you have me." She pulled away, but his grip held her in place. "Leave me be."

"I can't." He lifted her in his arms and carried her inside the bookstore. "Upstairs?"

Elizabeth nodded as she shivered against the warmth of his embrace. Soon she'd have to deal with what had happened, but not right now. Her life would return too quickly.

Steven finished placing the ointment on Elizabeth's cuts and bandaged her hand, but not before she fell asleep. Gently laying her hand next to her side, the urge to protect this woman raged, as it had the moment he'd seen her being pushed into the alley. Anger pulsated through his veins yet again. What would have happened if he hadn't seen them across the street—seen her?

Steven tried to force his thoughts in a different direction as he headed toward the kitchen, but the image of Elizabeth frightened—huddled on the ground—remained etched in his mind. Glancing at her as she slept on the couch, he rummaged through her purse. He pulled out her cell phone and noticed the bottle of all-too-familiar pills. He swallowed down the fear that knotted his throat. How could Chris leave her?

Steven stood lost in indecision. Could he have read something that wasn't there when Chris had leaned in and kissed Elizabeth's cheek at the hospital? The love he'd seen in the man's eyes? It seemed real. Could three weeks really change someone? Steven knew the answer, but he hoped, for Elizabeth's sake, Chris truly loved her. She needed him.

Stuffing the phone in his pocket, Steven glanced one last time to where Elizabeth slept. "God, please protect her. Thank You for allowing me to be there to save her from the unthinkable. And now, lead me to know what to do next, and protect me from myself."

He closed the door behind him and headed downstairs to the bookstore. The smell of coffee lingered in the air as he made his way down the last step.

Steven pulled out Elizabeth's cell, then fingered through her contacts. Chris's name remained in the phone, but with no number listed. He searched for Elizabeth's sister's number and dialed, but no answer. He needed advice. *Lydia.* Reaching into his other pocket, he phoned.

"Lydia?"

"Steven. How is Elizabeth?"

"Not sure. She's asleep."

"You're still with her?" Her voice was tight.

"Yes. No. I'm in the bookstore. She's asleep in her apartment. I tried to call her husband, but … they're separated. I called her sister, Samantha, but no answer. Someone should be here when she wakes up and remembers what happened tonight."

The silence in those moments stood between them, the questions, the unknown, and now the woman who slept upstairs.

Steven exhaled. "I should go if I plan to leave tonight."

"So you're saying you might stay with her? Do you think that is such a good idea?"

"What do you think I'm going to do? Come on to her after she was assaulted? I found something."

"What?" Lydia's voice rose with curiosity.

"Pills. The same ones."

"It doesn't mean—"

"No, but I'm going to make sure."

"All right, Steven. But if you need me, call."

"I will." He hung up. Steven had his own idea why Elizabeth went to the club—the same reason she held on to the pills he'd found in her purse. She wanted to forget, just like he had when his family died.

He scrolled through the names again until Samantha came into view. He dialed the number and waited. No one answered.

Elizabeth. That same familiar voice called to her. Soft touches slid across her face, her hand, and her shoulder. She stirred.

"Good morning."

Her eyes lifted ever so slightly to find Dr. Moore's handsome face peering down at her. She closed her eyes and raised her hand to her head.

"Be careful with your hand. If you can sit up, I'll give you medicine for your head."

She lifted herself with the help of a gentle hand on her back.

"Here you go. Open." He popped two tablets into her mouth and slid a glass of water between her fingers. "Now drink. That should help."

After a few gulps, she returned the glass. "Thank you. I feel like a train ran over me." She reached for her face, but Dr. Moore caught her hand and held it. She froze. In that moment, everything came back to her—the drinking, her purse, and a man. Tears welled in her eyes. She tugged her hand free and moved off the couch away from him, almost falling.

"It's okay. You're all right." He stood from the couch and walked in slow steps toward her. "You know me, Elizabeth. I'd never hurt you."

His dark eyes drew her. There was something revealing and familiar. She couldn't turn away. When he touched her, she flinched but didn't move back.

The blanket that enwrapped her fell from her shoulder. Dr. Moore's eyes followed, as did hers. Bloody gash marks crossed her right shoulder. As strong arms captured her, she hid her face and cried.

A tender whisper broke through her sobs. "'Even though I walk through the valley of the shadow of death, I will fear no evil, for You are with me; Your rod and staff, they comfort me.'"

It took every bit of strength Steven had to go over the events of last night with Samantha. And after he did, he couldn't leave. He found ways to be useful, even cooking breakfast. But the underlying problem remained as he now drove onto the interstate. Leaving Elizabeth tortured him.

Overcome by emotions, Steven drove. Destination, nowhere. His schedule, calendar, and obligations pressed him. He needed to leave, anywhere to get away from her, but he couldn't, not now. He'd planned to take a trip; maybe he could leave earlier. He dialed his friend.

"Steven. What has you calling at this time of day?"

"Hey, Mike. I need to come for a visit." His voice cracked, wanting to share everything that had happened, but he couldn't. It would have to wait.

"I take it it's not for pleasure."

"It's about Elizabeth."

"She's walked back into your life, and she doesn't remember you."

Steven cleared his throat. "I'm going to try to clear my schedule."

"Come earlier if you need to. Susan and I will be praying. I'll tell John and Nicole."

"Thanks, Mike. I…"

"I know. I'll see you soon."

Steven hung up. Mike's words plagued him. *"She's walked back into your life, and she doesn't remember you."*

Chapter Seven

Chris turned over the house keys to the realtor with carefully masked reluctance. He backed out of their driveway one last time, crunching his dreams beneath the tires. His chest tightened. His marriage to Elizabeth was over.

Speeding up on the ramp into reckless afternoon traffic, he snatched the cell from the car console and dialed. "Phillip, I have to talk."

"I'm getting ready to go somewhere." His voice was sharp.

"I can be there in ten minutes?"

"Fine. I'll wait."

Chris didn't know why, but he had a distinct feeling something was wrong, and Phillip was holding it back. Could it have been about the house? He'd overheard his mother and Phillip talking yesterday about his decision to sell. Everyone in the family assumed he and Elizabeth had separated because of Katherine's death, but what good would it do to share the truth? Elizabeth wouldn't take him back, the house would soon be sold, so there seemed to be nothing left.

With two deep breaths, Chris pulled into the driveway and exhaled as Phillip came out of the house, his mouth pulled into a frown, brows together. Chris's gut cringed as he opened the door and climbed out. A faint bark sounded in the distance as the smell of freshly cut grass filled his nose.

"Let's walk." Phillip passed him.

Chris slammed the door shut, glanced at the house, then back at his brother. This wasn't a walk for fresh air. He caught up with Phillip's long strides, sweat beading his neck. "Is Samantha all right? Juwonya?"

"They're fine." Phillip stared ahead.

Chris's stomach tensed. Something wasn't right. "What is it? What's wrong?"

"You and Elizabeth for one thing."

He knew this already. "What else?"

"Nothing makes sense. Now this."

"You've lost me."

"Elizabeth needs you." Phillip's steps slowed to a stop.

Brown eyes focused on Chris's face. *Tears?* "What is it? What are you not telling me?"

"She was attacked last night."

Chris grabbed his arm. "Samantha?"

"No, Chris. Elizabeth."

Elizabeth? Attacked? His heart sank into the pit of his stomach. "Where is she?"

"Samantha's with her at the apartment."

Chris turned and sprinted back to his car.

Phillip followed, shoving him out of the way. "I'll drive. Get in." The car beeped as it unlocked.

He slid into the passenger seat, unable to speak.

Phillip pulled out of the driveway. "This is what Samantha told me."

Chris's stomach churned as the dark stained door to Elizabeth's apartment swung open. "How is she?"

Samantha's eyes widened. "Chris?" She stepped back from the doorway, allowing him to enter. "What are you doing here?"

"I brought him." Phillip came in and took his wife in his arms.

"Oh, Phillip." She exhaled. With sagging shoulders, she buried her face in his chest, grasping the back of his shirt. "She's finally asleep."

"Come. Sit. You're barely able to hold yourself up."

Chris started for Elizabeth's room. Tiptoeing, he rounded the queen size bed to avoid waking her. He didn't like the odds of being welcomed if she awoke and found him there.

Sunlight filtered through the burgundy curtains, its rays caressing her soft skin. Her arm poked out from the flowered quilt she'd made with her mother. He reached to touch her, but stopped himself. Pale purplish marks pressed against her cheek. Tears filled his eyes as he knelt beside the bed. Markings of a struggle painted her features.

"God, please." His voice strangled from emotions deep within his soul. Where was that man she needed? His face fell to the carpet. "I love her."

"Please … go." A faint voice rose from the bed.

"Elizabeth." Chris returned to his knees and touched her arm. She moaned in pain. "Where are you hurt? Tell me. I want to take care of you."

"I don't want your pity."

"It's not—"

"Go, Chris. I don't want you here."

"I need to be here with you." A hand touched his shoulder, snapping Chris's concentration. Phillip stood over him.

"Why don't we make some coffee downstairs? I know Samantha would like some."

With a reluctant nod, Chris pushed himself up and glanced at Elizabeth shivering in bed. For the first time since they'd been married, he understood why she shook.

He'd seen it happen before, most of the time when it involved Katherine, but there were others, times that included him. "You're frightened."

"Come on, Chris." Phillip's stern tone resonated, prompting his immediate obedience.

Downstairs in the bookstore, Chris paced. Bile filled his mouth, and he swallowed as he moved to the closest shelf. A title caught his attention: *Hidden Keys of a Loving, Lasting Marriage,* and then another, *When The Vow Breaks.* Heat filled his veins. He hurled the books across the store. With each flick of his wrist, pain shot through him, and with each thump, guilt lay heavy on his heart.

"Stop! Chris!"

"Leave me alone!" Chris pointed at Phillip, who closed the distance between the couch and the near-empty bookshelf.

"I won't let you destroy this place. Samantha and Elizabeth worked too hard for this."

"What does all this matter anyway? My wife is up there, hurt, scared, and I can't hold her. I don't care about this place, only her. She's all I ever wanted." Chris chucked another book with all his might. Phillip grabbed his arms and held them behind his body. Chris struggled to free himself, but Phillip's hold tightened.

"I won't let you destroy their dream. It's all Elizabeth has, and I won't let you take that away from her."

"Let go, Phillip, or you'll regret this."

"Why are you fighting me? What has you captive that you feel you need to fight *me* of all people to be free?"

"You're the one holding me against my will."

Phillip released his hold, pushing Chris away. "If you want to be free, all you have to do is ask. God will set you free. He is the only one who can take away our sins and remember them no more. But you have to admit what you did. God already knows, but He's waiting for you to confess it. He loves you."

"How could He after…?" Chris ran his hand through his hair. He didn't want to think about it. Not now. Not ever. The guilt wrapped around his neck so tightly, he suffocated in turmoil.

"It doesn't matter. Nothing you do can take His love away from you. It's called grace."

"I don't deserve God's forgiveness. If only you knew what I've done."

"It's between you and the Lord. I'm here to tell you, He's waiting for you." Phillip turned and left him standing alone.

Chris's eyes roamed the mess. Taking a step, he tripped. Staring up from the floor lay a black leather Bible. He gritted his teeth. God wouldn't want him. Yet his heart burned, and a yearning he hadn't felt in quite some time tugged at him. Lifting the Bible, he turned back the bent pages, and read, *'Blessed is he whose transgression is forgiven, whose sin is covered.'*

His hands trembled. Tears stung his eyes. "Oh, God. Please, forgive me."

Steven fiddled with the pen on his desk, mind restless from the night before. His every thought revolved around the woman from his past, the same woman he had left a few hours ago. He never realized, looking at the hospital chart, Elizabeth Roberts was Elizabeth Manroe, the woman he'd known in college, until he walked into Katherine's hospital room and flicked on the lights. Everything spiraled within those moments. But when she hadn't recognized him, it made his decision to care for Katherine all the more sure. Now he knew why she didn't recognize him. Her fall had erased her past, everything they once shared.

Standing from the desk, Steven headed for the shelf next to the couch and lifted his family's photo. "How I've missed you." His index finger ran across his loved ones' faces. Memories raced to a time and place he wished he still belonged to.

"When you met me, Jess, you picked up my shattered heart and loved me in a way I never knew possible. There are so many times I wish you were still here, loving me, but I know God had a purpose for taking you so soon." He studied his son's face, a mirror image of his own, before resting the frame in its dust free spot.

"God, I have many questions to ask once I see You, but right now, I hope You'll answer these. Why Elizabeth? Why now? I'm so weak, Lord. Take these feelings from me. Your word says You will give a way out when tempted. Let it be quick. Allow me to leave for Mike's sooner. There needs to be a distance between us. Elizabeth's memory isn't good enough."

A nurse knocked and poked her head into the room. "Dr. Moore. There is a man here to see you."

Steven cleared his throat. "I'll be out in a minute." Margaret never interrupted him unless she deemed it important. In the office bathroom, he splashed cold water on his face, toweled off, and headed for the door, dropping the towel in his chair. Elizabeth's husband stood in the doorway.

"Chris?"

"I needed to talk to you about my wife."

His wife. "Please come in."

Chris nodded and melted into a chair. "I hope you don't mind me stopping by like this. I remembered the way to your office. I needed to see you."

Steven sank into the opposite chair.

"What happened to Elizabeth last night?" Chris stared at Steven with bloodshot eyes. "I have to know, Dr. Moore. We're separated. She won't see me."

Steven wanted to yell, *Fight for her. Don't give up!* Maybe if he'd gone after her, things would have been different. But then what about Jess and his son, Steven? His family. He never would have known what it felt like to be loved.

"Will you tell me?"

Chris's eyes pierced his heart. Steven might have had doubts, but no longer. Chris loved Elizabeth. "You'll need to tell me what you know first."

"She was attacked downtown. You saved her and called Samantha."

"I have to tell you up front, Chris, I tried to call Samantha, but she didn't answer. I didn't leave Elizabeth until her sister arrived this morning. I stayed downstairs in the bookstore last night."

"Dr. Moore —"

"Please, call me Steven."

Chris ran his fingers through his hair then jumped to his feet and began to pace. "She has markings all over her face, and she won't allow me to be near her."

"How is the gash above her eye?"

"I don't know. She hid her face from me." Chris paused and turned to him. "Tell me, where was my wife when you saw her?"

"It's not my place to tell you."

"Don't you understand? I love her, but I don't know how to help."

"She needs you." Steven moved to his desk, opened the drawer, and pulled out the bottle he had found in Elizabeth's purse. "I took this from your wife's purse. It's empty. I dumped the pills out." He placed the empty prescription bottle in Chris's palm. "This is the only part I didn't mention to her sister. I could tell she couldn't handle much more."

"What kind of prescription is this?" Chris rolled the bottle in his hand.

"Sleeping pills, a strong prescription, and with the number missing from the issue date, I flushed the remaining ones down the toilet. I feared —"

"You're not suggesting…"

"I am. I've never seen her this way." The words slipped out before he could retrieve them.

Chris's brows furrowed before his gaze lifted from the bottle to Steven.

"I'll tell you anything else you want to know but where I saw her."

"Did he force her to —?"

"No, I stopped him." Steven watched Chris's face relax. A slow exhale whistled through his lips. "This is the reason you came."

"I had to know if he…"

Steven stood in the middle of two lives he had no business being in, yet he couldn't walk away, nor did he have the strength to. "You said you didn't know how to help her. Pray for God's healing, for her mind, body, and her spirit. She's running away from God and I'm convinced He brought you here for a reason. You need to fight for your wife. Whatever happened that's pulled you two apart, don't give up. No matter if you're separated or not, you are united in God's eyes. You belong to one another. 'Let not man put asunder.'"

"Or woman."

Steven caught the implications of Chris's whisper. He needed to pray or he could fall himself.

Chapter Eight

Voices drifted into earshot—one her sister's, the other Steven's. His voice stirred conflicting emotions within her. Elizabeth wanted Steven as far away from her as possible, yet his presence drew and comforted her.

The bedroom door opened, and she tucked herself under the quilt, covering most of her body and face from view. Sam had mentioned she'd asked Steven to stop by with her medicine. She never said anything about him checking on her.

"Elizabeth, Steven's here. I'm worried about your pain."

Steven sat on the bed. His weight shifted her toward him. "I brought something to put on your cuts. If you let me, I'll start with the section above your eye. I need you to sit up for me."

Exhaling, she pushed up from the bed.

Sam stood behind Steven. "I'm going to call Phillip. I'll be back."

Disturbed by her cuts and the deep purplish blotches she'd seen on her skin earlier in the mirror, she avoided Steven's eyes by closing hers. A cool moist touch caressed her brow, then her cheek. Her skin tingled. A smile lifted the corners of her mouth, and she opened her eyes. Steven winced as his gaze roamed her scars. Her cheeks blazed.

She turned her face. She knew she looked hideous. "Finish what you came to do and leave."

Steven bowed his head and rose. "I can't stay. Your sister will have to finish. I gave her a prescription to help with the pain. Make sure you take it as directed. It's non-drowsy."

Tears seeped down her cheeks. Steven's frame filled the doorway, then vanished. She'd seen the marks, but if a doctor like Steven couldn't handle seeing her…

Elizabeth fought her thoughts as she slid back under her quilt. If only she could disappear.

Steven's heart pounded in his ears as he drove away from the bookstore, from Elizabeth. No amount of warning would have prepared him for what he'd felt while covering her wounds. The warmth of her skin had caught him off guard. He forgot to breathe. What a fool he'd been to think putting Elizabeth at a distance would keep temptation from him. It took only an instant for desire to burn.

But when the words *Leave now!* shot through him, he'd jerked back as if he'd been hit.

Had he been leaning into her? His mind spun. The hurt he saw in her eyes as he left wrenched his heart.

"God, please. Send me away."

Memories he'd pushed out of his mind years ago waged war within him.

In the darkness of the night, Chris tossed and turned. His niece had left hours ago, but the scent of popcorn still saturated each inhaled breath and pounded against his skull.

As he headed toward the kitchen for some medicine to ease the pain, Elizabeth's sleeping pills flashed through his mind. The empty bottle rested in his drawer. He would talk with her about them, but first things first—he needed to find a way to stay with her.

The cabinet squeaked as he pulled it open. He closed it after grabbing a glass. Chris popped two tablets in his mouth and washed them down with water. The cool liquid relieved his parched lips. He didn't realize how thirsty he'd become, not only for water but God's word. Was he really supposed to fight for his wife and their marriage? His time in the Word this morning gave him that impression. Right now he lacked faith in their future, but he believed in scripture, even if he hadn't lived like it for so long. With Jesus standing in the gap for his sin, Chris would need to trust and fight.

The clock on the stove read midnight. He couldn't stay still. His heart ached for his wife. Why not go to her?

As everyone slept, Chris plodded into his room, changed clothes, and packed a bag. If God told him to go, he'd go and stay, at least until he got thrown out.

With a duffle bag in hand, Chris sneaked from his parents' house much like he had when he was on a mission with his teenage buddies. Those were the days—rolling houses with toilet paper, staying up past daybreak, not a care in the world. But now, as he exited the front door, anguish dominated his world.

Chris filled his lungs with the crisp night air. Looking up into the sky, he blinked against the moisture filling his eyes. "Lord, help Elizabeth to be receptive when she finds me in the morning. Let her have compassion on me. I don't deserve it, but I'm asking for it. Give me the words. Amen."

A tiny voice cried out. *Katherine.* Elizabeth sat up in bed, sweat clinging to her skin. Heart pounding.

Her sister's light snore vibrated through the quiet room. Slipping out of bed, Elizabeth fought her wobbly legs into submission.

"Are you all right?" Sam rose and leaned on her elbow.

"Yes, now go back to sleep. I'm only going to use the bathroom." She gave her sister a weak smile, but the tightness from her face crushed her efforts.

Sam yawned and plopped back against the pillow. "I'll be here if you need me."

Elizabeth trudged down the hall. A noise stopped her. Turning around, she tip-toed into the living room. Nothing seemed out of the ordinary, but then she saw Chris sleeping on the couch.

Inhaling, she dashed across the room and hovered. Words formed in her mind like daggers aimed straight for his heart, a decisive blow to explode on impact. Eyes ready for a surprise attack roamed to the stubble a few days old on his face. She hadn't noticed it yesterday, or the dark circles under his eyes that mirrored her own.

The fierce words swirling within her thoughts quieted. Her arms slid to her sides. His chest rose and fell. Her fingers twitched to touch him. It had been so long. He didn't seem real. Really, their life didn't seem real after the accident. She dreamed of her husband at times, moments of happiness where she seemed cherished and protected, like nothing could pry them apart. But those dreams never lasted. She'd awaken to find him distant, yet here he slept.

Movement caught her eye as Sam moved in behind her. "Chris loves you," she whispered.

Elizabeth closed her eyes, tears catching in the back of her throat. If only that were true. How could it be? Had she become so unattractive her own husband didn't want her? And now, looking like this, she couldn't take any more rejection.

"Hang onto your marriage. It's worth fighting for."

"What is? More lies? Mistrust?"

Lines rippled across Chris's forehead. Hazel eyes met hers. She bit back a retort and dashed into her room. Footsteps followed close behind.

"I want to make things right, Elizabeth." Chris's voice trembled. "I need your help. I need for you to trust me again."

She whirled and faced him, balling her hands into fists. "Help you? How do you expect me to help *you* when I can't even make things right in my own life?"

"Let me stay with you … today, tomorrow, and the next day. We can get through this."

"I can't think about tomorrow or the next day when I don't even want to live past today." The words hung in the air like a thick fog. She didn't mean to say them, but there they were. The truth.

Sam came to her side and held her close.

Elizabeth shrugged off her sister's embrace and moved to the window. She wanted it all to go away. If she had her pills, she could relax.

"I'm sorry for leaving," Chris moved to stand behind her and whispered over her shoulder. "I should have been with you in the hospital."

"Please, Chris … don't. I can't talk about this."

"I'm not the same man, Elizabeth."

His breath brushed against the back of her ear. How her heart ached! She loved him. She couldn't deny it. However, there was another truth she couldn't deny. He'd given himself to someone else.

"Please forgive me."

She faced him. "I'm letting you go, Chris. It's over."

"No, it's not. It can't be." Chris pulled her against him. "I love you, Elizabeth. Forgive me."

She stiffened beneath his embrace. "You're hurting me."

"I'm not letting you go. I've missed you too much for this to be over."

"It is, Chris. I can't be your wife any longer. You can't love me the way I need to be loved, and I can't forgive you the way you want to be forgiven."

Sam stood next to them now. "Let go of my sister."

Chris's eyes pleaded as he searched her gaze. "Elizabeth. Don't do this."

Sam hurried away, but returned with Phillip.

Chris lifted his chin. "I'm not going, Phillip. I can't. I won't. I need my wife even if she doesn't need me."

"I do need you, but it's too late."

"It's never too late."

"I've already left you. I've filed for a divorce."

Sam choked, worry crossing her features. "Elizabeth, no … You can't."

Chris released her. His body slumped forward as he walked out of the apartment with Phillip close behind.

"What have you done? I need to catch him before they leave." Sam ran out the door.

Her sister's words slapped Elizabeth in the face. *What have I done? The Bible says I have every right since he cheated on me.* She went to the window. Outside they huddled together like a team planning their next move. But she wasn't willing to fight. There was nothing to fight for. After they dispersed, Chris got into the car and stared toward the window. He couldn't see her from the height of her apartment, but he stared. She remembered how his lips quivered when he'd said he loved her.

Phillip drove away. The door opened behind her.

"They're gone. We've decided since we're unable to run the bookstore right now, closing is our best option until we can hire several people. You shattered him, Elizabeth. You could see it on his face."

Elizabeth turned away, her heart in tattered pieces, knees buckling. If only she could numb the pain. "I'm going to lie down now."

"Yes." Sam sighed. "I think that would be best."

Back in her room, Elizabeth bent down and picked up her purse. She searched. Nothing.

She dumped the bag upside down, and everything tumbled out except for one thing. Her pills.

Chapter Nine

"You need to get ready."

Elizabeth stirred from her first peaceful night's sleep since the attack. Her eyes fluttered open and focused on the twirling fan, then on her sister who stood next to her bed.

"If you'd sleep at night instead of … oh, it doesn't matter. Just hurry."

Elizabeth closed her eyes once again and rolled over. "What are you talking about?"

"Remember Sarah? Your sister-in-law? She called."

She bolted upright. "I told you I'm not going. I can't go to Linda and Henry's. Chris will be there with the rest of his family."

Sam lifted her hand to her temple. "Then call Lindsey and explain why her aunt can't make it to her fifth birthday party. Don't you understand how much she misses you? When Katherine died, she thought you died, too."

Her stomach tightened. There were nights she prayed just that, and yet here she was, lying in bed.

"Call her before I leave." Sam flung the phone next to her pillow and left the room.

Elizabeth swiped the phone from her blanket, her pulse thumping in her palm as she slammed her hand against the bed. "Fine!"

She shook her head. It wasn't that she didn't love Lindsey; she did, almost like she was her own child, but that was the problem. Katherine was gone, and Lindsey wasn't hers. Every baby or young child reminded her of her loss, of the agony in her heart. "Why does every child in our family have to be a girl? What happened to having boys?"

She lunged to her feet, marched through the living room, and glared at her sister, stopping at an abrupt halt. "Why are you packing your things? Where are you going?"

"I planned to talk to you about this last night, but because you were so angry, it didn't seem like a good time." Sam grabbed her brush from the floor and met her gaze. "I need to go, Elizabeth. I miss Phillip and Juwonya." She pushed the brush in her suitcase, zipped it, and stood. Her mouth lifted into a smile. "Phillip and I want you to live with us. I've already packed everything you'll need. What do you say?"

"I'll think about it." Elizabeth's muscles tensed as she walked back into the bedroom. Two weeks ago she'd been attacked and hadn't dared to look into the mirror, not since Dr. Moore left. There were too many things she wanted to forget.

Chris whisked moisture from the misty mirror with his hand and leaned toward it. His two-week blond stubble had grown into a dark beard. He ran his hand along his chin. He needed to shave, but only if Elizabeth planned on coming. He'd given up hope after Samantha had called his mother last night. Mom didn't have to explain the conversation to him. When she sank into the chair, her body language had said it all.

"Chris." His father spoke from the other side of the bathroom door.

"Yeah, Dad. What is it?"

"Elizabeth is on her way. Phillip called."

He stared at his own reflection and ran his hand down his jaw. He looked like a cave man.

"Did you hear me, son?"

"Uh … yes." He fumbled around the bathroom hunting for a razor. No way would his shaver do the trick. Spying a bag of new razors, he slipped them out of the closet. "Pink. Great." *Beggars can't be choosers*. The cliché ran through his mind as he put women's shaving lotion in his hand, then on his face. With long strokes against his cheek, a smile lit his features. "Thank you, Lord."

After finishing, he hurried into the bedroom and dressed. His wife's voice carried as he entered the living room. Elizabeth wrapped her arms around Lindsey, and all he could do was gape. She was breathtaking the way her blonde hair hung long across her shoulders and how her blue dress brought out the turquoise in her eyes.

Sarah, his sister-in-law, slipped her arm through his. "She's beautiful, isn't she?"

Chris patted her hand. "Yes, and thank you."

"For what?"

He leaned close to her ear. "Phillip told me how everyone in the family has been praying for us."

Sarah grinned. "And I'm glad to see this change in you. It's like the old Chris is back."

"You mean since I shaved?" He smiled then turned to find Elizabeth facing his direction.

"Don't give up," Sarah whispered, before heading toward the dining room. Elizabeth followed, taking Lindsey with her.

The scent of vanilla cake teased his senses, and his stomach growled. For the first time in weeks, he looked forward to eating. The sound of laughter drew him into the dining room where everyone gathered.

Chris nodded a greeting to his brother, who nodded back with a wide grin. Timothy, the tallest of the three, stood with one arm around Sarah, a lighter in the other hand. He glanced at their five-year-old daughter.

"Are you ready, honey?" Timothy kissed Sarah's cheek then lit the candles on Lindsey's princess cake.

Sarah plopped Lindsey onto the chair, whisking a few hairs from the birthday girl's face. Dad held the camcorder to his eye with one hand. His other hand rose in the air to signal when to sing. Juwonya patted her hands.

Mom stood beside Chris next to the patio window. The sun highlighted the grey streaks in her hair. "Everyone ready? Henry, you're filming right?"

Dad lowered his arm.

"Happy Birthday..." Chris belted out. He'd avoided looking in Elizabeth's direction until now. Her lips barely moved. Her arms wrapped around her middle. Was she chilled? Should he get her a blanket? He studied her a moment longer. No. She trembled. His fingers ached to touch her, to hold her, to make her feel safe. Safe with him.

Chris stepped forward, but his mom blocked his path.

"Okay. I need a family picture around our birthday princess. Gather around." She herded everyone like cattle, but Elizabeth hung back, then turned through the patio door.

Should he go after her? Indecision held him a moment longer. He couldn't miss the questions swirling in his mother's eyes. It was hard enough to share his sins with Phillip; he would never breathe a word of them to her.

Once outside, his clothes clung to him in the humidity. Water trickling through the rock garden soothed his thoughts. He searched until his gaze landed on Elizabeth, standing in front of a concrete cross centered in a bed of white and pink roses.

He came alongside her, closed his eyes, and began to pray. "Dear God, be with us, Lord, as we are in such turmoil. Heal our hearts and our marriage. Take away the pain of our daughter's death."

Shuffling sounded beside him. Chris's eyes darted open. Elizabeth stood back from the rocks, but didn't walk away.

He moved slowly, afraid he'd scare her, like a frightened animal. With two measured steps, he closed the space between them. The berry scent of her shampoo drifted toward him.

As tears coursed down her cheeks, Chris's heart burned to comfort her even for a moment. *God, help me to know what to do.*

With the slightest movement, the tips of his fingers found hers. He inched the last step toward her and pulled her quivering body into his arms. She tucked into his chest, and her sobs broke the silence.

There was so much that needed to be said, but he couldn't speak. As long as he held his wife in his arms, God would take care of the rest.

Sin brought consequences, but seeing his wife deal with those consequences ate him alive. Whatever it took to make things right, and with God's help, they could work through this. God would teach him how to be a better man.

He kissed the top of her head and rested his face against her hair. He would hold her for as long as she allowed. *Please God, let it be for the rest of my life.*

Elizabeth shifted and moved from him as pools of unshed tears met his eyes. She averted her gaze and, with a shaky hand, touched his chest then turned and walked away.

Chris knelt where he'd found her. After he prayed, he headed back toward the house where Lindsey's party continued. Laughter filled the air, but his heart was no longer in it. He needed to be alone, to think.

Dad met him with a dishtowel hung over his shoulder. "She left."

He nodded. It didn't surprise him. "I think I'll go lie down."

"Son, wait."

"Dad, not now."

His father flung the towel down, dried his hands, and tossed it back over his shoulder. His brow creased as if he was deep in thought. "Do me a favor. Read Psalm 46."

Chris nodded then lumbered to his room and closed the door. Taking his Bible from the night table, he found the scripture. *'God is our refuge and strength.'* Peace settled into his heart. He read it again and continued. *'A very present help in trouble. Therefore will not we fear, though the earth be removed, and though the mountains be carried into the midst of the sea.'* He continued to read. *'God shall help her ... The Lord is Almighty ... He maketh wars to cease ...'*

"God, I understand I need to remember you're my refuge and my strength through this, but I'm not at war." His eyes focused on one line. *'Be still and know that I am God.'*

Chris fell back against the bed and rubbed his eyes with his palms. Rising up on his elbow, something on the dresser caught his eye. He threw his legs over the side and stood. Two white envelopes lay before him, stacked one on top of the other.

Someone may as well have punched him in the gut. He couldn't breathe. Allison's script ran across the top letter, the same one he'd lost. He'd looked everywhere for it and thought it must have fallen out of his pocket before he went to the hospital. He yanked the note out.

Chris, I happen to agree with you; money should be enough, but it's not.

~A

Crumpling the note into a tiny ball, he hurled it across the room. It sailed out of view on the other side of the bed. He thought of Elizabeth and froze. How did this end up on his dresser? He glanced at the other letter, thicker than Allison's but with no clues on the envelope to indicate who it was from.

Slipping the papers out of the legal size envelope, Chris's legs wobbled. He glanced at his closed door. If Elizabeth set this on his dresser … He eyed Allison's envelope. He tried to swallow the lump in his throat, but it didn't budge. Neither did the heading on the forms in front of him: R and R Attorneys At Law, LLC.

The warmth from the sun beat down through the car window and burned Elizabeth's skin, but she didn't move. It seemed right somehow, the burning, the heat, like the anger rising within her. She squeezed her eyes shut and forced the tears into submission. Sam seemed quiet since they'd left Henry and Linda's, but she couldn't stay there any longer. Elizabeth had known it would be a mistake to go, but never guessed how big.

She'd gone into Linda's garden to pray, but once she got there, no words came, only tears. She couldn't pray. No matter how much she willed herself, nothing happened. Just like when she tried to escape Chris, she couldn't move. Yet, when he pulled her into his strong arms, she collapsed, and her mind gave way. In those fleeting moments, she'd wanted him to never let go, to love her as he once did, to cherish her. But then her mind cleared, and reality set in. Her marriage and her daughter were dead. Everything she'd ever hoped for lay buried under dirt, rock, and sin.

"I know you haven't had much time to think about our offer, but Phillip and I would love for you to live with us. I have everything packed in my trunk, so we can go straight home." Sam shot her a pair of chocolate puppy-dog eyes.

"You know that only worked when we were kids, right?"

"What do you say?"

"There's something I should tell you." Elizabeth gazed out the window, eyes unfocused. Her mind prepared the words that surely would hurt her sister as much as it did her.

Sam pulled the car off to the side of the road, put it in park, and then met her gaze. "All right. I think I'm ready."

"I left divorce papers on Chris's dresser. Since we don't have any children and the house—the papers were more of a formality. The divorce should be final in the next few weeks."

Sam's face blanched. "There is one thing that you forgot to mention, Elizabeth. It's your commitment to—"

"Don't talk to me about commitment! Yes, I'm the one who left. But Chris is the one who broke our commitment. It was him. Not me! He's the one who had the affair!"

Sam grasped Elizabeth's hand. "I had no idea. Phillip never mentioned this to me. All I knew was he and Chris have been meeting every day for the past month or so to pray for your marriage."

"Now you know why I have to get a divorce."

"I know now why you feel you need one."

"He betrayed me."

"As I did years ago. What would have happened if you hadn't forgiven me? Where would we be now?"

"You're my sister. Of course I forgave you."

"And Chris is your husband."

"How can you say that? Are you taking his side?"

"I'm not on Chris's side. I'm on yours, but I've seen a change in him."

"He doesn't love me!"

"That's not true. I've seen how he wants to be near you and how he looks at you. And I caught you watching him sleep the other night. Admit it—you want to be with him."

"I'm done, Sam. I'm finished talking about this. And there's one more thing—I'm staying at my apartment, and we're not closing the bookstore."

Chapter Ten

Elizabeth stepped out of her bedroom into a cloud of smoke filling her apartment. In front of the stove, Sam yanked a pan of biscuits out of the oven. "I thought I smelled something burning."

"Oh, hush." Sam swatted the air with her hand. "I forgot to turn down the heat. Great." She stomped her foot. "Now the bacon is burnt, too."

"If I'd known you were coming over to cook, I would've gotten the key back from you." Elizabeth laughed and glanced around Sam's shoulder. "Yep. Fried bacon comin' up."

"Get out of the way." Sam bumped her with her hip. "Why don't you be useful and grab two plates?"

"Sure." She reached up and pulled out two yellow stoneware dishes from the cabinet, then set them on the table. "You still haven't mentioned why you came by."

"You know what, hand me those plates instead." Sam rotated and took them from her, then added eggs, bacon, and slightly burnt biscuits. "I needed to talk to you about Chris."

Great. She hadn't planned on discussing her husband. Now she'd have to force breakfast down. Hopefully it didn't have to do with the divorce papers.

Yesterday, in anger, she'd left *A's* blackmail letter on Chris's dresser. She wished she could have seen his reaction. She knew she'd hurt him. Why should she care? He'd hurt her plenty.

Elizabeth sat at the table and took several bites. Sam had yet to lift her fork. So Elizabeth began, "Tomorrow I plan to reopen the bookstore."

"Are you sure you're ready?"

"I like to eat. Besides, I have a business to run. This bookstore has meant everything to us, and I'm not about to let it go … because of Chris." He might have destroyed their life together, but not her future. She was in control.

"How do you plan to run the store? It took all of us."

"Chris hasn't worked at the store in quite a while. I'll do fine as long as you and Phillip can help out like before."

"That might be true about Chris, but he wants to come back to work. He's still part owner."

Elizabeth squeezed the fork between her fingers and placed it gently on the table, biting the tip of her tongue, keeping her mind and words in submission. She wouldn't work with him. How could she be expected to? "I'm not working with Chris. I'll buy him out."

It seemed to be her sister's turn to set her silverware down. "And how do you expect to do that when you're broke?" She crossed her arms against her chest.

"You and Phillip can buy him out. I can pay you back after we reopen the store."

"I don't think so." Sam leaned in. "Chris wants the marriage. He wants you."

Elizabeth rose from the table. "It's too late."

Chris paced the dimly lit bookstore. The shop had closed hours ago. Elizabeth should be here, but where was she? He glanced at the door in hopes of willing her to appear, but she still didn't return.

Samantha had relayed their earlier conversation to him, but he couldn't—no, he wouldn't—accept their marriage being over. He loved her, and God had told him to fight. He was in a war to win her heart, and he'd persevere no matter the cost.

Samantha's words still rang in his ear, though. "Maybe we should call Steven. He could find her. He always did. She trusts him."

With a deep breath, Chris ran his fingers through his hair, steeling his nerves. It was his fault his wife found comfort in Steven. In a way, it seemed Steven found that same comfort in her. Steven's comment still struck him as odd. "I've never seen her this way before." It nagged him, but right now he needed his wife to come home. If something happened to her again, he'd never forgive himself.

The door creaked open. Elizabeth wobbled into the bookstore. She smiled. Chris's arms caught her before she fell. Her breath smelled of rum. "Elizabeth, you've been drinking."

"Captain Obvious. Hey, you know what, Captain?" She touched his face. "You look like my cheating husband. It's not a good look for you." She giggled, her hands floundering.

"Let's get you in bed." He lifted and carried her up the stairs to her apartment. As he placed her in the bed, she grasped his shirt and spoke in a drunken cry.

"I loved you. Did you know that? You … I loved." She let go and waved her finger at him. "But you didn't love me. Nope. Didn't."

Chris's heart wrenched. How he wished he could turn back the hands of time, make things right. Tears filled his eyes. "I'm sorry. I'm so sorry." He tried to hold her, but she pushed him away.

"Go away." She rolled over.

Guilt covered him like a tidal wave, knocking hope of reconciliation from his mind. Breathless, he stood and headed down the stairs. He'd left the door ajar. Maybe that was a sign he should leave. Elizabeth had told him to go.

Chris glanced around, his focus stopping on a pair of ruby red slippers in the children's area of the store. He headed over to the wall and to the mounted shadow box where the slippers glittered in the store's lights. He could imagine Elizabeth as a little girl, clicking her mother's red heels together. Truth floated through his thoughts, words he'd once heard in a movie. He blinked away his raw emotions. There was no place he'd rather be. She was his home. But should he be here?

Chris walked to the door, locked it, and flicked the lights off, then headed upstairs. He still owned the title as husband, and he planned to care for his wife, whether she wanted him to or not.

Hours later, he awoke and strained to sit up against the back of the couch. Darkness still hung outside the window, but he needed to check on Elizabeth. She'd become sick several times through the night, and he did the only thing he could do—hold her hair out of the way. As his eyes opened, his gaze landed on the recliner next to him. Elizabeth cuddled with a quilt … asleep.

Surprised, yes, but did this really mean anything? Maybe she couldn't find her way back to bed. No, she knew this apartment; she'd lived here before. Elizabeth came to *him* last night. "Thank you, God," he whispered.

A smile tugged on Chris's lips. He wanted nothing more than to be with his wife but, sober, she couldn't stand to be in the same room with him. Chris looked over at her sleeping form again and rose from the couch.

Elizabeth's eyes fluttered open for a brief moment when he lifted her in his arms. They closed again, and her lips rose at the corners before she snuggled against his chest. When he reached the bed, he placed her alongside her pillow and fought the urge to trail his hand through several strands of her hair. He had to earn that privilege.

Back in the kitchen, he glanced at the clock. Only a few hours until they'd reopen the bookstore. He'd take care of what needed to be done and let his wife sleep. First things first—coffee. He headed downstairs to make the coffee and found Samantha had beaten him to it.

Samantha's head shot up. "I didn't expect you."

"Why not? Today's the big day."

Samantha measured a few tablespoons of coffee in the coffee maker. "Did you wake her up?"

"No, she's asleep and will be for a while."

Phillip came out with a pallet of merchandise. "How long has this been in the back? Whatever it is, it smells good."

"A few months." Samantha pushed the button to start the coffee brewing.

Chris ran his hand across the dusty boxes of candles. "Since you're both here, I should tell you I'm going back to Mom's tonight. I need to pray about moving in to stay."

"Fair enough." Phillip patted Chris's shoulder. "When will you be back?"

"Tomorrow, if that's all right. I'll leave after getting the store set."

"Of course. But if you decide you want to come back earlier…"

"I have a lot to pray about, Phillip, and if Elizabeth leaves again, I don't know what I'd do. I love her, and if this is truly an answer to our prayers, I don't want to do anything to push her away."

Elizabeth's heart thumped heavily within her chest as she looked through the window. Chris's car pulled away, and the breath in her chest escaped. She'd told him last night she didn't want his help or need him, but each time she became sick, Chris had showed her a gentleness she'd never seen in him before.

He must have thought she'd been asleep at one point in the night when he checked on her. She still felt his hand graze her cheek.

She forced herself from the window, determined not to care. He'd left her before and was doing it again. The sour taste of abandonment curdled on her tongue.

Head pounding, she swiped a red dress off a hanger in the closet and slipped it on. It fell over her hips and hung straight. In the last few weeks, her curves had vanished, but she didn't care. There was no one to impress. Right now, she had a store to run and a life to live. Later she'd numb the pain with a drink.

"Elizabeth." Her name seeped through the pulsating music. The smoke-filled club made it difficult to see as she glanced around the sea of dancers. Nothing. She turned, and a firm hand grabbed her arm.

"Steven? What are you doing here?"

"Looking for you."

"Why, do you want to drink with me?" She placed her free hand over her mouth, stifling a laugh.

"Samantha called me. Your family has been looking everywhere for you. I thought you might be here."

"Well, you found me, so you can go now." She yanked her arm and spun away to the dance floor.

Steven followed. "Elizabeth, come with me."

"Only if you want to dance." She said over her shoulder. "Otherwise, leave me alone." She continued through the crowd, and a man about Steven's height stepped in her path.

"Would you like to party, pretty lady?"

Steven stepped between them before she could answer.

"Excuse me." The man gripped Steven's shoulder.

Steven's eyes bore into hers. "She's with me."

"I am not with you!" She balled her fists.

"Right now, you are." He grasped her arm until they were almost outside. When his grip weakened, she jerked away.

"What are you doing, Steven? This has nothing to do with you."

"I won't let you do this. I don't care if I have to drag you out of here every night."

"Then you'll have to drag me out."

He raised a brow. "If you don't give me your hand, I will carry you out."

"Is that a threat?"

"Try me." He smirked.

She turned. Her feet left the floor. "Put me down!" She wiggled against him, but he only held her tighter.

"You're going home, and I'm making sure you get there."

Why did he come for me? Why can't he leave me be? But down deep, she wanted to be rescued. What was wrong with the desire to be cared for, cherished, and loved? Maybe that was also part of the happily-ever-after life—it only existed in movies and dreams.

She wilted against his chest, wrapping her arms around his neck.

When he finally pulled his car up to the bookstore, she climbed out but Steven still hurried to her.

"Hold on, I'm going to help you upstairs. Besides, I have your keys." He jingled them in the air.

They reached the top and entered the apartment, his smile radiating as he placed the keys on the kitchen counter.

She crossed her arms. Was he taunting her now that he'd won, dragging her out? What was with him? "What's so funny?"

"You drive me crazy, Lizzy. I've never been so upset at anyone."

She paused, studying him. Lizzy? No one ever called her that except for her sister, but it felt right somehow, as right as his strong arms holding her a moment ago. She realized she had been staring when Steven took a step toward her. Her gaze dropped to the floor.

"Elizabeth, look at me." He raised her chin with his finger.

What could she say to cover her thoughts or the pounding within her chest caused by his touch? "I'm sorry I fought you."

"I forgive you." He pushed her hair back from her face. "You don't know how hard it is not to comfort you."

His eyes turned dark, mesmerizing her. Her pulse quickened even more. Her husband didn't want her—he'd made that clear time after time. So why couldn't Steven comfort her? The divorce would be final in two weeks. "Will you hold me?"

"You don't know what you're asking." He pulled away. "Chris is the only one who should be comforting you. When I leave, I'm calling him."

"No! You can't." She shook her head. Did this man not understand? "He doesn't want me anymore."

Steven started toward the door. "Believe me when I say God wants me to leave. Chris is the man you need. If you want my advice, I suggest you get into the shower before he gets here."

"Steven, please."

"Lock the door behind me." He closed the door as he left.

Nervousness twisted her stomach as she turned the lock and trekked her way into the shower. If Chris did come, it was out of obligation because of Steven's call, not because he truly cared.

She'd finished getting dressed when Chris entered the apartment, his eyes red. "Are you all right?" He stood at the doorway.

"I am." She rounded the bed, hoping this would be over soon.

Chris followed. "Where did you go?"

She spun around almost into his chest and took a step back. "I went to a club downtown."

The corners of Chris's eyes crinkled, eyes almost shutting as if he'd been punched. He slumped down on the edge of the bed, shoulders caved.

She sat next to him, hesitant. "You really didn't need to come. I'm fine."

"I had to come, Elizabeth." He met her gaze. "I love you."

Then why did he leave earlier? "I overheard Samantha and Phillip talking with you about staying, but you left."

"Because I needed time to pray. I don't want to push you away. But when Samantha called asking if I'd seen you, I realized I couldn't lose you again. I know I have no right to ask, but I want to be your husband again. Will you take me back?"

"I can't, Chris. I'm scared you're going to leave me again. I'm scared to live without Katherine … I'm not the same person you married."

"Neither am I." He fell to his knees. "I will never leave you again. Every day I'm faced with the consequences of my sin when I see your pain and the sadness you're living with. I'm a sinner, covered in God's grace, and by His mercy, you're still my wife."

Chris's arms wrapped around her. She leaned into his chest, absorbing the warmth that radiated from him. Her body and heart knew they were home. But could she trust him?

Chapter Eleven

Elizabeth clamped her eyes shut. She swallowed the nausea bubbling in her throat. Chris's fingers caressed her cheek before gently sliding over her eyes. His soft touch sent shivers through her. Her eyes flung open.

"Good morning. Do you need me to get you anything?"

"I have a headache," she mumbled, the pain jabbing with each breath.

"I'll be right back." Chris rose from the bed and shuffled down the hall.

She inhaled, held her breath, then exhaled, forcing her thoughts from the pain to Chris. Could she do this? Could she trust him? Would he stay with her this time? The questions pressing against her skull were as painful as the headache. She didn't want to think, but when Chris returned, bringing the aroma of coffee with him, she had no choice. Each doubt flicked through her mind.

She accepted the tablets and water before meeting his eyes. "When did you start drinking coffee?" She tipped her head back slowly, swallowing the tablets.

"Since I've been meeting with Phillip to pray for us and our marriage. Would you like some?" He lifted the mug toward her.

She smiled. He knew how much she disliked coffee. "Are you trying to convert me?"

"If I could see that smile for the rest of my life, then yes."

"I should be getting up." Her smile faded, and she hurried from the bed to avoid a discussion about their future, but the movement ignited a jolting pain in her head. "Maybe I won't." She slid back onto the pillows, eyes closed.

"Rest, Elizabeth. I'll be here when you wake up." His lips brushed her cheek, and a moment later, the door clicked shut.

Elizabeth struggled to make conversation while Chris helped her get ready for the store to open. She grabbed the red sale signs from the counter and placed them over the clearance books. She sensed his gaze following her every move, but couldn't tell if he was condemning her or keeping an eye out for her protection. Either way, she wasn't his concern. Or was she? What had happened last night? What did it all mean? Her feelings were so jumbled she didn't know what to think.

As she pulled the register open and slid the till into the drawer, Sam entered the store with Juwonya propped on her hip.

"How are you?" she asked.

Elizabeth glanced toward Chris to see if he'd heard the bell as she entered. He must have, because he smiled at Sam, then turned back to the coffee maker.

Her sister tilted her head. "Do you want to talk?"

"Maybe later. I'm going outside to sit." Before Elizabeth could move, her sister placed her hand on hers.

"I'm here. Always."

With a nod, Elizabeth headed for the front door. The desire to get away made her mouth water. Whiskey, rum, she didn't care, anything to free her from her thoughts. The last time she'd stood in a garden, God hadn't answered her prayer. Had He left her, too, like everyone else who mattered to her? Sam had moved out at eighteen and never came back. When their parents died in a car accident, Elizabeth fought to survive her loneliness. Now Chris. *But when did God abandon me?*

Memories about her parents' death still brought a vague suspicion that something else had happened, something important, but her thoughts faded.

Elizabeth stared at the roses. Yanking a yellow bud from the bush, she plucked off several petals. Why couldn't she remember things? She felt certain her memory held the key to her life now. But her mind continued to go blank.

What did it matter? Her past couldn't have been much better. She tossed the half-torn flower on the ground, then kicked it into the bushes. Elizabeth moved on toward the opposite side of the bookstore entrance, where a concrete bench beckoned her. Water trickled from a fountain, spilling over the edge of a metallic bowl leading into the rock garden. A sparrow bathed, ruffling its feathers, and collected water in his beak, quenching his thirst.

Elizabeth dropped her head into her hands. She needed to talk; she needed her sister. The urgency made her spring from the bench, and with a hurried pace, she reentered the bookstore. She found Chris by himself, scooping books out of a box. "Where's Sam?"

"She went into the office."

Elizabeth again felt his eyes bore into her back as she headed toward the office. Yes, she needed to talk with her sister. Working with Chris was proving next to impossible.

Elizabeth rounded the corner and stopped at the sight of Juwonya running out from the doorway. She'd avoided her niece for months. Every time Sam kissed or hugged the little girl in front of her, it tore another piece from her soul. Katherine should be alive.

Juwonya looked up and smiled.

Elizabeth couldn't stand the churning within her chest, but it was too late. Her niece demanded attention.

As she snatched her up, Juwonya bumped her cheek with her own. Conviction pierced her core. She'd been so wrong. How could she withhold love from her own niece? Enveloping Juwonya in her arms, tears and love flowed like a dam bursting. Her niece's feather soft cheek pressed against hers once more, uncovering something she wasn't willing to admit—not to herself, not to anyone.

"Are you ready, sis? Do you want to tell me what's bothering you?"

Caught off guard, Elizabeth swiveled so Sam couldn't see she'd been crying. Maybe she wouldn't notice. Setting Juwonya down, she wiped her face with her hand. Juwonya ran off toward the bookstore. "What would you like me to tell you—that everything with Chris is happening too fast or that my memories keep vanishing on me?"

With a quick intake of air, Sam smiled. "Are you remembering things? Oh, Lizzy, that's wonderful."

She glanced off. "That's just it. That name. Why did you call me Lizzy? When did you start calling me Lizzy?"

"Mom and I used to call you that."

And Steven does. "I don't remember. That's what's so frustrating."

Sam's gaze fell to the ground before returning to her. "I'm sorry, but you said you're beginning to remember things. Maybe before long, your past will come back to you."

"In a strange way, I feel like it has, but I can't grasp it. Sometimes I wonder if it was better than what I'm living in now."

"Elizabeth, you can't live in the past. The past is gone, and God has a wonderful future waiting for you."

"I want to believe that, I really do, but I can't. The whole thing with Chris..." Her jaw tightened and her stomach knotted as thoughts of him crossed her mind, pulling at her hurt and mistrust. "I don't want to talk about it. That's why I go to the club and drink. I'm tired of feeling. I know you don't understand, but it's wonderful to feel nothing."

Her sister arched an eyebrow. "And how do you feel this morning? Anything?"

"Terrible. And I know where you're going with this. Do you know Chris stayed with me last night? When I woke up, he was fully dressed on top of the covers."

"He told Phillip he would never leave you again after last night. You've been broken to the point no one will be able to heal you except for God, but we will walk beside you."

"I can't trust Chris, Sam."

"Then don't. You don't need to right now, but trust God. Rely on Him. He'll never leave."

"How can you say that? I don't feel Him." She pressed her palm to her chest. "Where was He when Katherine died? Where is He now when I need Him the most?"

"He was right there with you. Still is."

"He should have stopped her from dying."

"He didn't stop His Son from dying on the cross."

"You know as well as I do it's different." Her voice faded, swallowing past the emotion in her throat. She walked into the store and caught Chris's gaze.

Sam came to her side. "It is different." Her voice softened. "But He understands how you feel."

"I can't talk about this anymore, Sam. I need to be alone right now." With moisture misting her vision, Elizabeth headed for the door.

"Where are you going?"

The tightness in Sam's voice made Elizabeth pause. However the look of concern on her sister's face saddened her more. "I'm going to be with Katherine. I don't know what else to do."

Elizabeth didn't expect it to take so long to get to the gravesite on foot, especially now with the clouds overhead growing stormy. Her mind lost focus as her feet grew tired and sore. She regretted leaving while the store was open, but she had to get away before she did or said something out of anger.

At a major intersection, a car pulled up next to the curb. Horns blared from behind.

"Get in." Chris's voice called to her.

Elizabeth turned to Chris waiting in the car, window rolled down. "How in the world did you find me? I walked through almost every yard and two shopping centers." A horn blasted behind him.

"I'll take you if you like, but I don't know if the guy behind me will let me wait for you to decide."

Elizabeth tilted her head and scowled at the driver in the other vehicle. A look she didn't know she had until recently. She'd learned a lot about herself in the last few months. Most of it she didn't like, but this came in handy.

A growl of thunder rippled through the air as she opened the door and slid into the passenger seat. "I think he got the point." She closed the door.

"Just in time. It's starting to rain." Chris drove off as heavy drops pounded on the windshield.

They arrived at the gravesite as the rain slowed to a sprinkle. The smell of wet dirt saturated the air, intensifying the heaviness in Elizabeth's chest.

Flowers once vibrant with new life now withered to brown, dropping blooms on the ground. Dead like the occupants of the graves. *Never again,* her heart yelled out. Sorrow, and now water, dripped from her.

Chris stayed alongside her in the rain.

Elizabeth shivered as Chris pulled into the driveway. He hurried to her side and opened the car door.

"Let's get you inside." He took her hand and led her up the walk to the bookstore.

"You both are soaked through." Sam hovered, helping Elizabeth inside.

Chris hurried back to the car, slammed the door, and ran inside, closing the door behind him, thankful it was after store hours. He didn't want to deal with customers. He glanced toward his wife's apartment, noticing Phillip in his peripheral view.

"Chris, wait."

"Yeah?" His body stood near the register, but his heart followed his wife up the stairs.

"Let's talk."

He exhaled. "Do you mind if I change?"

"Not at all. While you're changing, you need to think about where you'll be staying—in the apartment with Elizabeth or down here."

Chris remained silent, praying for guidance as he grabbed a dry set of clothes from his duffle bag and disappeared into the bathroom. Emerging a few minutes later, he felt at peace. "Downstairs."

"Then tonight I'll bring your things from Mom's."

"I don't know what to do, Phillip. She's going to be so close to me. It'd be too hard not to check on her. I don't know how to act around her, but holding her in my arms last night … We belong to each other."

"As soon as everyone has changed, I think it would be good to read scripture together." Phillip patted Chris on the back. "God will work this out. You'll see."

Chris climbed the stairs to the apartment behind Phillip, entered first, then leaned over the kitchen bar and grabbed the phone book. "What do you all say to pizza for dinner?"

"Sounds good to me." Samantha came out of Elizabeth's room alone.

Fear pierced him. He took several steps toward Samantha. "Is everything all right?"

She placed a hand on his arm. "She's fine. I think she needed some time away from me. She decided to take a shower. So pizza." She picked up Juwonya and nuzzled her with kisses. "Just you wait until you get older. You'll enjoy pizza like Mommy."

Chris's heart ached. He missed Katherine. Standing at her grave today shook his resolve. Seeing his wife slouched over the headstone, tears lost in the rain, he felt hopeless for the first time in weeks.

Phillip placed a glass of tea on the table in front of him. "You all right?"

Chris sat and forced a smile in his direction. "I will be."

"Take each moment at a time and remember God is in control."

Samantha cast a glance down the hallway, then turned her attention back to them. "Chris, did she say anything about where she went last night?"

"A club downtown."

"I wish I knew which one. If she runs off again, I'd go get her myself."

"You're not going down there no matter what your sister does." Phillip placed another glass of tea on the table and sat. "If anybody goes, it will be Chris or me."

Chris tensed. "Or Steven."

Sam touched his shoulder. "I had to call Steven. He's found her before, and if it wasn't for him ... God sent Steven for her. I know you don't want to hear this, but God is using Steven in her life."

"You don't think he's taken advantage of the situation?"

"The first time I saw them together, he had her Bible in hand with it opened. Steven cares for her—there is no doubt in my mind, but beyond that, I say no."

Chris fidgeted with the edge of the tablecloth. "It's hard to think of another man with my wife."

"I'm sure it's hard for my sister to think about you with another woman."

Elizabeth came up behind them. "Why are you huddled together?"

Samantha pulled her cell from her pocket. "After Phillip calls for pizza —"

"— this is the time Samantha, Juwonya, and I have our family time." Phillip took the phone from Samantha and dialed. "You're more than welcome to join us."

Chris cleared his throat. "Do you want to come sit?" His voice cracked like a teenager's, but what surprised him most was the nod that followed. She led the way, but sat in a recliner on the other side of the couch.

Hope, Lord. Please give me hope.

Elizabeth sat quietly, running her fingers through her hair.

Phillip sat down with his Bible. Samantha followed, placing Juwonya in her lap. "I thought we could read Deuteronomy 6:5-9 and maybe talk about what this scripture means to you personally. '*And thou shalt love the LORD thy God with all thine heart, and with all thy soul, and with all thy might. And these words, which I command thee this day, shall be in thine heart: And thou shalt teach them diligently unto thy children, and shalt talk of them when thou sittest in thine house, and when thou walkest by the way, and when thou liest down, and when thou risest up. And thou shalt bind them for a sign upon thine hand, and they shall be as frontlets between thine eyes. And thou shalt write them upon the posts of thy house, and on thy gates.*' Now, who would like to start?"

Chris sat up and caught Elizabeth watching him. "I don't know if I ever loved God that way until now. All that has happened has brought me closer to the Lord. I'm so thankful to God for His love. And with the second part of that verse..." Chris's gaze met his wife's. "I'm making a commitment to you and our children. That I will put God first and be the husband He has called me to be. I love you, and I'm looking forward to what God has for us."

Elizabeth stood. "I can't give you what you want."

Chris watched as her gaze swept from him to her hands. "What are you talking about? You're what I want."

"It has nothing to do with wanting each other." Elizabeth walked away.

"Then tell me." He almost yelled to stop her from going. He hurried to her side. "What does it have to do with?"

"I'm not having any more children." She faced him. "I have an appointment in July. If you want children, it won't be with me."

His shoulders slouched. "Elizabeth, please."

"I won't survive you leaving me again for someone else when you decide you'd rather have children."

"But it's you I want." He reached for her, but as she crossed her arms against her chest, his hand fell away. "I won't leave you."

"So you don't want children?"

"Of course I want children. You can cancel your appointment."

Her arms slid to her sides. "I won't have another child and watch them die in front of me. I can't. I won't. And if you leave me again … It's better that you don't stay here. The divorce will be final soon enough." She turned and bolted out of the room.

He shook his head, then threw his hands up in the air. "I need to go."

"Chris, wait."

"Not now." He hurried to his car, got in, and slammed the door. He pounded the steering wheel with the sides of his fists. His wife planned to divorce him and soon. They had nothing left together.

Chris didn't know where to go or what to do. He started the car and drove aimlessly, until it came to him. They did have one thing. Their house

Chapter Twelve

Chris replayed the previous day's events in his mind as he drove back to Elizabeth's, the sun barely rising above the buildings. Giving up his anger and hurt to the Lord, he knew the call God had given him—a call of sacrifice.

Chris climbed the stairs, unlocked the door to the apartment, and stood in front of her bedroom door. He sucked in his breath and entered, expecting to see his wife, not a freshly made bed. His heart fell as he hurried out of the bedroom and searched the rest of the apartment. He ran back down to check the bookstore. No sign of her. *Where is she?*

He doubled back to the apartment, but this time looking in the closet. Her clothes were still there. She hadn't left him. Did she go drinking? He headed once again downstairs and spotted half of his wife's body sticking out from the aisle in the children's area. *Please, Lord … don't let anything have happened to her.* He rushed to her.

Elizabeth lay on her side, head propped on her arm next to the bookshelf, eyes closed. He didn't see any new bruises or cuts, and her breathing seemed normal. Was she sleeping? Why here?

Getting on his knees, the words the Lord had spoken to him the night before rang in his mind. *Sacrifice.*

Lord, what am I sacrificing on my knees?

Pride.

A lump grew in his throat. "Elizabeth," he whispered, moving several strands of her hair from her face.

"Chris." She licked her lips. "I think my arm's asleep."

"Do you know where you are?" She had yet to open her eyes.

"I remember being locked out of the apartment last night after dusting the store." Her eyes fluttered open, and a smile lifted the corners of her mouth. "You came back."

With his face inches from hers, even in the morning, her breath smelled like peaches. The urge to kiss her overwhelmed him, but he resisted and smiled back. "I did … for you."

"Do you mind helping me up? I can't feel the left side of my body."

Chris grinned and took her hand, then her elbow, to help her stand. "Is that better?"

"Maybe once I walk around."

"It shouldn't be long now."

"It's already feeling better." She pushed those same pesky strands he had moved earlier behind her ear, but they rebelled.

He tucked them back behind her ear and slid his fingers along the length of her hair. Her eyes closed. Chris yanked his hand away. *What are you doing?* But with her eyes still closed, he allowed himself to touch her hair one last time.

"I want you to know, when I take my hand away, it's not that I don't want to touch you. I do, but it's not worth rushing you into anything you're not ready for. I will wait for you."

"You're staying? You've changed your mind about children?"

Her face registered confusion, so he continued. "No, I haven't. I still want children, but if I have to choose between children or you, I choose you."

"You're staying."

"With you forever. Until death do us part. If you'll let me."

Elizabeth stood on one side while Chris faced her on the other in the middle of Sam and Phillip's living room. Between them sat the shredder. She owned up to her end of the bargain she'd made with Phillip after Chris left. If he hadn't come back within twenty-four hours, Phillip agreed not to say another word about the divorce. But Chris had come back, and now she was shredding the divorce papers, giving her marriage a second chance.

Phillip separated the stack of papers in half and handed it to each of them, but before he moved, he pressed the on switch. He smiled as the sawing noise began.

Chris looked toward Elizabeth, stepped forward, and held his portion to the mouth of the machine. With a deep grinding sound, it disappeared.

"Guess it's my turn." She didn't mean to say that aloud, blinking twice. If you shred this, this is it; you're making a commitment. What about him? He doesn't keep his commitments. What happens if you need him again and he's—

"Elizabeth."

"Chris." She startled and glanced up and, there within a breath, she knew what she wanted. She wanted him. She moved forward, lowered her hand, and with the slightest touch, the papers were gone.

Elizabeth barely heard Phillip speak, "It's done." Even though she would still need to call her lawyer to stop the divorce proceedings, she was willing to try again. Last night when Chris left, it had devastated her. That's when she knew she wanted him still.

Chris bent over and snapped the shredder to the off position. "What would you like to do?"

Maybe it was time to go outside. "Can we sit by the swings?"

Chris led her by the hand through the back door, passing the taupe patio furniture. Memories were too hard for her. She could still picture her daughter in the red infant swing, giggling. She glanced at Chris from the corner of her eye. "I used to spend hours out here with Katherine."

His hand tightened around hers. "I didn't know."

She nodded and tucked her hair behind her ears, walking over to the slide. "Katherine and I would play under there. I tried to keep her shaded from the sun. Being out here feels like a part of her is still with me."

"I overheard Samantha tell Phillip some of your memories are coming back."

"I guess. They're trying to, anyway. You know the red shoes hanging in the store? I remember Mom giving them to me before she died. I like the color red, so I assume it's my favorite color."

"It is. Come sit in the swing, and I'll push you."

She waved her hand. "I don't know."

"Come on. I won't push you too hard."

"All right." She scooted into the swing. "I might break it."

"Hardly. You're as light as a feather. Wouldn't you agree?" Chris raised his voice to Samantha, who headed toward them.

Sam smiled and placed her hand on the slide. "I came outside just in time to catch this conversation. She is indeed. You've lost quite a bit."

"Look who's talking, sis. You're as slim as they come."

"I can't help it. I'm tall." Sam's laugh caught Elizabeth by surprise. She, too, began and couldn't stop. It was wonderful to laugh. She had almost forgotten what it felt like.

Later that night in bed, Elizabeth flopped to her side, tossing and turning like she had for the past two hours. She should have fallen asleep by now, but her mind kept her awake, thinking of the man downstairs in the extra office.

She stared at the clock. One-thirty. Slipping on a shirt over her pajamas, she tiptoed down the stairs and around the corner. She needed to see for herself that Chris actually stayed. Entering the second door through the hall, Chris lay upon a mattress, his features illuminated by the moon's faint glow.

She knelt alongside him.

He did stay. She smiled.

He'd wrapped himself in a quilt her grandmother had made for her as a graduation present. Hand-stitched sea shells decorated the front and back, set in ocean-blue fabric. Once, not long ago, Chris had compared it to her eyes.

Chris moved out from the quilt, almost facing her, but she didn't flinch. She stayed and watched him sleep. Before she went back to bed, she bent down and gently kissed his cheek.

"How long will you stay?" she whispered.

Chapter Thirteen

Chris stared at his reflection in the bathroom mirror and hesitated, reaching for the razor. If not for Elizabeth's comment, "You're scruffy," and that she almost touched his face but pulled back, he wouldn't have thought to shave. Maybe if he didn't shave, she'd reach for him again. However, if she didn't like the scruff…

"I'm going for a run," Elizabeth called to him.

His whiskers could wait.

He leapt through the bathroom door into the bookstore. "Would you mind some company?"

She wrinkled her brow and shrugged. "If you would like."

"Let me grab my shoes." He hurried to slip on his shoes and joined her at the door. "I'm ready."

"No socks?"

He hadn't done laundry the entire week. "I'm good. Where are we running to?"

"My goal is to run a mile and walk the next, but —"

"I'll run alongside."

Her step quickened.

Sweat beaded and slid down Chris's face as he jogged. Adrenaline rushed through him. He and Elizabeth used to exercise together before she became pregnant with Katherine. Playing tag after their run had been his favorite. He'd chase her for miles, never giving up because the reward was worth the wait. He smiled and wiped his brow. They were inseparable then. He needed to find ways to be with her again.

Elizabeth headed back to the bookstore at a brisk pace.

Something must have been on her mind. She hadn't said a word the entire run, but he'd take care of that. After dinner with Phillip and Samantha, he planned to surprise his bride.

They entered the bookstore, and Elizabeth headed upstairs. He headed to the bathroom. He had an evening to plan, one he hoped would place his wife's ring back where it belonged rather than in his suitcase.

Elizabeth brushed her teeth and readied herself for their night out. She couldn't deny a desire to be near Chris. The run this afternoon felt invigorating, but she'd planned to go at it alone to think. Having Chris alongside made her tense. She felt so confused. Yesterday she wanted to run her hand over his face to feel his whiskers, and today she wanted to be by herself.

"Elizabeth." Her sister stood on the other side of the bedroom door.

She opened the door. "I'm almost finished."

"Phillip and I will be downstairs. You look very nice in that red blouse and faded jeans. I have to warn you, once Chris sees you in that red shirt..." Sam laughed as she closed the bedroom door.

How did she look? She gripped the brush in her hand, unable to meet her reflection.

Her heart fell as she thought of her daughter, a mirror-image of herself. Everyone said so, and it was true, down to the small prick of a birth mark on her lip.

"God, You used to care about me. Are You there? I'm hurting. There are too many reminders of my little girl." How pathetic. She couldn't even stand to look at herself in the mirror. "What has happened to me?" She set the brush down. "I'm trying to pull myself back together, but I can't. I don't have the strength. Heal me. Quench these desires raging like a wildfire before they consume me." She wiped her tears.

"God, can You hear me? I don't want to think about my marriage, but with Chris here, it's all I can think about. How he's failed me, and I him. There are too many obstacles to overcome, God, and I'm the hardest. He wants something I can't give him … he wants a wife. Someone to love him, truly love him, and I can't when I'm…"

She bit her lip and grabbed her purse. She needed to stop her thoughts.

Pulling out her antidepressant she had refilled, Elizabeth unscrewed the lid and popped one into her mouth and swallowed. With a deep breath, she steadied her nerves. *Time to go.*

When she emerged into the living room, Chris's eyes widened. How long had she wanted to feel attractive—to have Chris notice her? But now she didn't want his attention. She wanted his comfort.

"You look beautiful."

"Thank you, Chris." She stared at her hands.

Twenty minutes later, Elizabeth entered the restaurant with Sam and Phillip and scanned the people milling around the hostess stand.

"Do you see Chris? He said he would meet us here." Sam rose on her tiptoes and looked across the dining room floor. "I wonder why he wanted to take separate cars."

"Right this way, please." A man with olive skin led them around other diners. He placed menus on a table beneath an artificial tree. "I will be your server today. My name is Carlos. Do you know what you would like to drink?"

"Excuse me." Elizabeth stood and hurried toward the restroom. Someone caught her eye, and her heart lifted.

Chris rushed into the restaurant. "I'm looking for a party already seated. Roberts is the name." Waiting for the maître d' to search the seating chart, Chris's eyes scouted out Phillip. Instead, he spotted his wife's radiant smile.

He patted his chest pocket. The bulge from her wedding ring set rested against his racing heart. How many ways had he envisioned slipping her ring back on? He'd lost count, but soon, he wouldn't have to imagine any longer.

"Right this way, sir."

Chris followed, eager to discover what lit up his wife's face with that smile, the one he missed so much. He rounded the corner, and his stomach lurched. Elizabeth was talking to Steven. Her smile belonged to him.

"About time you got here. We thought we were going to have to order without you." Samantha lifted her menu.

Samantha couldn't see Elizabeth and Steven behind her, but Phillip's eyes widened. Chris never imagined someone could lure his wife from him, but if that smile indicated anything, Steven could.

Phillip's gaze flicked to Chris before returning to Samantha.

"What are you both looking at?" Samantha twisted in her seat in time to see her sister returning to the table. "She looks beautiful tonight, doesn't she?"

"Are we ready to order?" The waiter pulled the chair out for Elizabeth.

"Thank you." She grinned, unfolded her napkin, and placed it across her lap.

After their orders were taken and the food served, Elizabeth shared her conversation with Steven. Chris praised God for letting him sit through it all without reacting. Anger and fear caught in his throat. If Steven was competing for her affections, Chris would win. Elizabeth was his wife, and he knew her better than anyone else, including the doctor.

"It's nice to get out of the house. Don't you think?" Phillip added to Elizabeth's last comment.

"Yes, indeed." Samantha patted her napkin against her lips. "You barely touched your food, Elizabeth. Are you not hungry?"

"I'm fine."

Wasn't she hungry? She barely ate today. Was it because of Steven? Chris took one final sip of his drink. "If you're finished, Elizabeth, would you like to take a walk?"

"You mean now, since you're getting up?" She chuckled.

"I know these two would like some time alone, since Mom has Juwonya." Chris patted Phillip on his back. "We'll be home later."

"Chris, can I see you a minute?" Phillip rose and guided Chris out of earshot from the girls. "I don't know what you're planning, but don't rush her into anything because of Steven."

"I'd already planned this before I saw Elizabeth with him."

"I'm just telling you, go slow."

"I want to take my wife away from everything and for it to be the way it was, but I can't. She doesn't want to be in the same room with me most of the time. She doesn't smile like that when I'm around. But I will not let Steven take her from me. I'll do anything to stop that from happening."

"She doesn't love him."

"I couldn't tell that, Phillip, and I don't think you can either. The girls are looking this way. We're going. Don't expect us for a while."

"Chris." Phillip placed a strong arm on him. "You better think about what you're doing."

"I did as soon as I saw them together." Chris thrust his arm away and headed for the table.

"Are you ready?" Chris held out his hand. She accepted.

Once outside the restaurant, Chris regretted letting his temper get to him, but he knew what was best, not Phillip. If he needed to help his wife see her need for him, so be it. One way or another, he would.

"Where are we going?"

"Do you remember the last time we ate at this restaurant? We laughed about your butterfly shrimp being tough, and after dinner, we walked across the street to the beach. I thought we could reminisce and walk for a little."

They strolled down the beach hand-in-hand for some time before stepping onto the boardwalk. Chris kissed the back of her hand as they passed several fishermen. "This is nice, being outside under the stars."

"It really is." She gave his fingers a small squeeze.

His heart quickened, and blood pulsated in his ears. Phillip's warning waved a red flag in his mind, but he ignored it and took her toward the edge of the pier where they could be alone. *This is it.* He scanned the ocean. The breeze blew her hair in his direction. *Everything's right, and her barriers are down.* Chris smiled to himself. *This is my wife.*

"I've always liked the mixture of sand and water between my toes. The breeze against my face."

"I know." Chris pressed her fingers to his lips. "And I know other things you like."

She stilled.

Chris lifted his other hand to twist the strands of her hair.

"Chris, don't," she whispered. He caught her breath in a tender kiss.

She stiffened and pressed her hands against his chest before relaxing in his arms. His kiss deepened. The taste he'd once lost, he reclaimed, stifling her words.

"Chris." She moaned while he nuzzled her neck. She stepped back, but he moved with her.

Recapturing her lips, his fingers burned to touch her, to feel her with him again.

Sacrifice.

His hand traveled down her thigh.

"I'm not ready."

He continued. Her body went limp. He kissed her again, but this time, salt mingled. "Don't." She pulled away. "I can't."

What had he done? He wanted her to trust him—to want him, not love him by coercion.

"I'm sorry, Elizabeth. I'm jealous."

"Jealous?" She backed away, looking at him.

"Of Steven. The way you smiled at him tonight. I want to be the only one you love."

"What are you talking about? You're the one who left me for someone else. Remember?"

"I don't want you to see him anymore."

"If it wasn't for him, I'd be dead. You should be grateful." She turned to the rail. "I'm leaving. Give me your keys." She spun and held out her hand, lips pressed into a fine line.

He slipped his hand into his pocket, wanting nothing more than to stop her from going, but he'd been wrong. He had to fix this. But how? "Elizabeth."

A tear fell from her chin. "Now, Chris."

Placing the keys in her palm, he made sure not to touch her. "Where will you go?"

Without a word or glance, Elizabeth left.

Chapter Fourteen

Steven had passed the Osceola Parkway exit five miles back. He'd be in Orlando in a few minutes. Unable to sleep, his anxiousness to get away had driven him to leave tonight instead of in the morning.

His phone rang. He glanced at the number he didn't recognize and answered.

"Hello?"

"Steven, this is Chris. Elizabeth's husband."

Steven's heart dropped to the pit of his stomach. He could barely talk. "Chris? I'm driving. Can you hold on a minute and let me pull over?" Slowing his vehicle onto the shoulder of the road, Steven took a deep breath. The car stopped. "What's happened?"

"Have you seen Elizabeth?"

"No, not since we spoke at the restaurant. What's wrong?"

"I can't find her. I thought—I thought she might be with you."

"She isn't with me." But oh, how he wished she were. He would have done anything to find her and never stopped searching.

"I know you care for her. I could see tonight when the two of you were talking, and I can hear it in your voice now."

His heart raced. Of course he cared for her. He was the one who should've been her husband. "I do."

"I had to know … I had to know if she was with you." Chris hung up.

Steven ended the call in a daze, but with a new understanding of why he felt anxious, of why he felt pressed to leave for Atlanta tonight. God knew he needed protection from himself.

Steven pushed speed dial for his old college friend. "Mike." His voice caught.

"Steven?"

"I'm driving in tonight. Elizabeth is missing. You've got to pray."

"And I will for you, too."

Steven hung up and allowed the tears to flow. Elizabeth was to have been his bride. He would have cherished her with all that was in him, all that he had. But she had chosen to leave.

The hours from Macon north to Atlanta dragged, but he finally pulled into Mike's driveway and parked his black sports car behind Susan's. He'd made it in one soggy piece.

He couldn't remember crying like that since his wife and son had died. And for that very reason, he knew there were some serious questions he needed to ask himself, and one seared his mind: could he still be in love with Elizabeth after all these years?

Right now, he could barely function, much less answer such a question. He hadn't noticed the lighter hue of the sky until he stepped out of the car. He grabbed his bag from the back seat and headed toward the house.

Mike met him at the door. "Hey, buddy, come in."

Steven dragged himself into the house, using all of his strength to stand upright. This wasn't how he'd intended to begin his trip, but at least he had friends who loved him, and whom he could freely love back.

"Set your bag here by the couch and come sit down. Have you heard anything else?"

Steven dropped his bag and sank into the loveseat. "No, and it's killing me. What happens if they don't find her, Mike? What happens —" A lump lodged in his throat.

"God is taking care of her."

"Like He took care of Jess and Steven?" He jumped up and paced, rubbing the back of his neck. "I don't know what's come over me."

"Steven." Mike patted him on the shoulder. "You've never stopped loving Elizabeth. We all knew that, even Jess. But God healed you and your heart. You were able to love again."

Wasn't this the question he'd debated as he drove? Was it clear to everyone but him? "I don't love her, Mike. You have to make a choice to love someone, and I haven't. I will not." The words spilled from his lips, and they were true. He hadn't chosen to love her and wouldn't. She wasn't his.

"All right then, can we say you care for her more than you care for most?"

Mike pushed for something he didn't want to admit. He did care for her and the dreams they had both shared. He still wanted children, a house full. But the Lord wasn't in it. Not yet.

Steven's head throbbed. Lost in indecision, he'd been pacing. "I do care for her more than most."

"I think while you're here for the next several weeks, we need to pray for the direction of your life. Where do you go from here? I believe this is one of the reasons God sent you now instead of before. We just have to remember, His timing is perfect."

"I know the other reason. Pray with me, Mike. I'm anxious. I have to pray for Elizabeth."

"I'll pray with you, too." Susan came down the stairs and kissed Steven's cheek.

Petitioning God on Elizabeth's behalf, Steven's limbs and mind continued to be numb. He needed to lie down. When they finished praying, he carried his bag to one of the spare rooms on the first floor. Sprawled out on the bed, he closed his eyes and prayed one more prayer. "God, let me know she's okay."

Moments later, it seemed, Steven jolted awake at the sound of his name. Mike stood in the doorway with Steven's cell.

"You have a call. It's a hospital in Miami."

Steven jumped from the bed, tangled in his clothes as he grabbed the phone. "Hello?"

"Dr. Moore?"

"Yes."

"We have a woman here. She's blonde, five feet six inches, and with no identification. She was admitted last night when someone found her on the shore. She's been in and out of consciousness for several hours. It looks like she's had head trauma in the past. We've asked her name, but she won't say. Just keeps repeating your name. Luckily your reputation precedes you, Dr. Moore. You weren't hard to find."

Relief and fear mingled in his heart. What had she done? "I believe her name is Elizabeth Roberts, and she lives in Coral Gables. How is she?"

"She's under observation, because we don't know if the lapse in memory is from her previous injury or associated with mixing prescription drugs and alcohol. I believe she'll recover in the next twenty-four hours. Do you know her family?"

Steven choked on the words. They refused to come out.

"Dr. Moore?"

"Yes, I know the family. I'll call them. Do me a favor? Send me her bills directly. Would you be discreet and not mention this? They've been through enough without the extra worry."

"Of course, Dr. Moore. I take it you're still at Mercy Hospital?"

"I am. Oh, one more thing. I would like to call her. What room is she in?"

"308."

"Thank you." He inhaled a deep breath. "You don't know how much I appreciate your call."

"I'm glad we found someone who knew her."

Steven ended the call and dialed. "Chris? It's Steven. Elizabeth has been found."

Chris held the phone with a shaky hand. "Steven."

"I know where Elizabeth is. She's—"

"Tell me..." Fear stole his breath, and he leaned against the wall, gripping the phone tighter. "Please ... Tell me she's all right."

"They think she'll be fine. They admitted her last night after someone found her. She's at Coral Gables Hospital, room 308."

"Will you tell her I love her ... tell her I'm sorry?"

"I'm not with her, Chris. I'm in Atlanta."

Chris wasn't sure he heard Steven correctly. He wasn't with her, this man who came to be Elizabeth's "knight in shining armor"? The one she smiled for?

"They might order a mental health evaluation."

He found his voice. "Why?"

"To find out if she purposely mixed her antidepressant with alcohol."

Was Steven implying...? Elizabeth wouldn't. Things were better. But what would happen if last night had pushed her too far? Chris's stomach soured. He needed to see his wife.

"I have a request to make. If it's all right with you, I would like to call and talk to her tomorrow."

Still processing what Steven told him, Chris said the first thing that came to mind. "Sure."

"Take care of her. You're the only one she needs." Steven hung up.

His words stuck in Chris's mind. *You're the only one.* Hadn't God told him those very words last night when he'd petitioned on his knees? His jealousy was a sin. God made it clear he needed to love his wife as 1 Corinthians said, and from this point on, Chris determined to be obedient to God's word. Weeks ago, God had called him to sacrifice. Now he knew what that meant. Sacrificial love, as Christ had for His church. His bride.

Once at the hospital, he pressed the elevator button several times and waited. Impatient, he took the stairwell instead and exited at the third floor, noting the signs and counting down until he found room 308. "Elizabeth." Her eyes slowly opened. A bandage covered the right side of her forehead. Her hair pressed to the back of the bed.

"Chris."

Her voice was low and rough, as if she found it difficult to speak. "Shhh." He touched his finger against her lips. "I'm sorry. I was jealous and wrong. I pushed you into something I shouldn't have."

Chris brushed her hair from her face. "I had plans for us, but not like that. I had your wedding ring in my pocket. I wanted to put it back on your finger." He rested his head next to hers.

Chris's tears fell onto the pillow. This was his fault. God had been working on his heart, especially last night, but He was going to have to do a miracle. Soon, they'd go back to the apartment, but how would Chris prove himself to his wife? *God, open the door for me. Open her heart.*

"I'm okay…" Elizabeth's raspy voice trailed off.

"Shhh," Chris hushed her softly once again. "Don't talk. Rest." Elizabeth's eyes closed, as if she'd been waiting for permission. He caressed her face until her breathing became steady.

Steven rose early the next morning, anticipating his call to Elizabeth. He stared at the beige walls decked out in memorabilia of his friend's travels to Ecuador. A picture of an active volcano nestled within the mountains caught his attention. If he'd been standing near the stream, the river would have flowed in his direction. He envisioned himself bending down, skimming his hand along the water, cupping the liquid to his lips, quenching the thirst that raged within him. Except the quenching he craved wasn't physical, but one of desire.

Clenching his eyes shut, Steven reined his thoughts in, giving them to the One who could quench those desires. Even as his mind called out for another, he fought for what was right and prayed for strength.

"Hey, buddy." Mike knocked on the door. "Are you up?"

Steven opened the door. "Yeah, I've been up for a while. I'm struggling, Mike. Do I call Elizabeth now and get it over with?"

"Why don't we go work out first, even though it doesn't look like you need it? Actually, it looks like you've been living at the gym."

"I have." Steven followed Mike into the kitchen. The sun shone through the window into his eyes.

"Because of Elizabeth?"

"Mostly."

"I'm listening."

"Not now. I'd rather go to the gym." Steven stood. "I'll change and be out in a few minutes." Steven entered the bedroom and shut the door, throwing on a pair of jogging pants and a t-shirt. The urge to call the hospital grew so intense, he gave in.

"Yes, room 308." The phone buzzed in his ear. No answer. He called once again. "Yes, I need room 308." The phone continued to ring. Fear crawled up his spine.

"Hello?"

"Is this room 308?"

"It is, but the woman who was here has gone home."

"Thank you." He gritted his teeth and hung up, then left the room and called up the stairwell. "Mike! I'll be outside. I'm driving." After snatching his keys and wallet, Steven headed to his car.

Mike hustled out to join him. "Susan held me up. I'm ready."

Steven revved his engine and pulled out of the driveway. Once the tires touched the street, they headed southbound.

Mike gripped the door as they squealed around the corner. "Tell me, Steven, what happened in the short time we were apart? And remember, you're a doctor, not a cop. You can get a ticket."

His friend glared, but Steven wasn't about to talk—not now, not ever. He would take what he felt to his grave. Except for his anger, which he planned to release in the gym.

The car came to a screeching halt in the gym parking lot, and Mike let out a breath. "If you're still like this when we come out, I'm driving." They both got out of the car and entered the double doors. "Go work off some of that frustration. I'll be around."

Several runners circled the track in front of Steven. He would do that later. Right now, he needed to bench press. It would be safer if his arms became tired, too tired to punch anything.

Scooting on fifty-pound weights, then adding two twenty-pound weights on each side, Steven set himself before lifting. One, two, three times, he continued to press up and down. *Lord, Chris said yes, and then he goes and takes her away. Why did You bring her into my life? What good can come out of it? Nothing. Only temptation.*

Steven pressed even harder. *God, scripture says You don't tempt, it's only from man's evil desires he is drawn away and sins. I don't know where I am, but Your word says You will provide a way out. You need to help me. And fast.*

"Steven, look who I found." Mike came toward him with someone who looked familiar.

He lifted the bar back over his head and rested it on the stand. Steven sat up and grabbed the towel next to his leg to wipe his face. "You'll have to forgive me, but—"

"George Summerton. It's nice to see you again."

Chapter Fifteen

Steven racked his brain, but the name meant nothing. "I'm sorry. I can't place where we've meet." He wiped another spot from his face before flipping the towel back on the bar.

"George Summerton. We met right after you guys graduated from Palm Beach Atlantic. I guess you can say we triple dated. It was about the time you got engaged."

"How can I help you?" Steven forced a steady tone as he rose from the weight machine. He didn't want to be reminded of his life with Elizabeth. He had a hard enough time with his own thoughts betraying him.

Mike patted George's shoulder. "George is now on the board of directors at the Children's Hospital in Atlanta."

"Congratulations." If Steven knew where this was going, he could wrap it up and get back to his workout.

George dropped his bag on the ground. "Your name and your research precede you, Steven. We on the board are looking to appoint someone with your knowledge and expertise in the field of apnea and bradycardia."

"George, I'm not interested in anything right now, but thank you." Steven's voice came out harsher than he intended. He should apologize. Instead, he returned to his seat on the bench.

"You know what, George? Do you have plans for tomorrow night?" Mike took a step in front of him.

"I'm free."

"Great. Why don't you come by tomorrow for dinner? You know John and Nicole from the hospital. They can join us, and we can talk then. How does that sound?"

"Fine. Tell Susan I'm looking forward to her cooking. See you then, Steven." George grabbed his bag and strode toward the exit.

Steven stared at the bar above his head, planting his hands firmly around the metal. "Would you like to explain? I don't remember him."

"I think you should listen to what he has to say. Tomorrow will be here soon enough, but in the meantime, get back to work. You're still too grumpy." Mike smiled and wandered off.

Steven did have things he needed to work out, but they weren't at this club. One woman came to mind, one who should have taken his name. He knew what needed to be done, but he didn't know how to let go. Could he be the one to walk away this time?

A few minutes later, he entered the changing room and stood in front of his locker, clicking it open. He slid out his phone and began to dial. "Lydia, it's me. I'm at the gym. Call me. I won't be at church on Sunday."

He slid his finger to end the call. No messages. Elizabeth hadn't called.

Making his way back into the gym, he grabbed water from the courtesy desk. If he didn't push himself hard, he wouldn't sleep. He needed this day to be over.

"Lydia?" Steven paced the bedroom, gripping his cell. He had called to tell her he was in Atlanta, but now she insisted on coming to meet him.

"Will you pick me up at the airport?"

Steven stopped and massaged the back of his neck. Lydia was his friend, but would her coming make things worse? He was confused about his life, Elizabeth, and his uncontrollable emotions, but as he'd prayed last night, peace had seeped through his prayers. Whatever George was about to offer, Steven sensed he needed to accept.

"I'll be there about five tomorrow evening."

"We're having company, though you're more than welcome to come. Just give me a call when your flight lands, and I'll pick you up."

"I will. And thank you, Steven. I'll see you soon." Lydia hung up.

Steven pocketed his phone and exhaled.

"Sounds to me she's coming," Susan said, from the bedroom doorway.

Mike grinned. "Looks like you've got a date."

He sighed. "She is and I don't see the humor." Steven grabbed his bag from the floor and dropped it on the bed, digging out his Bible.

"I know I'm giving you a hard time, but you've been here for less than thirty-six hours, and I've only seen you this way twice—when Jess and Steven passed, and Elizabeth…"

Heat rose up the back of Steven's neck as he met Mike's gaze.

Susan took her husband's hand. "Let's follow Steven's lead and grab our Bibles. I have a feeling it's going to be a late one."

Steven stepped into the kitchen and dropped the phone on the counter. "Lydia isn't answering. I wish she'd let me pick her up from the airport."

Susan slipped on oven mitts, opened the glass door, and pulled out a pan of chicken cordon bleu. "Well, the message said she'd changed her mind and would take a cab once she got here, so don't worry."

Mike leaned against the sink. "You've never been intimate with her?"

"Of course. Sitting on the couch in her office every week, pouring out my heart about Jess and Steven."

"You know what I mean."

Steven resented the question. Yes, he and Lydia were close. He always cared about her safety, but they were friends as far as he was concerned. He'd never guessed her feelings might run deeper until the last several weeks. "No. Not with anyone."

Susan slipped in another pan. "After all these years, you kept your commitment to the Lord."

"I wish I'd have made that commitment before Elizabeth." Steven ran his fingers through his hair. "We were just weeks away from our wedding when her parents died. I only intended to comfort her when one thing led to another. Do you understand how hard this is for me? This whole situation?"

Mike frowned. "Does Lydia know your past with Elizabeth?"

"No. I've never told her anything before Jess except, of course, about how our group met my first year in college. I never mentioned Elizabeth as part of the group. I didn't want to think of her again, the hurt."

Silence settled between them. Mike dropped into the nearest chair and cleared his throat. "I wonder if Samantha or Chris know?"

"I don't think so. Samantha never came around back then. She distanced herself from Elizabeth and her parents. Actually, the first time I met her was at her parents' funeral, but Elizabeth had already left me by then."

"Then it's us, John, and Nicole. Tonight, when George offers you the board position, you should take it. We've all been praying since you first called. I know you've been struggling with God's timing, but I believe it's now. You need to follow wherever He leads."

John's head poked through the doorway. "Hey. You guys must be in a serious conversation not to hear the doorbell. Steven, how are you?" John pounded Steven's back as Nicole reached in for a hug.

"It's nice to be home." Steven gave Nicole a squeeze.

"You know if you moved back..." Mike strolled to Susan's pot and pulled out a noodle.

"Let me have one of those." John laughed as Susan batted his hand. "I heard through the grapevine at work George is going to offer a highly-esteemed doctor a position on the board, plus a heavy salary."

Nicole elbowed her husband in the gut. "Don't mind John. He's in the know at the hospital."

"She's a good woman." John wrapped his arm around his wife's shoulders. "Whoever would have thought a man could have a tendency to gossip? I find myself needing to be reminded of God's word at times."

Steven laughed. He missed his friends, and through everything, they'd always been there for each other ... except for Elizabeth. His smile faded.

"You need a louder doorbell, Mike. I think someone's here." John tucked his wife's dark hair behind her ear. A smile passed between them before he headed for the door.

"I'll get it." Mike slapped John on the shoulder as he rushed past them toward the foyer.

Nicole grabbed several plates, and John handled the silverware as they followed Susan into the dining room. Steven's thoughts trailed them as Nicole and John left the room. Envy pinged within. He forced his thoughts to the back of his mind and focused on his watch. Ten minutes 'til six. Who would be first, George or Lydia? He rounded the corner and found Lydia standing with Mike. Her beauty would turn the eye of many a man. Someday someone would love and cherish her the way she deserved. But it wouldn't be him.

"Hi, Lydia."

"Steven." She stared at him for a moment before she smiled.

Mike cleared his throat. "It's nice to see you again, Lydia. I'll leave you two alone before George arrives."

"Thanks, Mike." Steven's eyes trailed him out of the room, then returned to Lydia. "How was your flight?" He led her into the living room.

"It was good." She sat on the couch and cocked her head to the side, short strands of her hair falling in her face. "I needed to see you."

"I gathered. I planned to pick you up at the airport."

"I know. I needed time to think. There's so much to say, and I'm afraid..."

He watched as indecision flashed across her features. She seemed vulnerable, and in that single moment, he wanted to protect that child-like vulnerability he'd never seen.

"I've fallen in —"

"I'm moving to Atlanta." The words shot out before he could realize he said them. Her brows furrowed. He didn't like knowing this hurt her, but he knew God was leading him to this decision, regardless of what George proposed.

She focused on her folded hands in her lap. "When?"

"Soon. I might have a job offer before the night's out."

"I don't doubt that." She raised her head to face him. "Anyone would be lucky to have you as their ... doctor."

He'd been a fool not to have seen her feelings for him; it shone from her eyes, but he'd never thought of her as more than a friend. He had female friends, Susan and Nicole, but as he sat there, Lydia *was* different.

She rose from the couch. "I should go."

Were those tears?

"I had to come. I had to see you and, now that I have, I can't stay." She headed for the door.

Steven followed her to the foyer. "Lydia."

She released her hand from the door handle and turned to him. Tears slid down her cheeks. "Ever since I met you, Steven, you've held people at arm's length, fearful they might leave you in one way or another. But I've never left." She wiped one of her cheeks. "I'll miss you." Lydia hurried out the door.

Steven fought the urge to run after her. *God* —

"There you are."

Steven spun around. "George." He offered his hand. "I didn't know you were here. Please forgive me."

"Not a problem. Do you have a few minutes so we can talk?"

Steven glanced outside. A cab pulled from the driveway and down the street. "Of course. We can use Mike's office." Steven shut the front door and shuffled into the office, closing the double doors. He sat in the opposite chair from their dinner guest. "What can I do for you?"

"I have a proposal to make. As I mentioned yesterday in the gym, we are looking to appoint someone with exceptional skill and knowledge with premature infants to fill an empty board seat. With your research on premature infants, I thought of you. Think of my surprise when I saw you at the club."

"What are you proposing?"

"Two years at Atlanta Children's working with apnea and bradycardia patients. Giving the hospital your name in any manner we see fit. And, if you accept, you will have a seat on the board as long as you stay."

"This seems a little strange, being offered a position on the board."

"True, but within the two-year period, we've planned a building project to expand the hospital. It will have a multi-million dollar face lift, but it will include a new wing for premature infants. If you decide to stay on with us, you would head up the new wing."

"So what you're saying is my name will bring in the funding needed for this project to move forward."

"That is exactly what I'm saying, and in return, we will present you with a seat on the board, as long as you practice here in Atlanta for a minimum of two years."

Isn't this what I prayed for—direction? A way out of my temptation? Thank you, Lord.

"Now, let's talk salary."

"It's all right. I have all I need to make my decision."

George gave a slight frown. "Are you sure? I think you'd be very pleased."

"I have no family, George. No wife or children to speak of, and everything I have is God's. Anything I need He provides, so money is no consideration."

"So what do you say?"

"When do I start?"

"As soon as you like. Do you have anything tying you to Miami?"

A memory of remarkable aqua eyes popped in his mind, and doubts crept through his heart. "I don't."

"Then the sooner, the better."

Steven nodded, and they shook hands. "Are you ready for dinner? Susan's chicken cordon bleu is wonderful."

"Then lead the way."

Mike met them halfway to the dining room. "I'm glad you two are finished. I was about to interrupt. Steven, you have a phone call. Susan laid it on the guest bed. Come on, George. Let's see if John's already begun to eat without us."

Steven nodded his thanks.

Elizabeth.

Chapter Sixteen

Elizabeth took her cell and a torn slip of paper from Chris's hand. She glanced at Steven's name and number scribbled across. "Are you okay with this?"

"It's fine." He kissed the top of her head and closed the bedroom door behind him.

With a deep breath, she dialed. Her stomach knotted.

"Hello?"

She hesitated, not expecting a woman's voice on the other end. Had she called the correct number? "I'm calling for Dr. Moore?"

"Hold on, okay?"

Elizabeth exhaled, waited, then heard, "Mike, get Steven. My pasta is sticking."

"Is it Elizabeth?" a male voice asked.

"Yes, now hurry. She's waiting."

Elizabeth pressed the phone to her ear. How did they know it was she?

"Hello?"

Her pulse raced. "Steven … it's Elizabeth."

A long pause filled the line.

"Steven? Are you there?" She switched to her other ear, gripping the phone even tighter.

He finally spoke. "How are you?"

"You were worried?" Her words faded as she sat on the bed. "I can hear it in your voice."

"I—you mixed alcohol with an antidepressant. You could have died."

"I didn't mean … It was an accident." She pressed her lips together, and her heart wrenched. "I'm not going to take them any longer. For the first time in months, Steven, I prayed. I couldn't feel God after Katherine's death. I didn't believe He was still there, but He saved me." She swallowed down the lump in her throat. "This seems so natural with you."

"You've lost me, Elizabeth."

"When we talk. When we're together. I can't explain it, but it's like I've known you most of my life." She laughed. "Okay, that sounded like a cheesy pick-up line, but I promise I'm not hitting on you. Never mind."

"Thank you for that. I'm smiling and I feel the same way, so don't worry. Our friendship is intact."

Elizabeth glanced around the room. She wasn't ready for the call to end, there were things she needed to tell him. But how? Her eyes settled on a silver frame of her and Sam as children. "My sister told me you're in Atlanta."

"I'm visiting friends, but actually they're like family … I would have been there. At the hospital."

"I know you would have. I think I'm starting to see things clearly. Well, as clear as I can, anyway. My past is still up in the air. I know my thoughts are jumping all over, but this isn't easy to say."

"Whatever you say will be fine."

"My sister also told me your name was the only one I remembered. I'm sure it hurt Chris. He's trying hard to be the husband I need, but if I'm counting on you, I'm not being fair."

"It has always been my prayer for the two of you to reconcile, and for you to turn back to God and trust Him again."

"Thank you, Steven, for being such a good friend. I wouldn't be here if it wasn't for you."

"It's been God the entire time. He simply used me to help."

"Okay, so now I know you can't take a compliment."

"You're smiling."

Elizabeth didn't realize. "How did you know?"

"I can see it."

"Steven —"

"Will you do me a favor? Will you call me every so often and tell me how you are? I would love to hear children's voices in the background."

Her heart pounded in her ears. Children? "I'm not having any more children."

"How does *Chris* feel?"

"He understands how I feel."

"Isn't part of loving someone considering them in the decision making? If you were my wife ... I would want more children, as many as God would allow. Don't take that away from Chris because you're scared. The greatest gift you can give God right now is your fear. Trust Him wholeheartedly. Give all of yourself to God and to your husband. The past is the past. What matters is the future."

It was as if his words knocked on her heart. "I ... I don't think I can do it again."

"You love children, and remember what scripture says, they are a blessing from God. Let God have His way." He cleared his throat. "I should go, Elizabeth. Please take care of yourself."

"I will. Thank you, Steven ... bye." Elizabeth pushed the end button. She needed to pull herself together before Chris came in and saw her watery eyes. Though she tried to hide it, Steven's words touched her deeply. She'd always wanted children, and if she did what she planned, would another dream die? Was a dream and the unknown worth so much pain?

She didn't know anymore, remembering Chris's words and touch only hours ago.

As long as my heart beats, I will love and care for you. You are all I need, Elizabeth, now and in the future. He'd held her hand against his heart.

She clenched the paper in her palm. *God, thank You for saving me. Help me to trust You and Chris wholeheartedly. Help me to let my husband love me again.* She glanced down at her hand and Steven's number. *Thank you.*

Placing her phone and the torn slip of paper in the end table drawer, she rose. How did Steven know she loved children?

Chris battled the urge to march upstairs into the apartment and listen to Elizabeth's conversation. Instead, he stacked enough books to make a pyramid on a sales table while a few children played in the kids' area. A little boy waddled in front of him across the floor, taking one step forward and two steps back, his mother's watchful eye trained on the child. Oh, how he wanted a boy to carry on the family name.

He stared down at the books in his hand, clenching them tighter.

"Here you go. The last case." Samantha placed another box of books by the end of the table.

"I'll stack these under the table." He set down the books from his hands and watched the mother scoop her toddler into her arms and place a kiss on his cheek.

Chris bent down and yanked out two hands full of books, placing them on top of the others. It wasn't long before he heard Samantha ask, "How's Steven doing?"

Chris glanced up from the floor as his wife came down the stairs. Samantha wasted no time with the questions. Maybe she was as curious as he was.

"Fine." Elizabeth walked toward Samantha.

Her sister measured out three tablespoons of coffee and glanced toward her. "That's it?"

"Basically. He's in Atlanta visiting friends, as you know."

Who cares! Chris forced his mouth shut.

"Maybe God led him there." Samantha puffed a loose strand of hair out of her eyes.

Elizabeth exhaled. "In a way, I believe that."

Chris couldn't keep quiet as he stood and moved toward her. "Why?"

Her face softened. A smile lifted her lips as he met her. She cupped his cheek. "For you."

The warmth of her touch filled him, but those two small words held a greater significance and made his mind soar. They meant everything. The urge to hold her stilled him. He wouldn't make the same mistake twice.

Her eyes searched his, but in that intimate moment, something happened. The intensity of her focus pulled away. She turned and headed for the office.

Samantha chuckled. "She almost kissed you. To me, it looked like she thought about it too much."

Chris wished that was true, but he knew better. He shook his head. "I don't think so. There's something else." The bell above the door rang, indicating someone had entered.

"You're back." Samantha put her writing tablet down and met Phillip on the other side of the counter. "Hi." She kissed him. "Juwonya is settled?"

"Yes." He returned her kiss, and lingered.

Chris glanced toward the office. Did he almost receive a kiss much like the one Phillip did? "I think I'm going to go for a drive."

"Wait." Phillip called out. "You can't. Elizabeth will need you to help run the store."

"Why? You both are here."

"We haven't mentioned this because we weren't sure if we needed to change our plans, but several months ago, we made a reservation to stay on the beachfront for a few days. Mom's watching Juwonya. That leaves you and Elizabeth to take care of the bookstore, starting in thirty minutes." Phillip looked at his watch. "Or fourteen to be exact."

Near the register, Samantha slid the yellow pad toward Chris. "Here are a few things that need to get done."

"Elizabeth doesn't know yet, does she?" How would she take the news of the two of them working alone?

Samantha shook her head. "Nope."

"What don't I know?" Elizabeth emerged from the office with receipts in her hands.

"That we're leaving for a few days. The store is all yours until we get back."

"Then maybe Mrs. Wait-until-the-last-minute can tell me what these receipts are for. I can't pay the bills until these are logged into the computer."

"Oh, I placed the list of items I bought at the store on the yellow note pad Chris has. You two can share." She gave them a wink.

Chris placed a gentle hand on his wife's back. "Can you believe they're taking off for a few days and didn't plan to tell us?"

Phillip laughed. "If you need us, we're staying at the beach. The same spot where I found your sister the day I came back from Africa. Tomorrow is our anniversary."

"Oh … Congratulations." Elizabeth hugged Phillip, then her sister, crinkling the papers in her palms. "I didn't know. I hope you both have a wonderful time."

"Thank you, Lizzy. I knew you would be happy for us. We should go. I don't want to miss walking along the shore tonight."

"All right, my love." Phillip placed his palm on the small of her back. "If you need us —"

"We'll be fine." Chris flicked his hand.

As the door closed, Elizabeth went back into the office.

An hour later, the door opened and Chris popped into the office. "I need to know if I've done something, Elizabeth. Earlier I thought —"

She narrowed her eyes at the computer screen, trying to forget what she'd almost done. She'd almost kissed him. But her thoughts had jumped to Steven at that precise moment. "Can you hand me our bank file?" The words rushed passed Elizabeth's lips. She wasn't about to discuss Steven with Chris. He wouldn't understand. Besides, she didn't know why Steven had popped into her mind when she held Chris's cheek. She'd never touched Steven this way. The only time it might have happened was when she had asked him to comfort her, but he had drawn back and left a few moments later.

The cabinet behind her opened, then slammed shut. Chris placed the file on the desk next to her. "Let's go somewhere. Tomorrow is Sunday. We're closed."

She looked up and met his eyes then. "Where?"

"I don't know. Fishing."

She laughed and spun around to him. "You're kidding, right? You know what happened the last time we went fishing."

"I take it you're talking about what happened to your line. I can't help it if you can't fish."

"Now that's not fair." She leaned back in her chair. "You're hitting below the belt. I'm not used to using a bait casting reel."

"You're not used to using any kind of reel." Chris laughed. "That's what we should do. Take a road trip to Lake Okeechobee and fish. Dad's got his boat. What do you say? How about tomorrow?"

"Do I need to remind you we have a store to —?"

"Or we can boat ride?" His eyes sparkled.

Her heart raced a bit faster. He was strikingly hand-some. "Sure, sounds fun." She sat up and swung her chair, facing the computer. She caught his smile in the reflection of the screen.

"Great."

Elizabeth tried to act as if something on the desk had her attention, but she couldn't pry her eyes from Chris as he stood behind her. What was he thinking? Why didn't he leave when she spun back around? She almost asked when he turned and walked away.

Chapter Seventeen

Elizabeth had packed everything for their excursion last night after dinner while Chris made their lunch. Now as they readied to leave, she still couldn't get over him contentedly doing something he'd always considered a chore. She glanced over at him stuffing food in his black backpack.

"Did you call your parents to tell them we are coming?"

"No. I didn't want them to feel they needed to be there since we're not staying." He zipped the bag and slung it over his shoulder. "I've got everything we'll need in here, including our food. I'll load this in the car if you're ready."

She grabbed the small cooler. "I am."

"Oh, do you want a blanket to sit on for a picnic? That is, if we find an alligator-free zone."

"We have those in Florida?" She chuckled.

"Let me take that." He took the cooler, loaded everything in the car, and came back in. "We're ready to go except for the blanket."

"I've got it right here." She snatched it from the couch. "Let's go."

They locked up the apartment, got into the car, and headed for Linda and Henry's.

When they arrived at Chris's parents' home, he unlocked the front door and held it open for her. Stone white and creamy yellows covered the walls. Brown furnishings accented the space. A bamboo fan spun above her head. Elizabeth sniffed the air; no paint fumes. Hadn't she just been here for their niece's birthday party a month ago? Even this couch wasn't here then. Her body tensed when Linda drew near with wide eyes.

"Elizabeth. I didn't know you were coming." Linda grabbed her in an embrace.

Chris closed the door. "I know. I didn't call. Elizabeth and I thought we'd go for the day on the boat."

"Oh, let me tell your father before he heads out for a deacons' meeting. He can help you. Which vehicle do you want?"

"My truck will be fine."

His mother's brows arched. "Son, did you forget?"

A puzzled expression crossed his features for a moment then disappeared. "Whatever you don't mind me taking for the day."

"I can prepare something for lunch if you like."

"I made sandwiches, but thank you. I'll find Dad."

Elizabeth teetered between dashing out of the house and hugging her mother-in-law again. Linda had taken the place of her own deceased mother before she and Chris began dating. She hadn't realized how much she missed her. Chris had told her how Linda fought with the doctor to see Katherine after she was born, while she herself lay unconscious in the hospital bed. The confrontation must have been with Steven. She smiled at the headstrong woman who stood in front of her. Elizabeth would like to have seen that battle live.

She reached over and took hold of the stout woman once more. "I've missed you, Linda."

"I've missed you, my daughter." Linda sniffled. "What does this mean, your being here with Chris?"

"We are trying. I called the lawyer to stop the divorce proceedings. Sam said you and Henry came to the hospital. Thank you."

"I love you. I've never stopped loving you. I tried to stay out of your marriage, and I prayed for you and my son to find your way back to each other. For God to heal you both."

"We have a long road ahead."

Chris opened the door and stuck his head in. "You ready, Elizabeth? Dad said Timothy took the boat out yesterday, so it's still hitched."

Linda rocked on her heels, lips curled in a smile. "Have fun."

"We will." Chris blushed as he placed his hand in the arch of Elizabeth's back. She settled in Henry's 4x4 truck. Chris scooted in, started the engine, and checked the mirrors. "I think we've got everything, and the spare."

"Do you think we'll need it?"

"It's about a two-hour drive, so better to bring it along in case." He pulled out of the drive. With a bounce from the front of the trailer and then the back, they were on their way.

"I've never noticed until now, but your family's tastes are eclectic. Your parents have a five-bedroom, four-bath home, yet your dad drives an older truck and leaves the new SUV in the driveway for anyone who needs a vehicle. Phillip is a missionary who could have gone pro golfing. Timothy is a lawyer by day, and at night, he and Sarah run a shelter for the homeless. Yes, I'd say very eclectic."

"What are we?" Chris glanced at her.

"Together."

"Chris! Hurry!" Elizabeth's sunglasses disappeared into the dark murky water.

On the pier several yards away, Chris laughed. "What happened? You're supposed to be holding down the fort."

"Not a moving fort. A boat drove by, and waves rocked me around. I couldn't hold onto the dock. My sunglasses fell into the water. And it's not funny." She threw her hands on her hips. "Those were my favorite pair!" She couldn't resist the humor of the moment. Plopping her bottom onto the boat seat, she laughed. "How am I supposed to get the boat back to you?"

"Maybe you should use the trolling motor."

Okay, she could do this. She rose and stood over the machine. Gently sliding the trolling motor into the water, she found the switch and planted her foot onto the lever and leaned it forward to head toward the dock. The boat lurched further toward the lake. "This isn't working."

"Play with it. Watch the direction." He sat on the dock, legs hanging just above the water.

"You're sitting. Thanks for the vote of confidence." *I'll show him.* Slowly she rolled her foot until the boat changed direction and headed for the dock.

Christ stood up. "You're doing it. Just a little closer, and I'll jump in."

She eased her foot off the pedal and headed toward the seats in the back when Chris jumped in. His weight tipped the boat to one side, throwing her off balance.

His arms snagged her from the boat's edge, pulling her against his chest.

Words escaped her. Their lips inches apart, she lost her breath.

"I have you."

"Yes, you do." She giggled and pulled back from him, watching her steps as she secured her footing. "I don't know if I should kiss you and get it over with or wait until later."

Chris jerked his chin up. "Well then, I'm anxious to find out what you decide."

"I'll let you know." She smirked and planted herself in one of the seats.

He leaned back into the driver's chair, turned the key, and cranked the engine. "Are you ready?"

She nodded with a smile. Within moments they were racing across the lake, spraying water, and leaving waves in their wake. Birds flew underneath a crystal blue sky. Chris would call it a blue-bird day with not a cloud for miles, but she'd call it beautiful.

Elizabeth enjoyed the wind rushing past her ears, flipping her hair behind her, but when the wind died down as the boat slowed, she twisted in his direction. "Where are we?"

"I have to check my map, but this looks like a great place to fish. I brought two rods. Would you like to give it a shot?"

"I'm game if you don't mind cutting out a nest again." She rose from the seat.

"Optimism." He leaned in and kissed her forehead.

She held his arm. "Don't move yet. Let me enjoy this moment." She felt his body hesitate, then with soft kisses, his lips traced her hair line. "You've left me breathless."

"I'm the one who's having difficulty breathing. I better get those rods." He took a few steps to the rod compartment and yanked them out. Chris shot her a smile before trolling over to the side of the lake in front of a cove opening.

"All right, stand over here." He pointed.

She started to hand him the fishing pole. "Do you want to cast it for me?"

"Why don't you try first?" He showed her how to hold the rod with her finger on the reel and line as she cast.

"Are you ready?"

Chris laughed. "You're not planning to toss me overboard?"

"No, but I suggest you stand back so I don't hook you."

Chris moved as she raised the tip of the rod. In one fine motion, she flung the bait and rod forward. It left her hand. She hurried over the edge of the boat as the fishing pole sank into the lake. A movement drew her eyes from the spot where the rod fell in, and she turned to see Chris splash into the water beside her.

"Chris!" He disappeared under the water. Did he hit his head? He wasn't wearing a life jacket. Alligators. Without another thought, she jumped in. "Chris!" She dove under.

"Elizabeth!" Her name sounded muffled through the water.

She popped up and tried to blink the murky moisture from her eyes. "Chris, are you okay? What happened? Did you bump your head?" She swam to him and searched for blood.

"No. I jumped in for the rod. That combo is worth three hundred dollars. I couldn't find it."

"That is the dumbest thing I've ever heard." She smacked her hand on the water's surface and swam back to the boat. "To think, I jumped into alligator-infested waters."

A smile lit his face. "You know what that means, don't you?" He helped her back into the boat, climbing up behind her, and shook his hair.

"What? I'm stupid?"

He tapped her chin. "That you love me. You're willing to risk your life for me."

He took off his shirt, socks, and shoes and laid them in front of the boat. "You could do the same." He grinned. "I'll get you the blanket."

"Um … I'm fine." Her eyes refused to turn from the man in front of her. Heat crawled up her neck when Chris met her gaze. Did he see her desire? Her heart pounded as she turned toward the water. She needed to focus on something else, but her thoughts went back to her husband standing inches away.

"Are you ready to eat?"

"Sure." When she turned back around, she forced herself to meet his gaze. She almost laughed at herself, at how hard she was trying not to notice her own husband.

Lord, I'm attracted to him. Help me to trust, because You know my heart.

"Here you go." Chris handed her a sandwich.

The heat returned to her cheeks. "Thank you."

They were about five minutes from Mom's, but Chris didn't want this day to end. Exhaustion traveled through his body, but to have his wife all to himself, he'd turn right back around and do it all over again. Now she leaned against his shoulder, arm cuddled in his lap. How wonderful it would feel to have her hold him again, to feel her body next to his as they slept.

He parked the pickup and boat trailer in front of the house, then moved his arm and brought her into his chest. "Elizabeth, sweetheart, we're here."

"I didn't mean to fall asleep on you." Her words sounded groggy.

"I didn't mind."

She sat upright and pulled the blanket off her lap. "I need to go inside. Do you think the door is unlocked?"

"I'll walk you up." He got out of the truck and helped her scoot out on his side, offering his hands. She gave a tired smile before tucking her arms against his chest as they heavy-stepped up the steep yard. "I'll be in as soon as I put the boat away."

She nodded. Juwonya's laughter met them as he opened the door.

Chris hurried back to the car and put everything the way he had found it before heading back inside. "Hey, Mom. Where's Elizabeth?" He flipped the water on in the kitchen and washed his hands.

"She's in the bathroom. I think I should have waited until you came in, but with what she said to me earlier —"

"What did she say to you earlier?"

"She stopped the divorce, and you both were working on your marriage. I thought telling her about the cruise —"

Chris lifted his hand. "Wait. What are you talking about?"

"The cruise your dad and I gave you boys for Christmas. It's in two weeks."

Chris lumbered over the table and plopped down. "The cruise. I forgot." He looked up at his mother. "She didn't take it well?"

"She didn't say anything. Just walked off to the bathroom."

Elizabeth reappeared, face solemn. "I'm ready to go."

Chris rose from the table and kissed the top of his mother's head. "I'll call you tomorrow."

They drove to the bookstore in silence. Maybe Elizabeth was tired? Maybe it was the cruise? He wanted to ask but kept his questions to himself, hoping for an opportunity later. When they arrived at the bookstore, she slipped upstairs to her apartment without a word.

Chapter Eighteen

Morning sunlight illumined the office where Elizabeth sought privacy. She pressed the phone against her ear and ground her teeth. "I've tried for two days now. Yes, I've already spoken with the nurse, and she sent me to you. I'm scheduled for a tubal ligation in three weeks, but I won't be able to make that appointment. I hoped you had something earlier. Tomorrow or next week even."

"I'll have to call you back, Mrs. Roberts. The doctor is out of the office, and I would need to check with her before I changed her appointments. Is this the number where I can reach you?"

"Yes. I'll have my phone with me." Elizabeth pressed the end call button. Her hand began to shake. *I'm doing the right thing.* Heaviness weighed on her as she slumped in the office chair.

She'd made it plain to Chris she wasn't having any more children, and he'd accepted the idea and chosen her anyway. So why did she feel the need to hide her actions and avoid him? But she had to do this, especially the way she had responded to him when they had gone fishing. She couldn't imagine them being intimate anytime soon, but she couldn't take any chances she'd become pregnant.

Sam's voice rang out through the bookstore. "We're back."

Elizabeth stepped from the office, stomach in knots. "Hey, did you have a nice time?"

Sam cuddled Juwonya in her arms, pressing a kiss on her cheek before setting her down.

"A wonderful time. Where did Chris go?"

Elizabeth scanned the bookstore. "Maybe still sleeping? We don't open for another hour."

"No, the car's gone."

How long had he been gone? "I haven't seen him since last night before I went to bed." Chris had been praying when she opened the door from the loft. She'd planned to do some work, but instead, she closed the door and went to bed.

Sam sighed. "Phillip and I hoped this time alone would have done you both some good. I guess we were wrong."

At that moment, Chris strode in. "It's nice to know you two are back."

Elizabeth pried her gaze from them. Knowing what she wanted to do, was going to do, and how it would affect Chris brought such conflicting feelings. She headed back to the office. She couldn't take the chance of having another child.

"Wait, Elizabeth. Phillip and I need to talk with you and Chris about something. Come sit on the couch."

Elizabeth sat on the couch, and Chris joined her, resting his hands in his lap.

Phillip cleared his throat and looked toward her sister. "Samantha and I made a few decisions while we were away and wanted to talk with you. We've decided to tear out the apartment and turn it into a Christian section for the bookstore."

Elizabeth gaped at him. Was he kidding? She was living there. "That's going to be a little difficult with me living there."

Sam looked between her and Chris. "But you still have the house."

Chris dipped his head. "She doesn't know. I never told her. I planned to tell her while you were away, but … I didn't have the chance."

"What are you talking about?" Now she glanced between them. "What house?"

Chris met her gaze. "Our house."

Elizabeth's thoughts spun. They had no house. "But I thought you sold it."

"I almost did. I realized it was all I had of you, and I wasn't willing to let it go. I'd hoped to take you back to the house while they were gone. And like when I asked you to marry me, I wanted to give you your home. Our home." Chris rose, put his hand in his pocket, and pulled out her wedding band and engagement ring. He set it on the table.

"I know it wouldn't have been like last time, but I hoped you would accept being my wife again and come home."

Tears filled her eyes. "Chris, I—" She jumped up and walked to the patio garden in front of the store.

"Elizabeth." He followed. "Talk to me. Please. What's going on?"

She spun around. "I want you, Chris. I can't remember a time I wanted you more than right now. To love me, to hold me, to be by my side every day of our lives, but I can't."

"Why not? I want to be everything you need and more. Let me be your husband again."

Her eyes closed, fighting against what she wanted when his hand rested along her cheek.

"Let me love you?"

With the only resolve she had left, she took a step back. "I can't." She turned from the moisture glittering in his eyes.

He reached for her arm, but pulled back. "Let me show you the house. You can do whatever you want with it. It's yours. But come see it with me?"

"Chris —"

"Go with me. Let me show you." He extended his hand.

Elizabeth straightened her hunched shoulders when they drove up to the main gate, steeling herself against what she knew was coming.

Chris rolled down the window. "Hi, Frank."

"Mr. Roberts." The security guard looked into the vehicle. "Oh, Mrs. Roberts, it's so good to see you."

"Thank you. It's good to see you, too. How's the family?"

"Doing well. Thank you for asking. You both have a wonderful day." He stepped back and nodded them through.

Chris drove slowly around the corner to their home.

Her ivy had grown considerably since she'd left. When Chris had given her the vine, he'd said it symbolized his love. No matter what they went through, they would weather the storm, and no matter what they encountered, their love would keep them strong and growing. The ivy had taken over the entire left part of the house, covering the brown brick and the top of the garage.

"Let's go inside." He wiped her cheek with his hand before getting out to open her door.

She avoided looking at him as they walked toward the house, knowing she'd come undone if she saw the tenderness in his eyes. "You put lights along the walkway."

"I wanted to make sure you could see at night."

Chris unlocked the door and held it open. She pressed her lips together. "I don't know if I can do this. Katherine…"

"Then we'll do it together." He held out his hand again. This time she grabbed onto it like a lifeline. His other arm wrapped around her back in support as they walked inside. She gasped.

Topiaries and a high-vaulted ceiling met them in the foyer. A few steps farther in, her mahogany furniture showcased the living area with newly added burgundy couches, giving color to the freshly painted taupe walls. She couldn't believe the changes. "Chris, the house looks beautiful."

"Let me show you the kitchen." Upon entering, he ran his hand over the new counter tops. "Do you like them? You can cut on these and not have to worry."

"I do." She drew her fingers across the smooth surface. "What is this?"

"Granite. I know how you like to cook —"

She glanced at the stove and dishwasher. "You bought new appliances. I like the black and stainless together."

"I picked everything out for you."

It seemed strange to be in the house, new, beautiful, and yet the memories of the last months so vivid. She recalled how many times he mentioned their lack of finances. "How could you afford all this? You reminded me more times than I can remember that we weren't making it."

"Come sit with me in the family room. I'll tell you."

By the stairwell, Elizabeth caught a glimpse of the shelf she'd placed along the wall. She and Katherine would take pictures every month. "Chris, where did that picture of Katherine go?"

"The one where you're wearing a turquoise blouse? I took it with me to Phillip's."

He was confusing her. This wasn't like him. "Why are you doing this? The changes? And how did you have the money?"

"God's been telling me to sacrifice, Elizabeth. I thought I understood, but later it hit me. God wants me to sacrifice like Christ did for His church. Jesus gave up everything, from leaving heaven to dying, so we could understand what true love really means. I still have a long way to go, but I finally understand. I would give up everything for you."

"But what does that have to do with this house?"

"I sold my truck and the gold coins my grandparents gave to me to fix up the house. I want us to live here again."

Chris got down on one knee and took her rings from his pocket. "Elizabeth, please be my wife again. Live with me in this house. Our home."

Her husband's hopeful eyes melted her heart. *God, please. Let me forgive him for the past, and let him forgive me for the future.* "Your mother reminded me about the cruise. I had a doctor's appointment during that time, so I called to reschedule for this week. I won't have any more children, Chris." She almost couldn't say his name. How many times could she crush him in one day? She jumped to her feet and headed out the door.

Chris dashed after her. "I want you! Don't you understand? I want us!"

His words reached her ears like a vise that squeezed and gripped her heart. She stopped cold.

He stood before her, his breath ragged. "I'd give up everything, even children. Isn't that what love is about? Not my way, but what God calls us to do. Sacrifice. If I have nothing left in this world but His love and yours, I would be the richest man."

Chris's eyes brimmed with moisture as he held his arms out to her. There on the sidewalk in front of their home, she gave up her fears and followed her heart, straight into her husband's arms. "I will."

With the softest of touches, he lifted her chin, lowered his mouth to hers, and kissed her ever so slightly. "I love you, Mrs. Roberts."

She looked up into his eyes. "My heart has been aching for you. To be near you. To let you love me. I'm so afraid."

"Then we'll go slow, but first things first." Chris pulled the rings out of his pocket and held them out. Her rings nestled in the palm of his hand. "May I?"

She bit her lip and nodded. He slid her wedding bands on her finger. She pressed her palm to her chest, meeting his gaze. "Oh, Chris."

"I hope you won't mind if I do this." Chris swept her up into his arms and carried her over the threshold. "We're home."

"I expected a better greeting than that." She threw her arms around his neck and kissed him passionately, drinking him in. From this point on, she intended to absorb every touch, taste, and breath, praying they would never take each other for granted again. Feasting on another kiss, she giggled. "Maybe you should put me down."

"I think you're right. I'm feeling a bit weak." He grinned and set her on her feet. "Would you like to see the rest of the house?"

Elizabeth glanced at the stairs. "I don't think I'm ready."

"Are you okay with moving back in?"

She turned back to him and touched his face. "I want to be here with you, in our home, together, but would you mind if we move our bedroom downstairs?"

"Of course." He kissed her hand. "It might take me a week or two to move the house around."

"Then we can officially move back in after our cruise."

"Yeah, I guess you're right." Chris leaned into her. "How about one more of those kisses before we head to Phillip's?" He kissed the edge of her chin, then her cheek.

"I'll make you a counter offer." She closed her eyes, fighting to keep her mind on track. "How about you hold off now and wait until later?"

He paused. "I'm not sure. I kinda like this spot right here." He kissed her lips, then stepped back. "What happens if something changes your mind and I miss out?"

"After I was released from the hospital, you held me every night. Will you stay with me again?"

"I'd be honored."

Chris's heart swelled as they drove to Phillip's house. Several times Elizabeth wiggled her fingers and held her rings up to the sunlight. He couldn't wait to tell his brother and sister-in-law the news. Once they arrived, Chris ran to Elizabeth's side and helped her out, kissing her hand.

When the door opened, Chris paused at Phillip's grave expression. "Come in."

Samantha met them in the foyer and frowned at her sister. "Did you tell him?"

Chris didn't know what was about to happen, but he placed a protective arm around Elizabeth's waist. She needed to know he loved her and he'd stand by her no matter what.

"What are you talking about?" Elizabeth looked up at him then back at her sister.

"You left your phone on the register counter. I wish I'd never answered it. The doctor called about a cancellation. Your tubal ligation is set for the day after tomorrow. You'll need to be there at six in the morning."

Elizabeth stiffened.

Chris's arm slipped from her waist.

Chapter Nineteen

Chris lay in bed, staring at the popcorn ceiling in the apartment. He wrestled with what he'd told Elizabeth the day before. He'd told her the truth. He desired her more than anything. Yet he still wanted a child. When he'd walked into Katherine's room for the first time in months, the emptiness had doubled him over. Tears stung his eyes, regret punched him in the stomach. He hadn't been there for Katherine or his wife. If he could do things over again, he'd be there loving them, cherishing them as precious gifts, as blessings from God. But if Elizabeth had this operation, he would never again know the joy of another child. His child. Their child.

Elizabeth rolled over in her sleep. He glanced at the door, got up, and left the bedroom, pulling the door closed. Time to show his wife he loved her.

After cooking, the smell of bacon saturated the air as he entered the bedroom and scanned the empty bed. Elizabeth peered out the window, arms wrapped around her middle. Did she worry about her appointment tomorrow? Did she mind him sleeping in her bed? Did she want him there? Chris shook his thoughts. If he didn't stop giving way to his doubts, he couldn't be the husband his wife needed. He walked over to the window and encircled his wife's stomach with his arms.

"How are you this morning?"

"I don't know." Her voice trembled.

"Do you want me to leave?"

Elizabeth swung around. "No. Don't leave." Her watery eyes pleaded. He would never leave her. Never again.

"I won't. I was planning to go to the house today with Phillip and Timothy, but we can wait. Phillip's here now."

She lifted her chin. "In that case, you have to go." A trembling smile appeared on her lips. "I'm ready to go home."

Chris lifted her chin a bit more with his finger and pressed a kiss on her lips. "Not much longer now."

"I can't wait."

Chris grinned. "Then how about we get dressed and have breakfast? The sooner I get over to the house, the sooner we can go home."

"I'd like that." She reached up and planted a kiss on his cheek. "I'll be out in a few minutes."

He nodded. The bathroom door closed, and he got dressed and headed out to the living room.

Phillip sat at the table. "I called Timothy. He said he would meet us there, but Sarah and the kids are coming."

"Thank you for calling them."

"I thought Elizabeth could use some company." At that moment, she walked out of the bedroom, running her fingers through the tips of her hair. "You might want to grab your dance shoes. Sarah is on her way with Lindsey."

Elizabeth stopped, looked at her clothes, and a spark lit her eyes. Lindsey, his five-year-old niece, always brought out the little girl in Elizabeth. She'd dance, sing, and play dress-up. Whatever Lindsey wanted, Lindsey got, if Elizabeth had anything to say about it. Maybe, just maybe, she was the one who could change his wife's heart.

"Um … Chris, will you help me with something?" She turned around and almost pranced into the room.

Chris shot his brother a smirk. "I like the way you think."

"God gave me the idea this morning." He chuckled.

Chris hurried after her. "What do you need help with?"

"What dress should I wear? Which one do you like best?" She swayed side to side with a plum-colored dress, then ran into the closet and exited with a teal gown. Now where had he seen that dress before? She twirled around.

"Which one?" She bounced, her lips lifting into a perfect smile.

Perfect for kissing. He couldn't help his thoughts and had to do something about it. "They're both nice. I don't think Lindsey would care."

"Thanks. Not exactly what I was going for." She dashed into the bathroom.

Wait a minute. He wanted a kiss, and besides, what did he say wrong? Lindsey wouldn't care what she wore.

"Chris, they're here," Phillip hollered. "I'm ready to go whenever you are."

"Elizabeth, they're here, so I'm getting ready to go."

"Wait, don't leave yet." She swung the door open. "I need you to zip me up." She spun around, cocking her head to the side. Her hair hung over her shoulder.

Chris's eyes drank in the delicate curve of his wife's back. Grasping the zipper, he pulled it closed, but paused at the three scars raked across her shoulder. *Where did those come from?* He almost asked as he moved her hair for a better view, but then it came to him: her attacker. Heat rose up his neck. He draped her hair back over her shoulder, hiding the past. A past he had caused.

"What is it?" Her hand rested along his cheek.

He couldn't bring himself to look at her. "I should go, Elizabeth."

Her hand slipped away. "Do you know what time you'll be back?"

"I don't." He kissed the top of her head, fighting his anger. "If I'm not back before you go to bed, don't wait up." He fled the room. The sooner their house was ready, the sooner their lives and marriage could heal, along with the scars.

"If I'm not back before you go to bed, don't wait up." Elizabeth swallowed hard. How many times had Chris spoken those words to her and never come home? How many times had she pretended to be asleep when he slithered into bed, minutes before the alarm went off? Why hadn't she seen the signs before? Maybe if she had confronted him. Her stomach rebelled.

"Auntie, I'm here." Lindsey pounded on the bedroom door. "Can I come in? I want to show you the dress Mommy got me. It's your favorite color. Do you remember what color that is, because Mommy says —?"

"Hey, Elizabeth, she'll wait out here."

"I'll be out in a minute, Sweetie." Elizabeth ran her hands down her dress, pressing out a few wrinkles. She had picked this dress for Chris. She'd worn it after the wedding for their honeymoon. It had pleased Chris then; she'd seen it in his expression in old wedding photos, but not today. He didn't seem to notice her or want her.

Taking a deep breath, she gathered her thoughts. God, my emotions are on a rollercoaster. Please take them before I lose myself in what my flesh wants. It's craving to get away. God … I'm scared about tomorrow and about Chris … Amen. Taking another breath, she opened the door.

"Oh, Mommy, look!" Lindsey ran up to Elizabeth and grabbed her hands and pulled her around in circles. "I want to be a princess like you. Can I? Can I please?"

Taken aback, Elizabeth laughed at her excitement. "I'm not a princess, Lindsey. You're my princess." She picked her up and hugged her.

"Let Mommy do your hair, then she can do mine. We both can be princesses." Lindsey swung her head around.

"Will you, Mommy? Will you help Auntie and me be princesses?"

"I sure will, sweet pea. Then you can dance at the great ball." Sarah curtsied. "At your service."

Elizabeth squeezed Lindsey in her arms and twirled with her. She'd put this dress on for Chris, but it was Lindsey who made her feel not only beautiful, but like a princess.

Dancing at the princess ball with Lindsey yesterday had brought Elizabeth such a sense of peace. Now, as she sneaked out of her apartment, doubts nipped at her. She sat in her car, not knowing what to do. Would having another child give her the same joy and love? Was the death of a child worth the risk?

She caught a glimpse of Chris hurrying to the car. He opened her door, breathless. "Elizabeth. You weren't going to let me know you were leaving? You weren't going to tell me goodbye?"

"If I did, you'd only try to stop me. You want another child, and it's ripping your heart out. I know you've tried to hide it."

Chris's knees hit the driveway. "I'm here for you no matter what, but I want you to be honest with me. Tell me, what is it you want? If you are a hundred percent sure you don't want another child, then so be it. But if you have any doubts, any doubts at all, don't do this. Give us a chance."

Did she really want to do this? "I need to go."

"Okay." Chris rocked on his heels, hands on his knees. "I want you to know something else. When you come back, I'll be waiting with open arms, no matter what you decide. I love you, and nothing you could ever do will change that." He stood, leaned into the car, kissed her brow, and walked back into the bookstore.

By the time Elizabeth pulled up to the hospital, nausea sickened her. She looked to her watch. Ten minutes before six. She was early. She got out of the car and slammed the door shut. She needed to hurry before she changed her mind. They'd prep her and hopefully put her under quickly.

A rush of air blew her hair as she entered the hospital. She ran her hands through a few strands, tucking them behind her ear while eerie silence accompanied her down the white hallways. Her pulse pounded against her chest and skull, deafening her as several nurses rushed from a corridor. A moment later, she found herself in the maternity ward. Her steps slowed as she rounded the corner, her gaze landing on a tiny newborn infant. Small fingers thrashed above a crib as lungs filled with air before pushing out the sweetest of cries.

Elizabeth pressed her hands against the glass.

Chapter Twenty

Steven returned to Florida yesterday, and now he had little left to do but pack up his office before returning to Atlanta. His feet seem to drag as he walked down the hospital corridor. How he'd miss this place. How he'd miss … *Elizabeth?* She stood staring at his nameplate on the door. "Elizabeth?" He grazed her elbow.

She spun around. "Hi, Steven. I wasn't sure if I should knock or bother you at all."

The more time they spent together, the more "Lizzyisms" Steven remembered. Like the way she twisted her hands. "Come in and tell me what brings you by." He opened the door and ushered her in. "Please, sit." He tossed his keys on the desk, then leaned against the edge.

She remained standing. "Would you like to go to lunch?"

"It's just past six in the morning."

"So, breakfast then?" She chuckled. A becoming blush flushed her cheeks.

"All right. Since I'm off today and haven't eaten, why not? But under one condition." He rose from the edge and slid open a drawer.

"What's that?" Her smile faded and worry wrinkled her forehead.

He took out a few bills and shut the drawer. "This is my treat. The food prices at the hospital are as bad as theme parks."

A grin spread across her face. "Deal."

After ordering, they sat down. A friend of Steven's stopped and congratulated him. Steven was aware Elizabeth's head turned slightly to the side as they spoke, listening.

She took a bite of her eggs, waiting for the conversation to finish, then eyed him before setting her fork down. "If you don't mind me asking, why did he tell you congratulations?" She lifted her water glass.

Steven moved his chair forward and paused. "First, tell me—why were you standing at my door this morning?"

She placed her glass down on the table and met his eyes. "I had a tubal ligation scheduled, but I didn't go through with it. I couldn't."

Steven sat back in his chair, confused. The distant memory of their plans for a family and her longing to be a mother raced through his mind. A life they should have had if she hadn't run away. She was still running. "How could you think of doing that?" Anger seeped through his voice. Before he realized what he'd said, Elizabeth rose from her chair.

"Excuse me. But I think this was a mistake." She turned and hurried away.

Steven jumped up, but let her leave. He needed to think and pray. Instead, he followed after her, yet she was nowhere in sight. She could have gone anywhere. He checked the parking lot and walked through the hospital, but couldn't find her. Back in his office, he sat at his desk, head falling into his hands. *God, what am I to do?*

The door opened. Steven jerked up.

Elizabeth stood staring. "Why are you so angry with me?"

He shot from his chair and coaxed her inside his office. As the door closed, he released her against his will.

"I feel like I've done something. Will you tell me, so I can make it right?"

"I'm leaving, Elizabeth. People are congratulating me because I've been offered a position at the Children's Hospital in Atlanta. I've accepted." He returned to his desk, but couldn't sit.

"Is that what's bothering you? It can't be. I feel … I don't know what I feel. Like I'm connected to you somehow, someway. Not just from Katherine but…"

Elizabeth's eyes pleaded with him for understanding. At that moment, it was enough for him, whether Elizabeth ever found out about her past and their life together or not. "Thank you. And if I may be honest, I feel the same way. I'm going to miss you." Steven enjoyed the blush tinting her cheeks once again.

"So … did you call Chris and let him know what you decided?"

"Not yet. I wanted to give myself some time before I headed home."

"Then would you do me the honor of joining me for breakfast once again since we barely ate? I'm starved."

Elizabeth smiled. "Sounds good."

Now at his desk, Steven fiddled with a few papers only to be distracted by the memory of the woman he'd spent the morning with. He wouldn't see her again. He hung his head and eyed his bare ring finger, then closed his eyes and thought of that last smile she'd given him before she drove away—one he'd remember and cherish forever. How her eyes had sparkled.

"Timothy, will you help me with this bookshelf?" Chris hollered from the master bedroom.

"Hold on, little brother. I'll be up in a second."

"Well, hurry it up then." Chris piled the books from the shelf onto the floor, keeping each stack in order. He'd worked enough hours in their bookstore to know how Elizabeth liked certain things organized, especially books. And if this simple deed would make the transition to another part of the house easier, he'd do it.

Timothy plodded through the door. "I brought you something to drink."

Chris took the mug and drank a few gulps. The fizz from the root beer popped on his nose. As he surveyed the nearly-empty room, Timothy laid a hand on his shoulder.

"It'll be okay."

"How do you know that?"

"I'm talking about your future and your marriage. What you've both been through together the last year with her accident, Katherine, and then fighting for your marriage, it's still somewhat hard for me to believe, but God is at work."

"I wish God would have stopped her from making this decision."

"God gives us the freedom to choose, but I'm afraid if Elizabeth goes through with this, she'll regret it. Sarah mentioned to me that she couldn't remember a time Elizabeth hugged Lindsey as much as she did."

Chris hoped she'd changed her mind, but she should have called hours ago. He set his mug down on the window seat and grabbed the side of the bookshelf. "Are you ready? Maybe Elizabeth and I can have a few days alone here before our cruise if I can get things done quickly enough."

Timothy nodded and grabbed the other side. "You sure there's enough room for this?"

"If not, I'll make it fit." They lifted the bookshelf, swung it onto its side and eased it out the door and down the stairs. They barely squeezed it through the smaller doorway into the downstairs bedroom.

"That was close." Timothy plopped on the edge of the bed.

Chris patted his brother's shoulder. "I wouldn't have been able to do this without your help."

"What are brothers for?" He stood and punched Chris in the arm.

"Don't tell me you're instigating a wrestling match. I have a room upstairs all ready to go, and the way I'm feeling, I'll take you down in seconds."

"Yeah, you wish. And about that room, not actually as finished as you think. When we flipped the shelf, I stumbled over a few books lying on the floor."

"Excuses, excuses." Chris smirked. "Next time."

"With witnesses, you mean." Timothy chuckled. "I should go. Sarah is expecting me home for dinner."

"Thanks, Tim."

"Anytime. If you need me tomorrow or Wednesday, let me know. I have a light case load until Thursday."

Chris walked his brother to the door and closed it behind him. With a deep sigh, he trudged upstairs to find his neatly stacked piles scattered. Raking up the last set of books off the floor, he carried them to the bedroom downstairs. Not only did his back hurt, but now every muscle ached.

With the last stack of books in place, his gaze landed on one of Elizabeth's yearbooks from college. He'd never visited Palm Beach Atlantic. The view on the cover of the intracoastal waterway invited him.

He settled on the bed, book in hand. His phone rang, and he glanced at the caller ID. "Hey, sweetheart. Are you all right?"

"I'm fine. Are you at the house?"

Our house. Chris listened to the humming of the vehicle through the phone. "Are you driving? I thought we agreed I wouldn't wait at the hospital while you had the procedure, but I would pick you up when you called. You're not supposed to be driving."

"I'm okay. I'll be there shortly."

"I love you, Elizabeth."

"I love you, too."

Chris hung up. The thought of feeling his wife in his arms consumed him. To keep his mind distracted, he flipped through pages, imagining the hustle and bustle of campus life. He'd graduated with two degrees, never leaving the comforts of home. As he glanced through the yearbook, he wondered if maybe the experience of college life was worth it. As he flipped the next page, something slid into his lap. A dead flower? Chris smiled. An old crush. He pressed it back into the binding of the book and turned the page. A small line under a picture caught his attention. *Steven Carrington and Elizabeth Manroe.*

Elizabeth pulled up to the house, unsure how she'd tell Chris. Her heart throbbed in her chest.

"Chris, I'm home." She pressed her lips together, stifling the giggles bubbling to come out. She stood in the doorway, her eyes focused beyond the stairwell to their new bedroom. Peace filled her heart. She wanted another child.

"Chris?" She'd expected him to be waiting for her, but when she entered the bedroom, Chris sat slumped on the floor. His brows furrowed together.

"Is everything all right?" She knelt alongside him, touching the side of his cheek.

He jerked away and stood. "I didn't hear you come in. Are you ready to go back to the bookstore?"

Elizabeth bit her bottom lip as she stumbled to get up. What had happened to the "I love you, Elizabeth"? Her fears were coming true. He didn't want her after all. She'd believed every word he whispered to her at night before she slept, the notes he left by her pillow when he worked on the house. How could she have been so wrong? The surgery did change everything. A lump grew in her throat. *But I didn't have the surgery ... and Chris will never know.*

Chapter Twenty-One

With his keys lodged in the lock, Chris swung the door open. Their house was a mess. He'd destroyed it looking for answers and, in two days, found nothing. One fact remained—the man with his arm around Elizabeth in the photo was indeed Dr. Steven Moore. Yet questions kept coming up. He prayed for answers, but none revealed themselves. He wanted to ask Elizabeth, but she had barely remembered him when she came out of the coma. How would she remember her life in college? He considered marching right over to the hospital and asking the good doctor himself. Instead, he called the hospital and left a message for Steven to call his cell. And yet, Chris was glad Steven hadn't returned his call, because the more he realized his fear, the more afraid of the truth he became.

The night he proposed, she'd bared her soul. She'd told him about a past relationship and how they were almost married. He'd never seen her cry until that evening.

Chris stepped over several books scattered along the floor, knelt down, and grabbed the yearbook. She looked so happy, and the way Steven smiled at her churned Chris's stomach. What if Elizabeth remembered him? Would she want him instead? He dropped the book and headed to the back patio for a swim. Maybe if he could tire out his body, his mind could focus on the house again. There wasn't enough time to move in two days before the cruise, but it must be ready when they returned. He needed to focus on his future, not Steven *Carrington's.*

Stripping down to his jeans, he jumped in. He lost count of the laps, but the exercise did its job. He pulled himself onto the edge of the step, panting. Water slapped against his calf. *God, please help me to be the husband Elizabeth needs.* He let out a deep breath, ran his hand through his wet hair, and stood to reenter the house. When he did, Elizabeth was staring at her scattered books.

"I didn't know you were coming." Chris's eyes scanned the floor for the yearbook. He knelt and began plopping books on top, water dripping everywhere.

"Sarah wanted to come by and see the house, but I guess there's nothing to see." She backed up a few steps before turning to leave.

"Elizabeth, wait." Chris jumped up, clenching the yearbook and other books in his hands.

She gripped the brass handle. "Sarah's waiting. Maybe I'll see you tonight." She pulled the door open and closed it behind her.

Chris hurried to the window and watched his wife enter the car. He'd just ruined what should have been their first night back in their home. A night of new beginnings.

Elizabeth sat silent in the passenger's seat, thankful Sarah didn't ask or say a word until they parked at the mall.

Sarah touched her hand. "Do you still feel like shopping?"

She nodded. "I need to. Sam and I usually share things, but..."

"How have things been for the two of you?"

"Sam and I? Not so good. She hasn't spoken to me since I went to the hospital."

"How are you doing?" Sarah took the keys out of the ignition and faced her.

Elizabeth shook her head and almost answered, but the words stuck. With her husband and sister avoiding her, she had no one. Days ago, hope seemed real, tangible in the way Chris held her, spoke to her. Now the shreds of her life that had started to heal began to unravel. "Do you mind if we don't talk about it right now?"

"Before we leave this car, I want you to know I'm here for you if you ever need me. And one other thing. Lindsey said since Grandma is paying, you have to buy a new princess dress while I'm shopping for one, too. I tried to explain you need a gown for the cruise, but then she explained to me—in her five-year-old way—you are always a princess no matter where you go."

Elizabeth smiled. "I'd hate to disappoint her, so we better get shopping." She'd find a dress her niece would love and, hopefully, one to draw her husband's attention. Her stomach clenched. Could she hold her husband's attention? She couldn't before.

Hours later, her shopping trip ended when the stores closed. It would have ended hours ago if not for Sarah.

Packages filled Elizabeth's hands and pressed against her chest, while bags dangled from her arms. She couldn't remember ever spending so much money at one time.

She dropped her bags on the bed, and sifted through the boxes in search of her "princess dress." She regretted spending so much money, but she couldn't allow Linda to pay for her things, except for one. She raised the dress to her neck, rushed to the mirror, and gaped. The powder-blue gown softened her eyes to a crystalline hue. Today was the first time she'd been able to look at herself in the mirror without the familiar taste of salt. Maybe this was the sign she needed to finally call the hospital and reschedule her appointment.

She grabbed a hanger from the closet, hung the gown, and swiped her phone from the dresser as she wandered through the apartment and headed outside to the bench in front of the store.

After her call, Elizabeth leaned back and tossed her phone, which clinked on the sidewalk. No openings until after the cruise. At this point, what did it matter? But it did to her. Everything mattered because she'd fallen more in love with her husband in the past months than ever before. Now, with Chris assuming the surgery had taken place, he acted distant. Her stomach gurgled. Fear. She remembered it all too well.

Her thoughts drifted. *Katherine.* Would time heal her wounds? Could she ever truly be whole again? "I miss you…"

Chris struggled to keep his eyes open on the way back to the bookstore. He should've come home to Elizabeth hours ago, but even working non-stop since she'd left, he couldn't get their house ready, no matter how hard he tried.

As he slipped into the apartment, all was still except for the refrigerator's incessant humming. Exhausted and dirty, he wanted to fall into bed and sleep, but even more than that, he wanted to hold his wife. He'd spent days wrestling with the past, neglecting Elizabeth, and now it was too late to move back into their home. The look on her face when he'd come in from the pool told him she needed reassurance, something he wouldn't have noticed before. Chris praised God for working in his life and their marriage. He climbed into bed, anticipating Elizabeth's warmth within his arms, only to find the bed empty.

"Elizabeth?" He hopped up and searched. Nothing. Heading out the door to the bookstore, he called again, but louder. "Elizabeth!" Still nothing.

"Lord, protect her and bring my wife back to me."

"Chris."

He turned and headed toward the couch where she sat. "Are you okay?" He touched her cheek.

She nodded.

"Why were you out here?"

"I felt alone."

"I'm sorry I haven't been around the last few days." He paused, searching for the right words. "I tried to get the house ready, but I feared losing you. I want to be the husband you need, but I don't know how or what to do except to rely on God."

"Why are you afraid I'd leave you?"

He enveloped her hands. "I've been thinking about the past, your coma. When you woke up, you didn't remember who I was. And when you came home, we were strangers."

She stood, her arms encircling her waist. "I've thought about all this and everything that happened. It's entirely my fault. All of it. I know I'm not the same person I was."

"Elizabeth, it's not your fault. No matter what happened between us, I broke my promise to you. It was my decision, my choice. I'm responsible for my own actions."

Chris tucked her into his arms. "And I'm sorry for not being here the last few days."

She pulled back without leaving his arms. "You never did tell me. Why are you afraid I might leave you?"

"You're piecing your memory back together. I'm not saying you don't love me ... but I want it to be in a way you've never known. When we take this cruise the day after tomorrow, I want you to fall in love with me all over again."

"I do love you."

"I know you do, but will you allow yourself to trust me wholeheartedly as your husband and give God our lives and our future?"

She turned and moved from him. "I want to, Chris, but I don't know if I can. You don't know what you're asking me."

"I do. Trust. Love. Faith. Hope —"

"I get the picture."

Chris closed the distance between them. "You can trust me."

"And that is where I struggle, with you and with God. How am I to trust when you've left me? And God ripped my heart out by taking Katherine. How do I get past the pain? I'm sorry, Chris, but right now … I can't." She headed back to the apartment.

Stunned, Chris found it impossible to move. His hope vanished. But he loved his wife and had faith in a mighty God. That would be enough for the both of them.

From his knees, he prayed God would provide the rest.

Elizabeth hid in the shadows of the bookstore and watched Chris kneel. She wanted to trust him. She almost had the day she came home from the hospital, but the distance he'd put between them made her glad she hadn't. Still, as she observed her husband praying, she ached. He was different. There was no denying what she'd seen these past months, but it wasn't enough to tell him the truth.

Chris's head rose slowly. Elizabeth hurried into her apartment. A few minutes later, Chris entered the bedroom.

"Elizabeth?" he whispered as he knelt beside her bed. "Are you asleep?"

"Hmm."

He ran his hand along her temple. "Will you do something for me? Will you sit up on the edge of the bed?"

"It's late."

"Please." He moved the quilt to the side when she sat up and scooted to the edge of the bed. "I love you." He almost bowed, laying his head down in her lap, arms around her waist.

She ached to touch him, but if she did … God, why are you doing this to me? Why did you send my husband to me like this?

"Are you ready for bed?"

Chris mumbled something before he rose, and he lumbered to his feet. "Lay down, and I'll cover you."

She did as he suggested, and his hand grazed her shoulder as the cover settled into place. Tears seeped from the corners of her eyes, down the bridge of her nose, running onto her pillow. *God, I'm sorry, but I can't.*

Chapter Twenty-Two

Elizabeth awoke wrapped in Chris's arms, on his side of the bed. Even in her sleep, she couldn't deny what she wanted, a fact she wasn't willing to admit awake. Pretending to be asleep, she enjoyed the warmth of his skin and the embrace engulfing her, but her heel began to tickle. Pressing her foot against his ankle, she relieved the itch.

"Better?"

She envisioned Chris smiling. "Yes. I guess I should get up." She began to move, but Chris held her tighter.

She closed her eyes and relaxed within his embrace. His fingers ran down her arm and up again, repeating the motion.

This was what she'd wanted after the accident—intimacy without being physical, allowing her to know and trust him. Why did it take losing everything and being crushed to have a moment like this? A moment that began to weave itself into the tiniest bits of hope, reaching out and sprouting through layers of rock built around her heart. It seemed the more Chris prayed, the more vulnerable she became. She wondered how long she could withstand Chris's appeal before her walls crumbled to the ground.

"What?" Chris's breath tickled her ear.

Elizabeth jerked her chin up. "Did I say something?"

"Something about the ground."

"Thinking about scripture. How Joshua, through prayer and obedience, won the battle."

"It's amazing how the walls fell down. You know, Phillip has a trumpet around here somewhere."

She snickered. "He would, wouldn't he?" She broke away from Chris's embrace, sat up, and looked around the room. "I think we need to start packing since we're leaving tomorrow."

He sat up and supported her back with his arm. "We have plenty of time."

"And what do you suggest we do with all this time we have?"

Chris leaned back and reached for his phone. "It's almost seven. If we leave in a few minutes, there shouldn't be too many people."

She twisted to face him. "Leave?" Okay, this wasn't what she had in mind. Her thinking ran along the lines of staying in bed and him holding her.

"The beach won't be as crowded as it is later in the day. You could show me this mystery bathing suit you bought."

She knew why she bought it, and regretted her decision. If her husband stayed with her, it was for love, not for any other reason. "It's going to have to stay a mystery."

"Then I look forward to discovering what's behind this bashful look of yours."

"There's not much to discover." *Literally.* She cleared her throat. "I would love to go for a run on the beach."

"Run?"

"Sure. Are you afraid I'll whip you again?" She threw the covers to the side and stood, planting her hands on her hips. "If you need, I'll give you a head start."

"Oh, will you now?" He came to her.

She chuckled and backed up. "Or if you need me to go slower..." Chris reached for her. She ducked away, hurrying for the other side of the room, but he caught her from behind.

"Not so fast, are we?" He tickled her.

"Stop." She gasped through her laughter, lunging for his waist, grabbing his side.

"I can withstand it, but you can't."

She pretended to lunge forward once again, but slipped from his hold, swiping a sheet from the bed to try to protect herself.

"And what is that for?" He stood smiling.

"One of these days, I'm going to tickle you for a change."

Before she knew what happened, arms were wrapped around her waist, and Elizabeth found herself on the bed, swaddled in the sheet. Chris grinned down at her.

"Now, I like this. Let's see … Where should I start?"

"Chris! Don't you dare! This isn't fair." She tried to wiggle her way out, but her arms were trapped in the sheet.

"I think I'll start here." He touched her lips with his finger, stilling her. "Which do you prefer? To be tickled or kissed?"

"What kind of question is that?"

"One that deserves an answer." He tickled her sides.

She rolled back and forth, giggling. "I surrender. I surrender. I'll tell you, if you'll stop."

"I knew I could make you talk." Chris leaned over her once again. "I'm listening."

"Hold on." She gasped. "I need some air. Will you undo me, please?"

"Not until you tell me." He brushed her hair from her face and gazed deep into her eyes. "You are so beautiful."

The intensity of his gaze grew. "I prefer soft, long kisses."

Chris rose and scooted her off the bed, standing her upright. He unraveled the sheet and dropped it on the floor. From behind, he shifted her hair to hang down in front and, with tender fingers, pulled her night shirt to the side of her shoulder. His lips gently kissed her scars.

She touched her forehead. A lump caught in her throat, and her skin burned from her husband's touch as the memories washed over her. In a half-whisper, she pleaded, "Don't." Then she pulled her shirt back over her shoulder and turned her face away.

He came to her and lifted her chin. "They are my reminder to treasure you. To care for you as I would for my own body, and to sacrifice my life for yours, if need be. God brought you to me as He brought Eve to Adam. Bone of my bone and flesh of my flesh, so these scars are mine."

She moved away, turned her back to him, and whisked away her fallen tears. "Do you still want to go for a run?"

"If you'd like."

She nodded.

Chris left and closed the door behind him.

She dragged herself to the dresser and snagged her running clothes, then threw them on the bed. She couldn't pray, but she could get out of this house. The beach and the roar of thunder as the waves pounded the sand would clear her head and emotions.

She headed out from the apartment and down to the bookstore where Sam gave her a weak smile.

Chris came up and touched her hand, slipping her the keys. "I'll meet you in the car."

"Okay." She headed for the door.

"Elizabeth." Sam's voice stopped her. It stabbed Elizabeth's heart that her sister had been avoiding her ever since her appointment. She whirled around.

"I have to apologize." Sam dipped her head. "It was hard for me to think you decided not to have children. That you didn't want them when Phillip and I can't."

"Hard for you? What was hard for you, sis? To have a husband who would die for you if he had to? Or having a precious little girl who calls you Mommy that you're able to hold at night? What I wouldn't give to have that. Nothing has been taken from you. God has given you everything. I don't want to hear how my decision not to have any more children has affected you. If I were you, I'd be praising God for your life. You wouldn't want mine."

She stormed out and paced in front of the car. "Ugh!" When Chris came out, he opened her door, but she didn't get in. "I'll be right back. I've got to run for a minute."

"Do you still want to go?" He yelled after her.

"Yes!" She stomped down the street.

Chris slumped into the driver's seat with his wallet in his lap, holding a photo of Katherine, Elizabeth, and him. His wife's words echoed in his mind. *"If I were you, I'd be praising God for your life. You wouldn't want mine."* What more could he do? What could he say to show Elizabeth he loved her?

Trust in Me, the words whispered in his ear.

Lord, I am trusting You … I have to. You are my hope. I know this because I'm a changed man. Even I know the difference between night and day, but I pray Elizabeth sees it. Guide me. Take my marriage so it brings You honor and glory, because in my hands, it sifts between my fingers like sand.

In the corner of his eye, movement caught his attention. Elizabeth headed back to the car. Chris slid the picture back into his wallet and turned the key. The engine came to life.

"Wow, I think I wore myself out." She closed the door, sucked in breaths of air, and gave him a smile he was tempted to kiss. "I'm so hot; I might jump in the water."

"I'm game, if you are." He hid his amusement as he backed out of the drive and down the street.

With a long exhale, she let out a, "Whoo. I might not let you have that head start when we race. I'm tired." She leaned into the vent. Strands of hair escaped from her clip and swung freely.

"No excuses. I'll give you the head start if I have to." He enjoyed the banter this morning, and seeing her smile now, he was glad they had this day before lifting anchor tomorrow for the Caribbean.

Chris stopped the car in front of the family's condo and glanced at Elizabeth. "Everything okay?"

She gazed out the window and nodded before getting out, waiting for him to join her on the boardwalk. "It's been difficult with my sister, Chris. When we get back, if the house isn't ready..."

"After the cruise, we're moving home."

Her brows furrowed. "Are you sure?"

Chris stopped at the edge of the boardwalk, one foot on, the other planted in the sand. "Whether the house is ready or not, we're moving back home."

"Let's run." White sand flicked through the air as she darted in and out of crowds, straight to the water's edge.

Was she running from the memories or the pain? It didn't matter. She'd asked him to be by her side, something he'd gladly do. While he ran, he prayed for the pain to subside, both hers and his. The knowledge that Katherine would be his only child brought him misery—the daughter he'd grown jealous of and neglected at the end of her life.

With a heavy heart, his steps slowed. Sea water swept into his shoes and sloshed up his socks.

"Chris! Where did you go?" Elizabeth bobbed around a couple strolling in the opposite direction and halted in front of him, smacking her hands on her knees. "I turned around, and you weren't behind me. Was I too fast?" She rose and laughed, but her smile vanished. "Do you want to tell me about it, or do I need to guess?"

"Guess what? I think I'm going for a swim." Chris shed his drenched shoes and glued on socks. His toes bathed in the coolness of the ocean. "Come with me."

"Will you tell me then?"

"It's nothing, Elizabeth."

"Don't keep secrets from me, Chris." Her arms hung by her side, one of her hands balled into a fist. "I'm scared to trust you. Don't give me a reason not to."

"This isn't the place." He bent down and grabbed his things. "Let's head back to the condo. We can talk there."

"No one's there right now?"

"Nope. Dad asked if I would check on it before we left for the cruise."

"Why doesn't he do it himself, since they're not going?"

"Two weeks ago he asked if I would oversee their rental properties, since he was getting too old. He said if I wouldn't take the job, he'd find someone. I didn't believe him until I overheard him asking someone on the phone for references. So I took it." Chris led her. "Here we are." He pointed, then lifted the keys from his pocket, and unlocked the door.

Chris flipped on the light and shut the door. "Let me put these wet things in the kitchen." When he returned, Elizabeth leaned against a cabinet etched with palm trees.

Her gaze met his. "Will you tell me now?"

"What do you want me to tell you? They're things you already know. I was a terrible husband. A jealous dad. Do you want me to list them?" He ran his fingers through his hair.

"Jealous of Katherine? Why? Our daughter was so fragile and needed us."

"I needed you, too. I prayed for five days, afraid you were going to die. You had to wake up, not for any other reason but for me. I couldn't live without you, and I didn't want to. But then, right before my eyes, a miracle happened. My wife opened her eyes and looked at me."

"But ... I didn't remember you," she whispered.

Chris sank onto an ottoman. "You didn't."

"And yet, when I saw Katherine for the first time, I fell in love with her." She knelt in front of him. "Oh, Chris, do you forgive me? I'm so sorry."

"Please. It's not your fault. None of this is."

Touching his cheek, she leaned her head against his. "If only you knew."

"If I knew what?" He pulled her back and gazed into her eyes.

She pressed her lips against his ever so softly. "How much I love you." She kissed him again, lingering. "You mentioned to me that once we were on the cruise, you wanted me to fall in love with you all over again. I understand now. But I can't imagine loving you more than I do at this very moment."

"I have to kiss you. If you don't want me to, you need to tell me." He searched her eyes, but hearing no words, he parted her lips with a kiss, inhaling her breath. Chris pulled her close, and she responded, returning his affections. He was hers, and she was his. Each touch and kiss grew in intensity he yearned for, yet sadness filled his heart. Did she trust him?

"We should stop," he whispered, inhaling deeply, caressing her. "I told you before I would wait for you. I want to earn your trust, and the only way I can do that is to keep my word." With one last kiss, he helped her to stand. "I need to look around and make sure everything is fine before we leave."

"All right," she exhaled.

Did he hear disappointment in her voice? Chris's footsteps pounded as he ran upstairs. He glanced at the bed. They could have ended up there, but it wasn't enough for him. He wanted her heart.

Returning downstairs, Chris found Elizabeth facing three black-and-white photos along the wall over the couch. Sea shells, always her favorite. "You took those."

She jumped. "I almost dropped this." She held a musical silver shell in her palm. "It's beautiful and the music … sounds familiar."

"Maybe because it's yours, and you've had it since before we met."

She turned back to the wall. "I took those?"

"You love the beach."

"I remember. I also remember you proposing to me at the beach."

"But you don't remember anything else about that night?"

She cocked her head. "No, should I?"

"Right outside this door is where I asked you to marry me. This is where we stayed for our honeymoon. Well, the first two days before we left for Hawaii." He smiled, then took the silver shell from her hand, set it down on the table, and claimed her in his arms.

"This place is ours, a wedding present from Mom and Dad. They've been holding onto it for us."

She groaned. "How can a person be a stranger in their own life?"

"You're not a stranger in mine. If you ever want to know anything about your past, you can always ask, and I'll try to help. I just hope when your memory returns, I'll be enough for you."

"You said something like that before. Why wouldn't you be? Did I give you the impression you weren't?"

"Never. I felt treasured, like the only man in the world for you."

She touched his cheek, meeting his gaze. "You are." Her lips grazed his. "Are you ready to go?"

Chris nodded and held the door, but in the corner of the room, the silver shell chirped a note. If he hadn't given it to her, who had? His heart dropped. *Could it be?*

Chapter Twenty-Three

As Chris drove to Phillip's, too many things didn't add up, beginning with the doctor's last name, and now the shell in their condo. After Elizabeth got ready for bed, he was determined to talk to the one person who knew his wife. Samantha. But wouldn't she have recognized Steven at the hospital or when he stayed with Elizabeth after her attack?

He pulled into their drive and turned off the car. Was he truly ready for answers? What happened if…?

He got out of the car, stopping his thoughts. His shoulders tightened as he strode to the door and knocked.

Phillip answered. "Chris, it's eleven at night. I didn't know you were coming by. Is everything all right?" He entered the living room where his sister-in-law sat reading a book.

"Yes, but I came because I need to ask Samantha a few questions about Elizabeth's past."

He caught her gaze, then sank into the loveseat. "Samantha, we were at the condo today, and —"

"You were?" Philip smiled.

"We were there to check on the place before we left. Did you know Dad was going to hire someone to take over the properties?"

"I did. I'm glad to see you took the job."

Samantha closed her book and set it on the coffee table. "What were you going to ask me, Chris?"

"There's a shell made out of silver in the condo that plays music and I can't remember where it came from. I wondered if perhaps you did?"

Samantha glanced to Phillip, then searched her empty hands. "Phillip and I were talking this morning about how I react when I become hurt or angry. I tend to push those I love away. I'm thankful my husband hasn't been the bearer of my stupidity."

She looked toward Phillip before focusing on her hands. "It's wrong how I've treated Elizabeth this last week, especially through the years. She's had to survive and if it wasn't for God, she wouldn't have made it. And by the look on your face, Chris, you have no idea what I'm talking about."

Samantha straightened her shoulder and took a deep breath. Phillip came and sat alongside her, clasping her hand. "I wouldn't know about the shell except for seeing it in the condo. I moved out of our childhood home the week after I turned eighteen and never looked back. I wasn't part of my sister's life except monetarily. Our parents couldn't afford to put us through school, so I sent money for her tuition. I took care of her the only way I knew how. When our parents died, I reached out to her, but she wouldn't return my calls. She never even came to our parents' funeral."

"What do you mean? She never showed? She told me when she looked over at you, you resembled Cynthia so much she became upset."

Samantha's brows furrowed. "I'm telling you, she wasn't there. I looked. Actually, everyone who was there gave their condolences after the funeral, since I didn't want a viewing."

Chris rose and paced. This made no sense. *If Elizabeth wasn't there ...* But she'd recognized Samantha. Questions grew by the second, and with each step, one question stood out from the others. "I know this is going to sound crazy, but … did you see someone who looked like Steven at the funeral?"

Phillip's forehead wrinkled. "Steven? He knew their family?"

"Not the family. Elizabeth."

Samantha's mouth dropped. "Dr. Moore?"

"Dr. Moore. Steven Carrington. I believe they're one and the same."

In his Atlanta apartment, Steven chucked the empty moving boxes outside, sending exhaustion ripping through his muscles. He scanned the three-bedroom apartment, plain walls, and remaining unmarked boxes. His newspaper still lay neatly folded on the counter, next to his cold coffee mug from this morning. His intentions to start the day with coffee and prayer had gone by the wayside when Elizabeth invaded his thoughts. His heart ached. Another move. Another day filled with emptiness—not only his apartment, but his life.

Mike's voice startled him. "You're better off here."

Steven glanced at the open door and shook his head. "I'm glad I'm in perfect health."

He patted Steven on the shoulder. "Your body might be, but your mind is in turmoil."

"After all this time, you know me so well."

"Doesn't the Bible say closer than a brother?"

Steven lifted another box and set it on the foyer table. "So what brings you by so late? If you've come to help, don't forget to shut the door." Steven smirked.

"Why don't you stay with us for a while? Until you get your feet under you?"

Steven glanced down. "My feet look to be in the right place. So tell me, why did you stop by?"

"Your secretary from Mercy called. She apologized. Chris called some time ago and wants you to call him.

Here's his number." Mike took out his wallet from his back pocket, slid out a piece of paper, and placed it on the table. "You know, you don't need to return his call."

"I know." Steven lifted the number from the table and stared at Susan's script. "And I know God has Elizabeth in the palm of His hand. I'm having a hard time facing the fact the woman I loved and the life I so desperately wanted slipped from my grasp." He crinkled the paper in his palm. "It's time to walk away."

Chris stood from the couch. "I should go. Samantha, do you mind keeping the yearbook with you? I really don't want Elizabeth to see the picture of the two of them together."

"Of course. But Chris, my sister loves you. Don't doubt that."

He nodded before heading back home. He knew his wife loved him. These past few months, he'd seen hope flourish and blossom, and though she tried to fight it at times, she was learning to trust him. Her heart opened to him, and he would be a faithful keeper for whatever she entrusted to him. But were her feelings enough? Would they stand against the brewing storm he sensed coming? The more Elizabeth remembered about that day and Steven, reality draped over them like a dark cloud.

Once home, he slid under the sheets and squeezed his eyes shut, praying for strength and courage.

"Hey," she whispered, turning to him. "Is it time to get up?"

"No." He pulled her into his arms and kissed the edge of her hair line. "I'm just getting to bed."

"Oh, is everything all right?" She lifted her head ever so slightly.

"I put all our stuff by the door."

She rested her head against his chest and fell back to sleep. Chris continued to pray, drifting into his own dreams.

"Chris … Wake up…," Elizabeth sang softly next to his ear, kissing his cheek after every use of his name. "I'm starting to think you're pretending to be asleep." An idea popped into her mind, and execution was the key.

Leaning over him, she kissed his chin, readying her hands for attack. With one final kiss, she sprang into action, clamping her fingers along his sides. Chris sprang upright, grasping for her wrists. Able to secure one free hand, she laughed until her sides squeezed in pain. "That was everything I hoped it to be." She taunted him with the other hand.

"I see how it is, taking advantage when a man's down."

"I had to do something. My man wouldn't get up." She leaned in to kiss him, but pulled back when Chris's smile fell from his lips. His hold lightened.

Something bothered him, but she wasn't going to let it get in the way of their trip together. She'd always wanted to take a cruise, and when Linda had bought her sons and their wives tickets, she'd started counting the days. Little had she known the mountains she'd have to climb to go on this trip with her husband, but she looked forward to it even more. A honeymoon of sorts, but one she would remember.

"Aren't you excited about today?" She tried her best game show announcer voice. "You and yours truly will be sailing from Miami for a seven days and six nights, all-expense paid trip to … the Caribbean." She stood from the bed. "We'll have the time of our lives, visiting Grand Cayman, Belize, and Cozumel. And the best part —"

"— We'll be together." Chris smiled and rose from the bed. At the knock on the door, he froze. "You've been saved."

Elizabeth plopped back on the bed and laughed.

"I was checking to make sure you were up." Samantha knocked again. "Lizzy?"

"We're up, sis, and can you please not call me Lizzy?" She huffed, getting up from the bed.

"All right. Timothy and Sarah should be here in a few minutes. Phillip is almost done with breakfast."

"Thanks, Samantha." Chris reached for Elizabeth's hand, then kissed it. "Why does that name bother you?"

"It reminds me I don't know who I am. Mom used to call me Lizzy. Well, that's what Sam tells me anyway."

"Has anyone else called you Lizzy?"

"That's a strange question." Elizabeth trotted over to the dresser and pulled out her clothes. She hoped to avoid answering, but Chris's expectant gaze told her otherwise. Was he testing her to tell him the truth? "Yes, someone else has."

"Do you mind me asking who?"

Her stomach looped into knots. This was not how she'd planned to start their trip together. "Steven … twice."

Chris came to her and slid his finger down her cheek. "Steven is a difficult topic for us to discuss, but I want you to know, you can talk to me about anything or anyone."

Elizabeth nodded, reaching up on her tiptoes, but Chris beat her to a kiss. Not just any kiss, but one that weakened her determination not to tell him about the surgery. She moved from his embrace and headed into the bathroom. The tables were turning. He was the honest one, and now she kept the secrets.

Lindsey's singsong voice carried as Elizabeth dressed. Opening the bedroom door, her niece hurled herself into her arms. How precious to feel the love of a child.

"Auntie, will you show me your dress? Mommy showed me hers. Can I see yours?" Lindsey turned to Sarah. "Mommy, you have my princess dress?"

"Yes, sweetie." Sarah pointed to the table. "Now come, sit down and eat."

Timothy plopped his hand on Chris's shoulder. "Are you all ready?

"Yeah. Let me load our stuff in the back of your car while everyone eats." Chris headed over to the suitcases by the door, lifted one, and looped his arm through.

"Here, let me help." Phillip pulled a suitcase by the handle and opened the door with his other hand.

Timothy caught Elizabeth's attention as he sat at the table. "Let's say grace." He dipped his head. "God, we thank You for this time we are about to have as a family. Thank You for Mom and Dad, who have provided for us all these years. Even as adults, we are still their children, as we are Yours. Amen."

Elizabeth pushed her food around her plate and glanced at her watch. Soon she'd set sail on her lifetime dream, but it seemed when she thought of that dream, an outline of a faceless man stood out of reach.

Twenty minutes later, they approached the port terminal, and Chris squeezed her hand. "So what do you think of the view?" His grin set her heart on fire.

She giggled. "It depends on what you're talking about. The ships, or you?"

"Are you flirting with me, Mrs. Roberts?"

"I daresay I am." She hid her blush, refocusing on the massive ships to her left, her eyes taking panoramic shots.

Small white boats with orange covers looked like dashes across the middle of their cruise ship. The red, blue, and white smokestack reminded her of a killer whale's tail stretching into the sky. Once they parked, got out, and headed into the terminal, little fingers captured hers. Her niece's blue eyes peered around.

"Come here, you." Elizabeth swept her up into her arms.

Lindsey leaned into her and whispered, "I'm scared, Auntie. Mommy said we'll dress like princesses when we get on the boat, but I don't wanna be a princess now."

"Oh, you will have a fun time. Don't you worry. As soon as you get on the boat, you'll see." Elizabeth hugged her. Following everyone else's lead, she pointed out blue flags hanging from the ceiling, and once in line, they played their own game of Guess Who. However, when the winding line lingered, Lindsey's eyelids drooped then shut. Elizabeth handed her into Chris's outstretched arms. He laid her head against his shoulder and cradled her back. Pink shoes dangled beneath her polka-dotted dress.

Elizabeth took note of how Phillip grazed Samantha's arm. Her sister stepped back into his chest. They acted like characters in a romance novel, except their life was real. With a deep breath, Elizabeth turned her attention to Timothy, who reached for several papers from Sarah. She touched the rim of her glasses and smiled. "You guys are next. I'll take Lindsey from you."

Chris placed the girl's limp frame into her mother's waiting arms. They were up, passports ready.

After receiving their passports, papers, tickets, and their cruise cards, Chris directed her to their luggage.

Elizabeth glanced at Chris as he walked beside her to the ship. If she had to use one word to describe him, oddly enough, it would be faithful. He'd stood by her through everything and had never given up on God or her. He wasn't the man she'd known before. Even as her memories of them were returning, she realized he was different now. Last night, as she was falling asleep, her heart had cried out to God for her marriage and the ability to trust Chris fully, but it was the spirit within her that yearned for God's presence, and as she continued to pray, tears had rushed to her eyes. Beside the bed, she had fallen to her knees before her Father. The Father who had never forsaken her but drew her. His prodigal daughter had returned breathless, in tears, but knowing she was loved to her very soul.

Chris snatched her hand and stopped her. His forehead wrinkled. "What is it, sweetheart? You're crying."

Her gaze fell, her fingers whisking away tears. "I'm happy, Chris."

He raised her hand to his lips and kissed it.

"Come on, love birds. There's something not right with the tickets." Sarah hollered to them, her hair swinging across her shoulders as she turned back around. Lindsey's pink shoes plopped against her waist.

Chris shuffled his feet in the elevator as Timothy and Phillip discussed the room situation. After visiting the service desk, there was nothing they could do. They weren't assigned a room which they had paid for—a mistake on the cruise line's part—but luckily, they found them another room. The elevators opened on the Empress deck.

"Our three rooms were supposed to be together." Timothy pushed their luggage out of the elevator and into the hall; Phillip and Samantha filed out close behind him. Sarah followed, cradling Lindsey in her arms.

"Chris, we'll come to your room before heading down for the drills." Phillip's words floated in before the elevator doors closed.

"Verandah room 8277, right?" Elizabeth gave him the sweetest smile.

"At least it has a balcony. Here we are. "Chris handed her the card for the room, then grasped the handles of the suitcases and tugged them out of the elevator, following his wife's lead.

Elizabeth unlocked the door, entered, and tried to hide a giggle as he came in.

"Oh, no." Chris let go of the suitcases next to the wall. "Those twin beds are coming together."

"Don't worry. I can sleep here, and you can take the bed over there." She pointed, still fighting laughter.

"I can handle a smaller room, but there is no way I'm sleeping without you. You don't take a cruise with your wife just to enjoy the ocean air."

Elizabeth fell onto the bed.

Chris leaned over her, planting both hands on the comforter. "I'm serious. You want to help me convert this to a king?"

When a knock sounded, Chris smiled and kissed her forehead. He walked to the door and opened it with a swing of his arm and a playful bow. "Brothers, you've come to check our humble abode. Welcome."

Timothy entered first and glanced at the beds. He chuckled. "So which one are you sleeping in, little brother?"

Phillip followed and, without a word, began moving the bed frames together. "We need to get the girls and head down for our safety meeting. There you go."

Timothy glanced out the balcony window. "At least you have a nice view." He turned to leave. "Are you going to come with us, or would you want to meet us down by the elevator?"

"We'll meet you by the elevator." Phillip gave Chris and Elizabeth a smirk and closed the door behind them as they left.

Chris pointed to the bed. "There. That's more like it."

"Are you tired of waiting for me?"

His gaze jumped to hers. "Where did that come from?"

She lowered her head. Her blonde hair fell across her face and hung down her black linen blouse. "I don't know."

He took her hand from her lap and placed it in his palm. "I want you to trust me, Elizabeth, and when you do, then I'll have your heart. Nothing is more important."

"Except maybe heading downstairs?" Her turquoise eyes peeked up at him.

"You could have a point." He gave her a peck on the lips and ushered her out the door.

Chapter Twenty-Four

Saturday—Miami, Florida

Elizabeth glanced at Chris as they headed back to their cabin. She pressed her lips together, stifling the laughter at the back of her throat. When the crew had asked everyone to put their head between their knees during the ship's drills, Phillip followed orders like clockwork—Mr. Straight-and-Narrow, unlike his two brothers. If Chris and Timothy weren't in competition with each other, they were making a commotion. How two grown men could act such a way, she'd never know.

"What? You have to admit it was funny." Chris smiled. "Dad taught us that song. He said he used to watch videos when he was a kid during the Korean War. A turtle, wearing a helmet on his head, would duck and cover from a nuclear bomb. When tornadoes came through, he'd sing that song to us. We just thought of it at the same time."

"But singing it so everyone could hear?"

"You have to admit, when some of the passengers began singing about ducking and covering right along with us —"

"Oh yeah, I can see it now." She stopped and swiped her hand through the air above her head. "Our cruise line presents, Timothy and Chris Roberts singing…"

"Don't be jealous." He took out their room card, unlocked the cabin, and let her pass, touching her arm.

Shivers raced up her body. She bit her lip and glanced around their small quarters. What was she thinking? This cabin was the size of their bathroom back home.

The cruise line's newsletter caught her attention. Swiping the pages from the bed, she searched for tomorrow's agenda. Buried in the red, white, and blue papers, she read the same paragraph three times, scanning the big bold print. 'Sea Day Tomorrow.' That will be fun." She tossed the paper back on the bed and quickened her pace to the door. "Are you ready to eat?"

Chris caught her arm. "Why? Are you in a hurry?"

"I'm hungry. Aren't you?" Well, she was a little, so it wasn't a lie.

"Ah, not yet but, if you are, we can go. Let me call the guys so they know we won't be joining them for dinner." He walked to the phone and picked up the receiver next to the mirror. Elizabeth sighed, strolling over to him. She slipped the phone from his grip and placed it on its cradle.

"Maybe I can wait. Would you like to walk around the ship?"

"Of course." He took her hand and rested it in the crook of his elbow as they left the cabin. "Where do you want to start?"

"The lobby." She stepped into the elevator and willed herself to relax as she stood alongside Chris. Being this close to him set her nerves on end. She needed to calm down, enjoy herself, and take in the scenery. She glanced at him. His cologne intoxicated her, and the way light reflected in his eyes when he looked at her, she might have a heart attack if her pulse didn't slow down.

Chris lifted her hand from the crook of his arm and pressed her knuckles to his lips before releasing her. She avoided his gaze and, thankfully, the elevator doors opened.

"I wonder what this place is." She walked through a set of elegant wooden doors into a theater.

Lights dotted the high ceilings. Bold patterns of gold, maroon, and navy blue were scattered throughout. Stadium-style seating spread from the right to the left. Poles wrapped in gold and blue, like candy canes, stood on both ends of the stage.

"Chris, look at that curtain." She pointed and strolled closer. "I used to watch a presidents' show when I was a kid at a theme park with a curtain similar to this, but it was red velvet. This place is beautiful. We'll have to come for a show." She spun around right into Chris's chest.

Chris cleared his throat and secured her within his arms, eyes darting to several people who entered. The corners of his mouth lifted.

If she didn't get herself loose, she might find out what was behind her husband's mischievous smile.

She pushed from his arms. A clear head was what she needed, and standing this close wasn't helping. She clasped his hand. "Come on."

Within a few steps, music drifted through the air. "Let's go this way." Chris tugged on her hand, entering some type of lounge with maroon high-back chairs and white oval tables. A man played the piano against the backdrop of a glass wall. The glass stretched around the open area. "That's nice."

"The music is nice."

"No. The wall." He tugged her forward, then released her to run his hand across the glass. He smiled. "I did something similar to this."

Her stomach soured. Was it wrong for her to feel jealousy toward the first thing that stole her husband away? Because if it wasn't for *that* job, maybe his heart and body wouldn't have left her.

She turned away. The music drifted behind her, as did the art gallery she passed. She strolled toward the exterior deck of the ship. They were leaving Miami. Skyscrapers stretched against the skyline like children's building blocks. *Katherine.* A pointed building with jagged edges caught her eye. She swallowed hard. The spear in her heart from her husband's affair had been removed, but she still bled from time to time and right now, if she didn't stop her thoughts, she'd drown.

"There you are."

She didn't need to turn around to know Chris's voice, but the image of him with another woman made her sick.

"I couldn't find you. I'm glad you didn't go far." He rubbed her arm.

Elizabeth took a step. The trace of his fingertips burned her. Nausea scorched against her throat. She wasn't the only one he'd touched. Glancing at the shore one last time reminded her there was no way off this ship, nowhere to hide.

"Chris, I need to go lay down."

"You're not feeling well? Do you think you're seasick?"

The concern in his voice made her turn to face him. His expression should have eased her mind, but it didn't, and she wasn't in the mood for his twenty questions.

"I'll be in the cabin. Why don't you go see your brothers?" She pasted on a smile.

"You don't want me to come with you?"

"I'm good." She turned and headed for the elevator.

Once inside, she glanced at the man and woman who stood in front of her. He wore a polo shirt and denim jeans. She, on the other hand, wore a tight thigh-length dress with three inch heels. Was that the way a woman needed to dress to keep a man's attention? Because it was obvious, by the fixation of the second man in the elevator, she had his attention, too. But the second man's wife was focused on their child. If people looked at her and Chris, was that what they would see? She didn't know how to be a wife or keep her husband's attention. Oh, right now she had it, but what about later, when she gave her heart and soul to him? Where would she be then? Alone and childless. She searched her empty hands, glancing at the little girl grabbing her mother's pant leg with one hand and sucking her thumb with the other.

The doors slid open. Promenade Deck. Three decks shy, but she had to get out. Following the couple in front of her, she veered left, then past the garden atrium. She inhaled and knew immediately she needed to turn around and head to the cabin. Something else called to her. Could she smell the scent of alcohol? She licked her lips and breathed in again. Drawn to the door nearby, Elizabeth glanced in. A sports logo held a dominant position above the arch-style bar. Television screens stretched the length. A few steps inside the door, she saw people huddled around the tables and swivel chairs, clinking glasses and yelling.

"Are you meeting someone?" A man's voice startled her.

She jumped and faced the palest eyes she'd ever seen. "Ah, no."

"I'm sorry. I didn't mean to scare you. Can I buy you a drink?" He led her to the bar. "What would you like?"

The question was, what was she doing? But before she could answer, he handed her a frothy glass.

"Here you go."

The smell intoxicated her. One sip, that's all she'd need to ease the pain.

Chris wasn't concerned that Elizabeth didn't show up for dinner until he entered their cabin and the bed hadn't been slept in. Now he hurried, exiting the elevator onto the promenade. Which way would she go? Each deck he searched with no signs of his wife, he found it harder to breathe. He glanced in both directions—to the left was the lounge, to the right a piano bar. He weaved through the striped wingback chairs, but his hope faded as he entered the piano bar. How many places on this ship served alcohol?

He sat on one of the black-and-white stools.

"What would you like?" The bartender slapped a cocktail napkin down in front of him.

"Information. Have you seen a blonde woman with eyes that look like window cleaner?"

"No, man, I didn't. If I did, I'm sure I'd remember."

"Thanks." Chris rose and left.

Another bar and two dance clubs later, Chris felt weak. They shouldn't have come on this cruise. At home, he knew where she was—safe.

Phillip and Samantha came toward him. Samantha sprinted ahead. "Have you checked down there?" She nodded in the direction he just came from.

"Nothing." Chris ran his hand through his hair.

"We finished off this floor then." Phillip grabbed Samantha's hand and pulled. "We'll go to the next deck. Why don't you check the room and see if she returned?"

"All right," he huffed. But he'd still do a quick walk through. "Let me know."

"We will."

Chris waited for the elevator doors to close before entering the casino. The place busted at the seams. Slot machines lined one wall. Blackjack tables lay scattered about, and stark grins governed the player's faces. Elizabeth wasn't here.

A sports bar was next. His eyes widened at the multiple screens. He fought to keep his mouth from gaping as he approached the bar.

The man behind the counter smiled. "Nice, isn't it? I see reactions like yours all the time. It makes this job amusing for sure. What can I get you?"

"A soda." Chris inspected the screens encased in silver. Maybe in the future, he'd redo one of the bedrooms into a theater room and do something similar to this—minus all the screens but one.

"Here you go." The bartender set the glass down.

Chris swiped the soda and drank it down, fizz and all. "Hey, maybe you can help me. Have you seen a woman with blonde hair —?"

"Yeah." The bartender chuckled. "Every cruise."

"Sure, thanks." Chris wasn't in the mood for games with his wife missing. He handed the bartender his room card, stood up and straightened his back.

"Here you go, guy." He handed the card back to him. "You should have been here about an hour ago. There was this chick that came in with these eyes. You should have seen them. She was a hottie for sure."

Elizabeth. "When did she leave?"

The bartender checked the time on one of the screens. "About an hour and a half ago. Why?"

"I'm trying to find her. Thanks." Chris dashed out toward the elevators. Rounding the corner, he jammed his finger on the arrow button. Several people waited beside him. The doors opened, and he rushed forward before everyone flooded in.

Fatigue wrapped around his muscles and squeezed as he leaned against the rail. He needed Elizabeth to be safe in their cabin. Then he could let go of his fear.

"Is this you?" A grey-haired woman smiled.

He glanced at the numbers above the door. "No, ma'am. Thank you. Guess I was in such a hurry I entered the wrong elevator. I should have gone up, not down."

"That happens to me every time I get on one of these things." Chuckles erupted behind him as she pressed the glowing Main Floor button.

The elevator stopped, and a few people exited. Chris mashed the button, then rubbed his temples. He'd never intended to take a joy ride on the elevators tonight. With one more stroke on his temple, the doors finally opened to their floor. His energy reserves kicked in as he ran out. *Just five doors. That's as far as I have to go.* He slid his card out from his pocket, placed it against the lock, and entered.

Chapter Twenty-Five

Sunday — Sea Day

Chris sat on the balcony, staring out over the ocean, lost in a sea of questions. He'd found Elizabeth's clothes last night, hidden in the closet. They reeked of alcohol. How much did she drink? And didn't she care someone could have taken advantage of her? His stomach rolled.

"God, I can't take care of her. I've tried … I'm trying, but no matter…" Chris sat with his head in his hands. What was he supposed to do?

"Hi."

He jerked his head up, but couldn't face her. He didn't want her to see him struggling with the disappointment, the hurt. He needed to pluck it out before it took root. "Do you want me to order breakfast?"

"I'm not hungry right now. Thank you."

After a moment of silence, Chris turned around. The doorway was empty. What do I do, Lord? How do I help? As he stood, verses weaved through his mind. Love is patient, kind, it always protects, hopes, trusts, perseveres and never fails.

He inhaled and entered the room. Elizabeth sat on the bed, leaning against the headboard and hugging her knees.

"Do you want to talk about it?" He sat alongside her.

"I went to a bar last night."

"Why?" Chris reigned in his tight retort. He wanted her to talk to him, not shut down.

She avoided his eyes. Her knuckles turned white against her knees. "I wanted to forget."

It didn't take a genius to figure out what she meant. Him and Katherine. The two events were so tied together, one didn't come to mind without the other.

"I was heading back to my room. I didn't intend to go to the bar. It drew me."

"What did?"

"The scent. Once I smelled the alcohol, I could taste it. Like the Bible says, what I don't want to do, I do. My flesh was fighting against me. Was that the way you felt with her?"

Chris jumped up, shaking his head. He didn't want to go there. God had molded him into a new man, a forgiven man. All he wanted to do was forget. "Please, Elizabeth. Don't."

"Scripture says love keeps no record of wrongs, it trusts, and never fails. I want to, but every time…" She met his gaze and rose from the bed. "I'm trying to understand. I'm trying to figure out how to hold on to you so you won't leave me again." She lumbered over to the balcony window and clenched her arms around her waist.

How could he reassure her in a way he hadn't before? How? He fell silent.

"I was hit on last night. He asked if I wanted to…"

Fear crept up his spine. *No.* He took a step toward her. "You're my wife, no one else's."

He needed to get out of there. Walking over to the dresser, Chris yanked a t-shirt out of the dresser and pulled it on. He needed to find this guy.

She'd asked Chris how to hold on to him, and he hadn't answered. What was the sense of fighting for a husband and a marriage if she couldn't hold on to him? She knew she wasn't pretty enough or skinny enough. If he didn't want her, she'd wanted to make sure he knew someone else did. But that had been a mistake.

"God, I didn't. I could never..." Her voice trembled as a thought flashed in her mind. She'd asked Steven to comfort her not too long ago. What would have happened if he hadn't walked away? Deep in her heart, she knew the answer.

Elizabeth crumpled to the ground. "Lord. I want my husband. Only him."

Chris marched back into the bar, fists clenched. He found the same bartender from the day before, pouring someone a drink. He could help him find the jerk. "My wife told me a guy hit on her yesterday."

"Hey, man. I guess you found her. And those eyes belong to you? Lucky man." He turned over a few glasses and filled them.

"I need to find this guy. Do you know where he is?"

"Listen here." The bartender leaned in. "You're on a ship. You may never find him with all these people. I'd let it go and take care of that hottie of yours. Besides, I think your wife has enough fire that no man would mess with her unless they wanted to get burned."

"What are you talking about?"

"She didn't tell you?" He laughed. "When your wife walked in here, a young buck went to her like she was a doe in heat. He pushed a drink under her nose before she could object."

"What did he say to her?"

"They talked for a bit, but I had to take care of other customers, so I'm not sure. But when I came back, he whispered something and whatever it was, it was a big mistake.

She took this full glass of beer in her hand and poured it over him. She made a huge mess, but you should have seen the look on his face. He was mad, all right. Stomped out of here in a hurry."

"Did they leave together?"

"Nope. She stayed. Grabbed a few napkins to wipe off her shirt. Glanced up at the screen a few times, but you could tell she wasn't interested."

"Hey, Mack!"

The bartender snaked his neck. "Yeah, I'll be right there." He flung a glass in the air and caught it. "Gotta go. Duty calls."

Chris didn't know whether to laugh or cry. The pent-up tension in his shoulders and neck eased. The blood in his hands began to flow once more. He inhaled and exhaled, relief lightening his mind and heart. A clock on the wall caught his attention. They had an hour before meeting everyone for lunch. Every emotion told him to stay locked in the room with his wife to keep her to himself for the remainder of the trip. But that wasn't going to happen.

When he entered their cabin, Elizabeth met him at the door, eyes brimming with tears.

"I couldn't resist the temptation to go into the bar, but that's all I did." She touched his cheek. "You have to know, you're all I want."

He bent down and caressed her lips with his. "I love you."

A wave of fresh tears slid down her reddened cheeks. He wiped them away with his thumb. "I was afraid."

"I love you, and only you." Her head rested against his chest.

Chris's heart pounded in her ear. She absorbed her husband's love, strength from his comforting arms, and God's peace flowing over her.

"Do you want to stay here?" he whispered, running his fingers through her hair.

She smiled. "I'd rather, but we should go. What time are we meeting them?"

"Lido Deck at one. I think Sarah mentioned they stay open until two-thirty."

"I guess I can't wear these." She tugged the bottom of her shirt and strolled to the dresser. She craned her neck to see what Chris wore. He had on a pair of khakis with a navy blue polo. "Is that what you're going to wear?"

"Is this not okay?" He patted himself in a mocking gesture.

"Yes, you're fine. As handsome as ever." She turned to gather her clothes, but Chris rotated her to face him.

"Are you still attracted to me?" He tucked a few strands of hair behind her ear, avoiding her eyes.

She studied him. Did he not know?

"That bad, huh?" He lifted his gaze to hers.

"If only you knew. When you come into a room and notice me, my heart skips a beat, but I also feel pride. I've seen how much time you've spent down on your knees with the Lord. You're the most handsome man I've ever met."

Tears threatened as he swallowed. He raised her hand to his lips, then his cheek. "Thank you." His voice broke.

She reclaimed her hand, desiring nothing more but to remain there, so close she felt his breath against her face. "I should get dressed."

Chris nodded. "I'll take a quick shower. But before I go, I want you to know I praise God every day for His mercies." A tear traveled to his lips. He turned and headed for the bathroom.

Elizabeth laid her clothes on the white sheets, then knelt down at the edge of the bed. "God, thank You for your mercies to us every day. But mostly, You know how I feel. Scripture says the Lord gives and takes away. Please forgive me, but I'm not Job in the Bible. Help me in my weakness and in my fears." She rose quickly and got dressed.

Twenty minutes later, they raced out of the elevators and into the restaurant.

Chris grabbed her hand. "Help me find them." He drew her along, weaving through blue tables and down a path of maroon-and-blue diamond carpet. Sarah stood waving.

"There's Sarah and Lindsey." Elizabeth pointed. Timothy rose with a scowl. As they got closer, it eased.

"Auntie! Auntie!" Lindsey squealed as they rounded the corner, flinging her arms wide as Elizabeth grasped her in a hug.

"We didn't think you were coming." Timothy sat down. "What ever happened to Mister Punctual?"

"God and Elizabeth dictate my time now." Chris shot her a smile and held out her chair. She hesitated before setting Lindsey down in her chair, then took the offered seat. Elizabeth let out a breath and glanced at her niece, smiling wide from across the table.

"Are you all right?" Sam whispered as she bent down to snatch her bag from the floor and plopped it in her lap. She fished in her purse and tucked a tissue in her hand, passing it to her.

Elizabeth reached out, snagged it from her fingers, and blotted her right eye. The moisture matted her lashes together, but she hoped it would dissipate on its own. She nodded her thank-you.

Phillip stood, patting his stomach. "I'm ready to eat."

"Come on, Lindsey girl. Let's go with Uncle Phillip." Timothy and Phillip escorted her to the buffet.

Chris turned to Elizabeth. "Do you want to go now?"

She tucked her hair behind her ear. "In a minute."

"Okay." Chris followed the others to the buffet.

Elizabeth couldn't help but notice how Timothy helped Lindsey with her plate. She wanted to be the one waiting in line, piling food on a plate for Katherine. Holding her in her arms and feeling the warmth of her embrace. She took a deep breath, and exhaled slowly. She willed herself not to cry by biting her lip. She'd draw blood first.

Sam's and Sarah's eyes locked on her. "Are you two okay? I thought this trip would be good." Sarah rubbed her back.

"It is. Believe me." Did she think if she said "believe me", it might convince them? Talk about God—that always works. Wasn't He always the answer? Something within her agreed. "God has everything in control."

After lunch, Elizabeth glanced up. "What about the bookstore?" Lindsey came to sit with her, handing her a crayon.

Phillip leaned back in his chair. "Several weeks ago, Sam and I mentioned a few changes we would like to make to the bookstore, but never finished the conversation. I asked Chris what he thought we should do about the apartment."

Chris sat up and folded his hands above the table. "And I told him we were moving back right after the trip. Straight from the car to our home."

Her heart lightened, and relief washed through her at the thought of moving back to their home. "Yep, that's the plan. Why?"

"Samantha and I, with your permission of course, would like to tear down the apartment and expand the bookstore. The timing is perfect, and since Chris knows all about designing and blueprints, it would only make sense to hire the best in town."

"I can't do it." Chris breathed.

Elizabeth stared at her husband. He had told her he would help run the store. Did he plan to go back to his old job after all? She knew they needed the money, but...

Phillip sat up. "We could really use your help with —"

"You're not going back," Elizabeth said, snapping Lindsey's crayon between her fingers.

"Auntie, you broke my purple."

Elizabeth glanced down. Two pieces of purple crayon rested in her palm. "I'm sorry, sweetie. I'll go to the gift shop and see if I can find some more for you." She rose.

Chris clasped her hand. "I won't be the one to take the apartment away from her."

"Can I go with you, Auntie? I want to come." Fingers wrapped around her pinky.

"I'll take you." Sarah stood and snagged her daughter in her arms. "Are we still on for mini golf?"

Timothy stood. "Wait, I'm coming. And of course we're on for mini golf. It's couples against couples."

"Sounds good." Phillip grabbed his glass of water, took a few sips as they left, and set his glass back on the coaster. "We're not trying to take anything away. We've been praying about the bookstore and what to do. If we expand, we can make the upstairs a Christian section, bringing in new business."

Sam nodded. "This is something you asked me to do before we opened, but I didn't know the Lord then. Now, I think it's time. Not only for growth, but for you. If you give us the okay, it's one step closer to healing and letting go."

Elizabeth studied her index finger in silence. If she gave her apartment to them to do as they pleased, what would happen if things didn't work out with Chris? Where would she go? It was the last thing she owned that was hers alone. No, she shouldn't think this way. She needed to look toward the future and let go of the past, fears included. Her sister was right.

Chris ran his palm along the back of her neck. "You don't need to decide now. It's up to you. Your choice. Okay?"

She tilted her head and caught a glimpse of a smile. He'd been so patient and loving with her. She wanted to say yes to please him, but her lips pressed together.

"Think about it for me." Sam rose from her seat and grabbed her bag from the floor.

Phillip followed his wife's lead. "Are you ready for a little friendly competition?" Laugh lines wrinkled around his eyes.

"Me?" Standing, Elizabeth shook her head.

"Don't play coy, Mrs. Roberts." Chris chuckled as he lumbered to his feet. "I know that look. We better watch out."

"So the poker face has made its way into mini golf, has it?" Sam laughed. "We'll see who wins."

"I've never known a family to be so competitive. Are you sure it's healthy?" Elizabeth chuckled. She loved this. It's what she'd wanted growing up, but everything had shattered once Sam left. An image of Steven played in her mind. *You always wanted a family.*

"Are you ready?" Chris's hand rested on the small of her back.

Her eyes jerked to his. "Yes."

Chapter Twenty-Six

Sunday—Sea Day

Chris kept his palm on Elizabeth's back until her focus reached him. The poker face she'd worn a moment ago now masked something he didn't recognize. Was it worry? Could she be thinking about the bookstore? He had told her the decision was hers. What mattered most was getting his wife back home and starting their lives over again. He'd wasted precious days before they left, consumed by the past. That's where he hoped the memories of Steven would stay—lost.

He stepped onto the Sun Deck in time to see Timothy swing his club. He almost smacked Phillip as he and Samantha walked by. He chuckled and placed a hand on his shoulder. "You can't take out the competition that way. Of course it means you'd forfeit and I'd win, but then again, I'm a natural-born winner."

Timothy laughed. "Talking smack, are we?"

"Listen to you—your urban slang. Hanging out with the youth down at the shelter has done you some good. You're loosening up. Thank them for me." Chris grabbed a putter as Elizabeth joined him and lifted an orange ball from the bucket.

Samantha leaned on Phillip's shoulder as the wind picked up strands of her hair and blew them across her cheek. She tucked them behind her ear. "Where is Sarah?"

"She and Lindsey went to check out the children's play center. There they are." He nodded in their direction.

Sarah reined in her *princess* by the hand before she danced away. Elizabeth's face brightened, and a giggle escaped.

Why did she have to have the surgery? If she'd waited until after the cruise—who knows what could have happened? And if nothing else did, spending this time with Lindsey might have changed her mind.

He kissed his wife's cheek. None of that mattered now. The deed was done.

"Who wants to go first?" Timothy pointed to Lindsey then placed her ball on the green. She trotted over to the marker with her putter. Sarah lined the ball with the hole and quickly jumped out of the way.

"Can I go now, Daddy?"

"Go ahead."

Chris inhaled. Lindsey held Timothy's heart. And if Katherine … He shook the thought out of his mind. He couldn't change the past. That was something he was learning, but he did have control of his actions, specifically loving his wife. He'd enjoy doing that for the rest of his life.

With the sixteen tries it took Lindsey to put the ball into the hole, Timothy waved the rest of them to play through.

"Go ahead, Chris. I need to practice my swing." Phillip swung the putter and hooked Samantha's bag, pulling her toward him.

He glanced back to the course. Elizabeth met him with a smile. "Do you want to go?"

"Sure." She stuck her ball in a groove, lined her shot, and swung. Hole in one. She trotted down the lane and grabbed her ball, cocking her head to the side. Long strands of blonde hair shimmered in the sun. "You're going to lose."

Hmmm. This should be fun. "There needs to be a prize for the winner, prize for best score, and…" Chris met his wife's eyes dead on. "…if I beat you, I get to choose my reward."

"That's only if you win, but don't count on it." She planted one hand on her hip and pointed with the other at the hole. "Are you planning to hit the ball?"

"Are those our terms?"

She laughed. "If you win, you choose, and if I win, I choose? Does that sound about right?"

"Better start accepting defeat." Chris walked over and took his turn. His ball sailed over several greens.

Phillip choked out a laugh.

"Whose ball was that?" Timothy joined them, looking from Phillip to him. "I heard you say something about winners and losers. I'm trying to root for you Chris, but that stunk."

"It's the wind's fault. Besides, what's that saying? 'It doesn't matter how you start the race but how you finish it.'"

Samantha smiled and leaned into Phillip. "We're rooting for you, Chris."

Elizabeth walked from the other side of the course. "Are you all talking about our deal?" She handed Chris his ball.

"Yep." Samantha pressed her lips together and prodded Chris. "Go, slow poke."

Chris laid the ball on the ground once again, but this time, when he swung, the ball slid into the hole. "Not too shabby." He winked at his wife and she blushed. Yes, indeed, this would be fun.

Elizabeth tapped her chin while Chris recalculated the score card. He ran a finger down the left side of the paper. She loved winning. "Um, let's see. What can I ask for?"

He glanced at her. "This can't be right. There is no way you beat me."

"You have the proof right in your hand." She pressed into his shoulder and pretended to study the totals when her sister walked over to her. "Hey, Sam, do we still have those extra frames at the store?"

"Yeah. Do you plan to hang the score card?"

"Of course. Right on Chris's side of the room. Maybe over his dresser."

"You're killing me." Chris carried their clubs and golf balls to the counter.

When he turned around, his body slumped, and his gaze fell to the ground. He looked like a little boy who had lost his dog. Those green eyes looked up, and she had to laugh. "You are not getting my trophy no matter how much you pout."

"It was worth a shot. I had big plans for us."

Elizabeth smiled. "What kind of plans?"

"You'll never know."

A tiny hand tugged her fingers, and Elizabeth looked down to see her niece staring up. "Mommy's going to take me to the kids' place. Wanna come?"

Elizabeth dropped to one knee. "Sweetie, I'm going to stay with Uncle Chris this time, but the next time you want me to go, I will. Is that a deal?"

"You promise?"

"Yes, I promise." Elizabeth hugged her.

"I love you, Auntie." Small arms encircled her neck. Lindsey kissed her cheek before she rushed off in her ballerina slippers.

Like Katherine, she was there one minute and gone the next.

Chris helped her to her feet. "You'll have to tell me her secret."

She blinked. "What secret?"

"How'd she secure a date with you?"

"It's easy. She asked." Elizabeth bit back her laughter and turned from Chris's view. She felt his hand slide around her, and her breath caught. Her cheeks warmed. Thankfully they lagged behind the others. Embarrassment didn't suit her.

"Where are we going exactly?" Chris tightened his grip for more of a possessive hold once they entered the elevator. She loved feeling him claim her as his own. *"Bone of my bone, flesh of my flesh,"* the verse sang through her heart.

Sam pushed the button, and the elevator descended a few floors. "We can meet you at the pool. It shouldn't take us long."

"Sure. We can use a cool-down." Chris chuckled under his breath.

The doors opened. "All right, we'll see you in a few." Phillip escorted Sam out.

"So, we have the elevator all to ourselves." The doors closed. "What would you like to do?" He squeezed her close to his side.

She remained silent, thinking about what to do about her swimsuit, when Chris bent down and caressed her lips with his. The doors sprang open.

"After you." He winked.

It was time to tell Chris about the swimsuit. She waited until he slapped their card on the table by the phone, but before she could mention it, he grabbed his swim trunks and dashed into the bathroom.

Okay, how would she tell him? What would she say? *"Oh, I bought this so you'd keep your eyes on me."* There was nothing wrong with a wife wanting to keep her husband's attention, but it wasn't something she could wear in public. Did she dare show him?

The best thing to do was wear a t-shirt the entire time. She changed quickly, slipping on one of Chris's long shirts, and grabbed a ponytail band.

"Are you ready?" Chris hustled around the room.

"Yep." Her voice came out mousy.

He turned around. "What are you wearing? Is that my shirt?" He stood in front of her, brows crunched together.

"I hope you don't mind." She took the ponytail band from her wrist and pulled her hair back.

"No. I don't think I've ever seen you wear my shirts before." He looked her in the eyes. His mouth opened and shut before he spun around. "I'll get the sunscreen. I don't want you to burn your fair skin."

"I'm going to keep your shirt on so we won't have to bother with the sunscreen this time. I don't plan to be out there long anyway." She twisted her head back and forth quickly to blur Chris's expression. Her hair flung side to side.

"Elizabeth?"

"Yes?" She snatched the towel from the counter and walked to the door. "I'm ready." Now if she could get through this without taking her shirt off or answering his looming questions ... This next hour couldn't be over soon enough.

Once out of the elevators and onto the Lido Deck, Chris clasped her hand. "There's Samantha in the spa."

Sam waved and pointed to the pool. Phillip's head popped up. Air and water blew out of his mouth like a whale, spewing on Chris.

"Hey, man, that's some nasty water to be putting in your mouth."

"If you'd seen some of the water I drank in Africa, you would drink this all day long. Get in. I'm surprised there's not many people here yet."

Elizabeth's hold tightened on the neon-striped towel. "You go ahead. I'll join my sister in the hot tub." If she stayed with her sister, the hour would pass by quickly.

They set their stuff down and parted directions. As soon as Chris entered the water, Phillip began discussing the bookstore and her apartment.

A couple in the hot tub climbed out, leaving her and Sam alone. Maybe her sister had an extra bathing suit she could borrow. Sam's eyes were closed when Elizabeth held her shirt down in the water and sat on the ledge. Jets and bubbles massaged her back. With a deep breath, she allowed the warm water to ease the tension she didn't realize she'd been carrying. "This is nice."

"Feels great, doesn't it?" Sam's eyes opened. "I would love to have one of these."

"I think that would be a great idea. Not a bad perk for being your sister. And speaking of, did you bring an extra bathing suit with you?"

Sam sat up taller. "Did you forget to bring one? Is that why you're wearing that shirt?"

"Oh, no, I brought one all right. If you can call it that."

"What about the new one you got for the trip when you and Sarah went shopping?"

She looked toward Chris, then ducked her head. "I bought it to attract my husband. I wanted his eyes to be on me and only me, but now I'm too embarrassed. What happens if he doesn't like what he sees?"

"I'm going to say something here. Please don't take it the wrong way. Yes, it's important that a husband and wife are attracted to each other, but it's more than attraction. It has to do with love and commitment. You won't always have the looks you have now. They are fleeting, but who you are in Christ is beautiful, and as scripture says, worth more than gold.

"Thanks, sis."

"That's why I'm here. Now, let me see this bathing suit."

"Are you serious?" She laughed, glancing around to find Chris and Phillip leaning against the pool wall.

"They're not looking."

With half of her body in the spa, Elizabeth took off her shirt.

Sam's eyes widened. "If that's the top, I can imagine what the bottoms look like. I wish I had another swim suit, but I don't."

"That's all right. I can hear Betsy from church now. 'Girl, don't you know modesty is hot? Go put some clothes on.'" Elizabeth laughed and righted her shirt. "Speaking of church, I'm ready to go back."

"Oh, Elizabeth, that is wonderful!" She yanked her into a hug and released her quickly. "Chris is coming."

Sam helped her drape on her wet t-shirt, but as her head pushed through, Chris's focus wasn't where she thought it would be. He stared into her eyes. She pulled her shirt down.

"Are you ready to go?"

"Are you?" She could barely speak.

"I'll get you a towel." He turned on his heels.

Sam touched her arm. "He loves you. Only you."

"Why did he seem upset?"

"I think you should ask him that. It would be good for you two to talk, and I mean really talk."

Phillip stepped into the hot tub and slid next to her sister.

"Here you go." Chris held out the towel like a screen. She stepped out and shivered from the breeze, tugging her shirt down past her waist. Strong arms wrapped the towel around her and held her in an embrace. "I'm kidnapping my wife for the rest of the day, so we'll see you tomorrow."

Phillip laughed. "Have fun."

Sam splashed him. Her sister's giggles followed them to the elevator.

Stepping inside their cabin, her stomach churned. "Are you upset?" She set the towel down on the counter.

Chris came to her and grabbed the edges of her shirt. "Lift your arms."

With her arms up in the air, her shirt came off and dropped on the floor. Cool air kissed her damp skin.

"Why don't you change? When you're done, meet me on the balcony."

She nodded. Her gaze sank to the floor, but Chris's hand caressed her cheek.

"Please don't misinterpret my words or my actions. If you knew my thoughts right now, you'd know how desirable you are."

She lifted her head, and a smile played on his lips. "Will you kiss me?"

His smile faded.

"You asked what I wanted from winning, and this is it."

With a closer step, he lifted her chin and lips to him. With the first touch, heat flooded her chilled body. With the second, she felt lightheaded.

He rested his head against hers. "When will you give your heart to me? When will I be yours again?"

"Don't give up," she whispered.

"I'll never give up on us." And with one last kiss, he left through the balcony door.

Darkness began to fall, but the image of a man gawking at his wife stung Chris's memory. With a deep breath, another image took over: Elizabeth standing before him in nothing more than a few strips of fabric. Yes, keeping her all to himself was what he needed to do, even for one night.

Leaning back in his seat, he propped his feet onto the other balcony chair. The ocean stretched beneath the sky. The door opened behind him, and the smell of coffee drifted out. He sat up.

"I ordered room service since you said we were staying in. I had them bring you some coffee." She set the mug down on the table.

"Thank you." He took a sip. With Elizabeth safely beside him, coffee never tasted so sweet. "Would you like some?"

She chuckled. "No thanks."

"Here, sit with me." He set his coffee down, arms outstretched.

"With you? There's not enough room."

"Sure there is." He took her hand and pulled her into his lap. She laughed, but to him it was perfect. He wrapped his arms around her.

"Wow, it's dark, isn't it?" She intertwined their fingers.

"Can you picture Adam and Eve holding each other in the dark, like we are?"

"Almost, but they would be slightly less dressed than I was earlier. I need to know if you were upset with me when we headed back to the room."

"Not with you, sweetheart."

"Are you sure, because the way I saw it —"

"The way you see it is not the same way a man sees it. Men are visual."

She lifted from his arms. "I bought it because I wanted to be the only one you noticed, but by the time I thought about taking it back, it was too late."

"And that's why you wore the shirt." He pulled her against him.

"Sam wanted to see what it looked like, so I showed her. I didn't mean to draw anyone's attention."

"Well, you definitely caught mine." He laid his face against her hair. No matter how much he tried to deny it, fear of losing her found its way into his thoughts.

She chuckled. "Why did you moan?"

"I did?" He ran his finger through her hair. "I'm sorry if I was being overprotective. It's just ... I don't want you to be hurt again. I've asked you to trust God, yet I'm finding it a bit hard to rely on God right now to keep you safe and in my arms."

She kissed his hand, clasped it, and rose. "Let's go inside. The food is getting cold."

Her soft hand rested in his palm as she led the way. Setting him down, she placed two silver trays on the bed before finding her spot next to him.

"So, what do we have here?"

She lifted both lids at the same time and smiled. "Steak and potatoes. I told them to fix it the way you like."

"Still mooing?" He laughed, cutting into the meat. The pink steak had lost some of its heat, but it melted in his mouth. "Thank you. This is nice."

About halfway through their meal, Elizabeth set hers aside. "Where are we going tomorrow?"

"Cozumel."

"Can I ask you something?" She clasped her hands together.

"Anything."

"Will you stay at the bookstore or find something else?"

The comment she'd made earlier in the day came to him. Did she think he was going back to work in West Palm? *Back to…?* He tried to swallow, but his food got caught. "Water," he choked, plopping his fork down.

She handed him a glass. "You all right?"

He drank the cool liquid. "Yes. I'm fine." He coughed a few more times. "Our business. Together. I don't care about anything else. Christ and you. God will provide." He inhaled a deep breath. Never would he go back to his old life and to being the man he once knew.

"Will you read scripture to me tonight?"

"I'll read right now. Can you get my Bible out of the drawer?" Chris stood and carried their plates. He stacked them on the tray and placed them outside the door. Washing his hands, he prayed. *Father, I know You will provide. Please keep Elizabeth safe, and take away my fear of losing her.*

Elizabeth had slipped under the sheet by the time he returned to the bed. His Bible lay by her side. Sitting next to her, he opened to Ephesians.

Later that night, Elizabeth fell asleep before Chris had a chance to say goodnight. He slipped under the sheet and thanked God for His grace, but prayed for peace.

Chapter Twenty-Seven

Monday—Cozumel, Mexico

Elizabeth and Chris squeezed into the elevator. "Do we have everything?" Elizabeth whispered, placing a hand on her bag draped over her shoulder.

"I'm missing one thing." Chris planted a kiss on her lips and smiled. "Now I have everything I need."

She leaned into his chest. "This is not the time to be romantic."

"No one is paying any attention to us anyway. I can't help it if I find my wife irresistible."

"You won't once I smell like a horse."

"Didn't you know? I just love the scent of grain and hay."

"Stop." She elbowed him in the ribs and shook her head. The elevator doors opened, and everyone filed out.

Chris pointed. "There they are."

"Are you all ready?" Timothy swung Lindsey up on his shoulders. Sweet giggles bubbled into the air.

"Giddy up, horsey. Look at me, Auntie. I'm up high."

Elizabeth chuckled, loving being a part of this family she held so dear, and especially claiming a precious spot in Lindsey's heart. "Yes, you are. Giddy up, Daddy."

"Giddy up." Lindsey nodded up and down in exaggeration.

Timothy shook his head. "Don't encourage her." He trotted away.

Sam huddled beside her while they all ventured off of the ship. "How are you doing?"

"Chris and I are doing great." She glanced at him and Phillip. "What do you think they're talking about?"

"Probably the same thing we are."

"Hey, what are you girls whispering about?" Sarah joined them. "I want to know."

"Men."

"Oh, I gave that subject up after Tim. He still keeps me guessing, and we've been married sixteen years."

Sam pointed. "Look, the excursion buses. Hey guys! Are we doing the ruins first, then going shopping?" She grabbed both their arms and hurried them to catch up with the men.

"That sounds good to me," Chris said. "I told Elizabeth this morning how much I like horses." He turned to her and winked.

Sarah laughed as they veered to the buses. "I saw that wink. I wonder what it means."

Elizabeth grinned. "That Chris likes the smell of hay." She couldn't help chuckling at how ridiculous it sounded, but she liked having something only the two of them shared. It had been so long.

When they arrived, Elizabeth followed Chris off the bus. Everyone huddled together, like the horses tethered to the rail. Orange straw huts lined both sides of the road. Some of the huts were filled with green, yellow, and orange plastic tables and chairs for the tourists.

Elizabeth scanned the people milling around. Some filed into a line a few feet away. One man came out, pulling a horse by a white rope. "I've never ridden a horse before today, and I have to admit I'm a bit nervous."

"You'll do fine. Besides, I don't think any of us has ever ridden a horse. Let's go over here." Chris shadowed the crowd to the end of the newly-formed line. Phillip and Sam came over and stood with them.

"Where did Sarah and Timothy go?" Elizabeth searched the crowd.

Sam pointed to a line of travelers coming from the building. "To the bathroom for Lindsey. Speaking of, I might need to go before this tour."

"I'll join you, Sam."

Chris kissed her cheek. "Hurry, we don't want to miss the tour."

As she and Sam stood in the restroom line, Elizabeth inclined her head and fought back a smile. "Oh, I forgot to tell you, I've decided to give up the apartment."

Her sister's eyes widened. "That's wonderful, Lizzy!" She engulfed her in a hug. "Sorry, forgot about the name."

"It's okay, now. I remember Mom calling me Lizzy."

Sam moved her at arm's length. "When did this happen? What all do you remember?" She took several steps forward.

"I'm not exactly sure. It's wonderful, but I still feel like there's more I don't know."

"Well, once you do, I need to ask you something." She said over her shoulder, taking several more steps forward.

"What did you want to ask?"

"It's nothing, really." Sam was next in line.

Why did it seem like Sam was holding something back from her? Perhaps it could even help her remember the missing pieces of her memory. Elizabeth grabbed her sister's arm. "You want to ask me something, go ahead."

"This isn't the right time." Sam glanced around.

Elizabeth's initial impulse was to pull her sister from the line and demand she tell her what was on her mind, but before she could think, her sister moved forward into the restrooms.

Once Elizabeth exited, she found Sam walking toward Phillip and Chris. She hurried to catch up. "Sam."

Her sister turned and smiled. "Ready? This should be fun."

"Not yet." Elizabeth met Sam's gaze. "Ask me. Whatever it is. I'll be fine."

"It's not the time."

She frowned, planting her hands on her hips. "Sam."

"Fine." She glanced back at the men and leaned forward. "Chris told me something about our parents' funeral that I'm confused about."

Elizabeth's hands slid from her waist. She wasn't expecting this. "Go ahead."

"He said you were there at the funeral, but I never saw you."

"I remember being there. It stunned me seeing you after all those years, especially how much you looked like Mom."

"Where were you?"

Elizabeth thought for a moment. "Hidden behind a tree."

"Stop!" Chris's angered voice caused them to jump.

Elizabeth turned to her husband, his face blanched, while Phillip pinned Sam with his gaze. *What had just happened?* "Hey, I'm sorry," Elizabeth apologized, hoping to ease the tension she now felt. "We just started talking and lost track of the time."

Chris clasped her hand and held it against his cheek for a moment. "Nope, doesn't smell like hay yet. We better get going." He smiled, but it didn't reach his eyes. She looked toward Sam, but Phillip had already moved them toward a set of horses.

When Elizabeth saw the height of her horse, she swallowed hard and tapped her fingers against Chris's chest. "I'm going to need your help if I'm to climb this beast."

"You can do it." Chris untied the reins from a rail and hopped onto his horse like he'd been riding for years.

"You're kidding me, right? You think I can get on that?" She pointed. "He's huge!"

"I want to see you try at least."

"Oh, thanks." She held the top of the saddle, put a foot in the stirrup, and while fighting with the horse to stay in one place, she threw her leg over, missing her mark.

Chris climbed down and held her horse's reins. "Try again. You have long legs. It should be easy."

"So you noticed my legs." She smiled, catching the amusement in his gaze. She was rewarded with more assistance than was required into the saddle.

Chris climbed back onto his horse, and the two of them trotted over to where everyone had been held. A few others gathered before they were given the okay to go. Several people hurried off. Some made clicking noises to encourage their horses to walk a bit faster. Chris moseyed alongside her in the back of the pack. "Look, Timothy and Sarah are coming this way. Lindsey's waving."

"I hope she hangs on tight. I can't believe the people who run this tour allow us to take the horses out on our own."

"She'll be fine. Sarah has her. Do me a favor—if your princess asks if she can ride with you, say no. You're not exactly stable on that horse."

"Thanks for the reminder."

Timothy trotted back and forth next to Chris like his horse ran on caffeine. "I challenged Phillip to a race. Are you in?"

"I'd rather stay here right now. Besides, we're just passing the last set of buildings. There will be plenty of time."

Sarah trotted over to them.

"You're riding really well, Sarah. How did you pick it up so quickly?"

"I've ridden horses before. I was a teen then, but I haven't forgotten. Those were some good times. When Lindsey gets a little older, I would like her to ride."

"Does that mean I get to ride horses too, Mommy?"

"I don't know, but we'll see."

Lindsey pointed ahead. "Look, Mommy, a little castle. Are we going to go through it like everyone else?"

"Yes, we are. Ready?"

Lindsey nodded. Sarah sped up to an empty spot in line and entered through the narrow arch. Timothy followed close behind.

Two walls made out of stone stood on both sides. What looked like lattice work carved in rock accentuated the doors. An arch connected the two sides. Though she knew she wouldn't hit her head, she ducked. That silly song Chris and Timothy sang on the ship came to mind. She turned around. "Don't sing it. I know, I know. I ducked but I didn't cover."

Chris smiled and trotted to her. "I love you, Mrs. Roberts."

"That was out of nowhere."

"I wanted to make sure I told you before my brothers came to steal me away."

She grinned as Phillip and Timothy galloped straight for them. "Yeah, the three *amigos*," she said as they neared.

"*Hola*." Phillip chuckled.

"Timothy, you can take him now. Thanks for sharing him with me."

"If you want him to stay..." Phillip rode next to Chris.

"No, go ahead," she assured.

"Then let's go. Oh, and Elizabeth, Sarah said to trot up there with her and Samantha so you're not by yourself."

She nodded.

"You'll be all right?" Chris's forehead wrinkled.

"Yes. Now go." She enjoyed the clippie-clop of the horses as the guys raced off. She followed the men's lead, though at a slower pace, catching up with Sam and Sarah when she noticed something odd. A horse next to Sarah's seemed to be pushing her to the edge of a ravine.

"Your horse bit me!" Sarah pointed at the woman's horse, and she stopped abruptly. Sam hopped off her horse and rushed to help Lindsey down. Sarah clenched her leg.

Elizabeth dismounted, frowning at what she had just seen. "What happened?"

"I don't know," Sarah said, grabbing her leg. "The lady's horse wouldn't let us by. She kept nudging us when it turned around and bit my leg. Look at this." She uncovered the bloody area. "I have teeth marks."

Sam reached in her bag and pulled out a pack of tissues. "Here, take a few to stop the bleeding. We need to get you back. It looks like you're going to need stiches."

Elizabeth looked up. Where was Lindsey? Quickly scanning the area, her princess bent down to look at something. "I'll be right back. I'm going to see how Lindsey is."

"Thank you, Elizabeth." Sarah stood. "Will you take her? I'm going to go with Samantha. When we pass the guys, I'll explain what happened and tell them to come back for you."

"We'll be fine." Elizabeth glanced at Lindsey once again. She had walked some distance from them, almost making it impossible to see her. She turned her attention back to them. "Be careful." She waved them off. When she turned around, Lindsey was gone.

"Come on, sweetie, it's not time to play hide-n-seek. We need to follow Mommy back." She checked behind several stones. Nothing.

"Lindsey!" An eerie sound sang through the rustling of the trees. A chill crawled up her spine. Panic suffocated her.

"Lindsey, sweetie, please! Where are you? God, where is she?" What was that? She stilled. Small, faint, whimpers floated to her ears. *Lindsey.*

She ran back to the first place where Sam helped her off the horse. Hurrying to the sound, she found Lindsey sitting against a boulder, her head hanging to her chest as she cried.

"Hey, there, my princess. What happened?" Elizabeth lowered herself on one knee and focused on the blood oozing from her niece's ankle.

"I fell down, and it hurts."

"I'm sure it does. Do you think you can walk, or do you need me to carry you?"

Lindsey's arms reached out and hugged Elizabeth's neck. It was all she could do to keep from tearing up herself. Her niece meant the world to her, and feeling her arms around her awakened a desire so deep, she never knew it existed. But she couldn't deny it. She wanted another child. Not one, many. God was giving her a second chance at love and a family. She felt alive.

Elizabeth hugged Lindsey to her chest and thanked God for His blessings. Her niece was safe. But before she could finish her prayer, Chris and Phillip galloped toward them.

Chapter Twenty-Eight

Thursday — Grand Cayman, Cayman Islands

Elizabeth giggled from the corner of the bed. She couldn't tear her eyes from Sarah as she stood with her hand against the crack of the door, trying to push Chris back into the hallway.

Sarah glanced at her with a smile then refocused her attention back to the door. "And who says men aren't high maintenance? I'm sorry, Chris, but the longer you keep me standing here, the longer it's going to take for you to see Elizabeth. Timothy can tie your tie."

Chris slipped his hand around the edge of the door and opened it a little wider. "I can see it now, my brother sliding a noose around my neck. I plan to spend the evening with my wife, not being thrown overboard and buried at sea."

Lindsey squeezed her head through the doorway where Chris waited. "Auntie looks beautiful. I have a new dress, too. Do you want to see it?"

"Yes, I do."

A few days ago Lindsey had favored her ankle when they returned to the ship, but now her niece smiled, and all was forgotten, scrapes included. But not for Elizabeth. It was the beginning of a wonderful future, as soon as she told Chris the truth.

Sarah glanced down. "Later, honey. Uncle Chris needs to find Daddy to help him with his tie. I'm not done with Auntie Elizabeth's hair." She pushed her glasses to the bridge of her nose. Her focus returned to the opening. "Bye." Chris's hand fell quickly and disappeared as Sarah pulled Lindsey from the door and shut it.

Sam sat in a high-back wooden chair, running her fingers through her hair. "Do you really like it, Elizabeth? What do you think Phillip will say? I can't remember having it this short."

Elizabeth had always thought Sam was beautiful, more so than anyone else she knew.

Sarah walked past her and touched Elizabeth's shoulder. "He will love it."

"It's such a big change. Seven inches."

"Elizabeth…" Sarah waved her hand in front of her eyes. "Don't tell me you're daydreaming of Chris. You'll see him soon enough." She released one of the hot rollers in her hair.

"I was thinking about how gorgeous my sister looks. You did a great job. The cut enhances her pixy features, and her hair looks beautiful draped over her shoulders, down her eggplant-colored gown. And Sarah, emerald is a lovely shade for you."

Sarah took out two rollers. "Thank you. One thing's for sure, we gals are going to be stunning coming down those dining room steps. You don't think Chris will really wear a tie, do you? Didn't he bring a tux?"

"Yes, but the rental only had clip-ons."

Samantha laughed. "I'm not sure Phillip will wear his, since he doesn't like anything around his neck. It might hang loose." She chuckled again. "He's handsome no matter what he wears."

"You crack me up." Sarah smiled.

"Mommy, are we almost done? I don't want to color anymore." Lindsey shook a piece of paper in the air.

"Yes, sweetie." Sarah took out the last roller, placing it in her holder. She grabbed her brush, ran it through Elizabeth's hair, then sprayed. "Finished. See, I told you we were done."

"Thank you." Elizabeth stood from the corner of the bed, looking behind her in the mirror. The powder-blue gown wasn't as bold as the others, but as it hung against her frame, it looked quite feminine. She slipped on her white gloves, strolled to the glass, and stared at her own reflection. *God, please give me the words to tell him.*

"Let's go, Auntie. Will you sit by me?"

She looked down at expectant eyes. If it's your will, Lord, may I have another daughter?

Chris fumbled with the fork on the table. A pinch grew in his neck from staring at the top flight of stairs cascading into the dining room. Never had he seen a room so extravagant, including the chandeliers. He might have been attending a royal ball, rather than a ship's dinner.

Timothy leaned back in his chair. "I wonder what's taking them so long. I've already downed my third soda."

"They'll be here." Phillip folded his hands. "How's the shelter going? Did you hire a new cook yet?"

"Yes, but he won't be able to start for another three months. Louis's last day is Monday. I need to find someone fast."

Chris glanced up once more, but the girls on the stairway weren't the ones he was waiting for. "How many days does Louis cook?"

"On Mondays and Thursdays. Why?"

"I think I would like to do it."

Timothy let out a howl. "Are you kidding me? When have you ever cooked anything in your life?"

"I didn't know you had certain qualifications for the job, since you have no one at the moment."

"He's right. What do you have to lose?" Phillip stood.

Timothy rose from the table. "Nothing. If people are hungry, they'll eat anything I guess. Even Chris's cooking."

"Thanks for the vote of confidence. Besides, this is something Elizabeth and I would like to do." By the time Chris stood, Samantha proceeded down the stairs. Was her hair different? He turned to Phillip, who wore the most ridiculous grin he'd ever seen. "Close your mouth before you drool."

Breaking the trance, Phillip weaved through several tables to the last set of steps, took her palm, and placed it in the crook of his elbow.

"He's making us look bad." Timothy smiled, before heading toward his family.

Elizabeth had yet to descend the stairs.

Everyone came to the table and began to sit. Chris glanced at them. "Did you forget someone?"

"She headed back to the room." Sarah kissed Lindsey on the forehead before Timothy scooted her to the table. "I'm sure she'll be here any minute."

"I'll go check on her." Samantha spun and headed back toward the stairs.

Chris hurried after her. "What is it, Samantha?"

"She was right behind me. I don't know what it is, Chris. Something is wrong. While we were on the elevator, Lindsey got off on the wrong floor and headed around the corner. Elizabeth went to get her. When they came back into the elevator ... she was hugging her middle. I don't know, maybe the thought of losing Lindsey?"

"She went back to the room?"

"That's what she said."

"Thanks." Chris bounded up the stairs, taking two steps at a time. When he entered their cabin, his heart raced. All the lights were off.

"Elizabeth." He flicked on a lamp. She stared out the glass door with her back to him. The pale blue gown curved with her figure. Her hair hung in ringlets down her back. She didn't turn.

"Sweetheart?" He walked over to her and stood. "Didn't we have a wonderful day?" He rubbed a curl between his fingers.

She nodded.

"I have the whole evening to admire Sarah's work. The back looks beautiful. May I see the front?" He wanted her to look at him, to tell him what was wrong. But when she didn't move, he wrapped his arm around her waist and leaned in. "Talk to me," he whispered against her ear.

She pulled away, shaking her head. "There's something I did, Chris. I wish…"

"It will be all right. You can tell me anything." Hadn't she realized she could trust him?

Trust in me.

Chris's hair stood on end.

"Lindsey got off on the wrong floor." Her eyes watered and darted away. "I went after her."

"Samantha told me."

"There was a bar and, for the first time, I wasn't tempted. Not one bit."

"There's nothing to be sad about." He lifted her chin and wiped a tear with his finger. Several others followed.

"I remembered something. Something someone said to me. 'I will drag you out of here every night if I have to.' I thought it was funny, because I realized God was healing me and I wasn't tempted anymore."

Chris's stomach knotted. She was talking about Steven? He was the only one who had gone after her. Fear and anger seized him. "I'm not talking about Steven." He dropped his hand from her cheek and clenched his fist.

"But Chris —"

"No!"

"Please. You have to know about … Steven and me."

Chris met her gaze. She knew.

"I…"

What was she trying to say—*"I'm sorry, I'm leaving you?"* He ached to touch her, but if he did, would it cause her to leave? He took a mental picture; she was breathtaking. The dress accented her curves. Her hair flowed down to her chest. Her eyes paled against the blue hue of the gown. A small tear left a trail to her chin.

"I knew him. We were close."

"I don't want to hear this." He turned, yanked the clip-on from the tux, and threw it on the bed.

"I need to talk to you." She went to him.

How could he stop this? *God, please.*

"Part of my life that I've tried to bury for years has come back, not only in my memories but —"

"Leave him there. Bury the memories. I don't care."

She grabbed his arm and turned him to face her.

"You almost married him. I know. I put it together after I saw the yearbook on the bookshelf. And from what you told me when I proposed, I know things went too far."

"I couldn't handle what happened. The death of my parents, and then the intimacy sent me running."

"Stop."

"What I did was wrong, Chris. I ran from him two weeks before we were to be married. We made promises to each other, and I broke those."

"What do you want me to say—I'm sorry? Because I'm not. If you would have married him, you wouldn't be my wife."

"I have to see Steven. I have to ask for his forgiveness. Not only his, but God's."

He almost reached out for her, but stopped himself. "You can ask God for forgiveness, but I'm not letting you go." Chris stormed out of the cabin.

The door shut, and Elizabeth wiped her face. What was she going to do? She needed to apologize to Steven.

All this time, Steven had never said a word. She remembered how he had held her after her attack and how she felt for him when she had asked Steven to comfort her. Her stomach lurched. *Chris knew about Steven.*

She walked to the mirror and stared, heart pounding against her chest. For the first time since the accident, she could recognize herself. She remembered everything. Slipping on her mother's red shoes and playing dress-up. Braces. Having Daddy-time when she bought her first car. Attending college. Meeting Steven. Leaving him. She wanted to smile at her long lost friend, Elizabeth Cynthia Manroe, but she couldn't. Her past needed amends.

She noted the furrowed brows of the woman looking back, the woman she had ended up being. Mrs. Elizabeth Roberts had everything, even the family she had always dreamed of, but one thing seemed to be missing since her parents died.

Several locks of hair covered part of her cheek. She pushed them back and inhaled. "Lord, I haven't been faithful to You, but You've been faithful. You never left me, though I ran from You. It's been so clear, but I didn't realize it until now. I feel You again, Lord. You are so close to me."

Her eyes watered. "Show me what I'm to do. You brought Steven back into my life. I need to ask for his forgiveness and Yours, Lord." She bowed her head. "God, forgive me for breaking my promises to Steven, and walking away from him. But mostly, for breaking my promises to You. I will never be like Job in suffering and pain. I will ask why. However, I've come to know You are worthy to be praised in all things, even when I can't peel myself off the floor. God, I will trust You."

Laughter broke through her tears. "God, I trust You!" She inhaled and exhaled. "Yes, Lord, I trust You."

Chapter Twenty-Nine

Friday — Sea Day

Elizabeth grabbed the card-key from the table and stuck it in her purse. She glanced in the mirror before heading out the door. The elevator opened onto the Empress Deck, where she stepped off and headed to her sister's room. Hopefully Chris had been there. She stood in the hall, took a deep breath, and knocked.

Sam opened the door and drew her into the room. "I knew you'd come."

She glanced around. "Is Chris here?"

She nodded and pointed to the balcony. "How are you?"

Elizabeth took a deep breath and shot another look to the veranda where the men were possibly discussing her. "I'm okay. Did he tell you?"

"Last night. Have a seat."

Elizabeth sat in one of the chairs at the small table, while Sam yanked a chair near the foot of the bed and set it next to her.

"When he came back to the cabin, he went straight to bed. He didn't say a word or hold me. I know that sounds

crazy, but I have to remind myself to trust God with this."
She fiddled with her purse. "You asked me before why you
didn't see me at the funeral."

"Do you know?"

"I hid because Steven was there. I watched from a set
of trees as he waited in line to speak with you before I left."
She hung her head. "I hurt him badly, Sam. How will he
ever forgive me?"

Sam reached over and gave her hand a squeeze. "I
think he already has."

"I have to apologize. There is more to this than having
peace after all these years. I was reading scripture before I
got ready. In Matthew, it says if you are offering a gift to
God and remember that a brother has something against
you, to leave it at the altar. To go and be reconciled, then
bring your offering."

"God convicted me of the same thing when I came to
you years ago."

"Then you understand."

"More than you know." She patted Elizabeth's hand
then stood. "Have you eaten?"

She hadn't thought about eating. "Not since breakfast
yesterday."

"I'll tell the guys we're going to get a bite." She
tapped on the balcony door.

Elizabeth jumped to her feet. "Wait!"

"He's not angry—he's afraid he might lose you." Sam
slid the glass open and poked her head out. "Elizabeth and
I are going to get something to eat. We'll be back shortly."

Elizabeth waited until she returned and lowered her
voice. "How did he seem?"

"It will be okay, Lizzy. Now, tell me, where would you
like to eat?" Sam tucked her card and phone into her jeans.

"How about that burger place?"

"Sounds good."

Once inside the restaurant, the aroma made Elizabeth's stomach growl. She touched her belly. "I didn't real-

ize I was that hungry." A lady walked by with a tray of fries and burgers. The smell lingered. "Are you ready?" Her sister was texting, so she nudged her forward. Sam slipped her phone into her pocket and placed her order.

Elizabeth ordered soon after, then found them a seat. The décor reminded her of a restoration she'd seen of an old store. Tin advertisements hung by the register along with license plates from various states. She glanced at a vintage soda pop sign when Chris entered. His shirt was untucked, his blond hair tousled, and his brows furrowed. Phillip pointed to her, and Chris caught her gaze. His face remained stoic, his eyes locked on hers as he approached.

"Hi. I didn't know you guys were coming." Chris's brows dipped slightly. He pulled out a chair and sat alongside her. She bit her lip and scanned the line for Sam. Phillip turned around with their food. Sam carried their drinks.

"I'm starved." Phillip placed the tray on the table, then helped Sam with her chair. He sat, brows raised. "So, what are your plans for the day?"

Elizabeth took a huge bite of her hamburger. They hadn't talked since yesterday. She didn't know.

Chris ran his fingers through his hair. "I thought we could go to the shops. I know this trip isn't what we expected, but I would like to get her something to remember the good times we've shared."

The hamburger caught in her throat. She grabbed her glass and drank. Her mind reeled. Chris had mentioned losing her. Sam had said the same thing this morning, and with him knowing about Steven … Did he think because she remembered Steven, she'd want him instead?

She set the glass down and grabbed his hand. "I love you."

"Is your love for me strong enough?" Chris stood. "Will you meet me in front of the main lounge show in twenty minutes?"

She swallowed hard. "I will."

Chris kissed her cheek and left.

Her gaze followed his drooping shoulders out of the restaurant. "I need to borrow a dress, Sam."

"Then let's go." She popped up and grabbed Elizabeth's arm.

"What about me?" Phillip smirked. "Go. Twenty minutes goes by fast."

Once upstairs, her sister tore outfits off the hangers for her to try on. "Wait! What about this one?" She lifted up a red halter dress. "I bought this, but haven't had a chance to wear it. It ties around your neck, but I really like the length." She held it against Elizabeth. "It's right on your knees. Perfect! Here you go." She pushed her toward the bathroom.

Stepping into the dress, Elizabeth looked in the mirror and tied it on. "Very nice!"

"Let me see."

Elizabeth came out of the bathroom, and Sarah waved a brush. "I heard you need a hairdresser."

"Oh, that looks wonderful." Sam twirled her, then planted her into a chair. "Get going, Sarah. She's got ten minutes."

Elizabeth giggled like a school girl. "I can't imagine what might happen if you both lived next door."

"Now that would be fun, wouldn't it?" Sarah laughed as she wound Elizabeth's hair around a curling iron. Finishing the last touches, she sprayed her hair, then hugged her. "Now go."

Sam pushed her out the door. "Hurry."

Chris paced in front of the theater. Phillip had reassured him Elizabeth made the right decision to take responsibility for her actions, no matter how much time had passed. Chris wanted his wife to move on from her memories with Steven, and if seeing him one last time would do that ... But was it necessary? What if his worst fears became a reality? His heart pounded. *Has it gotten hotter in*

here? He pulled at his collar and looked around. Elizabeth hurried out of the elevator, ran her hands down the sides of her red dress, and caught his gaze before smiling. He met her halfway.

"Hi. Sarah insisted on doing my hair. Have you been waiting long?" She pulled on a strand.

"How about a stroll? We have an hour."

She nodded. "May I hold your hand?"

They walked in silence. He ignored her glances. A decision had to be made, but his mind fought with his heart. Halfway around the deck, he'd decided. He needed to tell her now so they could enjoy their evening—not only tonight, but from now on. Steven would no longer be part of their lives.

He slowed by the garden atrium and led her to a row of chairs, then sat alongside her. "Elizabeth." He met her expectant gaze. "We need to talk. I know you're wanting to see Steven and —"

"I knew you would understand." She dropped her head and wrung her fingers. "This is going to be so hard for me, but I need this closure whether he accepts my apology or not. Sometimes God has us do things we know will be hard." She took his hand again and kissed his knuckles. "You'll pray for me while I'm gone?"

Chris rose. "I didn't say I wanted you to go."

She frowned up at him. "I know you don't *want* me to go." She stood.

"No. I mean you're not going. I was trying to tell you."

"I'm not going? But I thought you and Phillip were praying?"

"Phillip and I, what?" He gritted his teeth. "Yeah, we've been praying, but God didn't tell me to let you go."

She looked away. "Have you been listening?"

Chris spun around. Had he been listening? His muscles tensed. How many times had the Lord led him to do something and he did it? Countless! He'd become a servant to his wife, loved her like his own body, treasured her in every way, and asked for nothing in return but love and trust.

His stomach soured. Wasn't God asking him to do the same? To trust? Elizabeth stepped back from him. He grabbed her arm. "I'm sorry. Don't leave. Let's go to the theater, okay?"

She eyed him. "I wasn't going to leave."

He took her hand and placed it in the crook of his arm. He needed to think. Fear churned his stomach. Was she right? Could God be sending her to Steven?

They entered the theater and slid to the end of the row. She glanced at him. The lights went dim, and the red curtain drew back.

His mind raced. *God, what am I supposed to do here?* He looked toward her, but she didn't notice. All he wanted to do was fight for her. How could he send her away?

He prayed, waiting for the Lord to answer, to give him a sign, yet none came. Beyond the fear, his soul cried out.

Trust in Me.

After the show ended, the lights flicked on and Elizabeth stood. He exhaled and rose, clasping her waist. She was everything to him, and now God asked him to let her go. "Wait, we can't leave."

"Why not?" She glanced around the theater.

"Please, sit. Can we talk?" He swallowed the bile in his throat and pulled her toward the seat.

"What is it?" Her forehead wrinkled.

He took a deep breath and pushed the words from his mouth. "I have to say this now, before I change my mind. You should go to Atlanta."

Her lips gaped open. "I'm confused." She released his hand and rested her arms in her lap. "You want me to go?"

"Yes. No. That's not what I mean. When do you plan to leave?"

"Um, as soon as possible."

Could the feeling of being punched in the gut get any harder? "Then you should go whenever you feel you need to leave."

"I think I should call Steven to let him know I'm coming."

"Do you think Sam still has the number?" He stood and helped her up.

"I don't know."

He plastered on a smile, hoping she couldn't see through it. This was killing him. "I imagine Phillip and Samantha are still up."

She nodded.

On the way to Phillip's floor, Elizabeth stopped him. "I love you, Chris. Seeing Steven won't change that."

He wanted to believe nothing could change her love for him, yet he knew their past. The one he wished never existed. "And I love you. Always."

Within a few feet, Elizabeth was the first to reach the door and knock.

Phillip swung the door open and glanced at him, then smiled at Elizabeth. "Samantha is on the bed surfing for something to watch. Go on in." He waited until she was out of view. "What's going on?"

"She's going to be leaving soon to see Steven." He ran his fingers through his hair and turned from the doorway into the hall.

Phillip shut the door behind him. "How are you?"

"How should I be? I just told my wife it was okay to see an old lover. How do you think I feel?" Chris paced, clenching his hands. "She won't come back."

"Why do you say that? She's married to you. Of course she'll come back."

"But if she could choose…"

"She already chose you, remember? Everything you both fought for and have been through is a testimony of God's grace and mercy. She's not going to walk away. Samantha told me Elizabeth shared a verse the Lord put on her heart. God is telling her to ask for Steven's forgiveness. You're going to have to trust her and, most importantly, trust God. Maybe you need to finally give Elizabeth and your marriage wholeheartedly to the Lord. He knows what's best."

Phillip placed his hand on Chris's shoulder. "Let's go inside. I'm sure the girls are wondering where we are."

With a deep breath, Chris followed his brother into the room. Elizabeth held Samantha's phone to her cheek.

"Steven, this is Elizabeth. I'm coming to see you. I … I remember."

Chapter Thirty

"Dr. Moore, 1539." A nurse's voice blared over the hospital intercom system. Walking down the hall, Steven patted his pocket. No phone.

Mike caught up with him and glanced at his watch. "Are you ready for lunch? I've got about an hour till I'm on."

"I need to release an infant before I go. Will you do me a favor?" Steven pushed his white coat to the side, stuck his hand in his pocket, and pulled out a set of keys. "Can you try to find my phone? It should be on the desk or in the drawer." He handed his friend the key ring.

"Isn't 1539 George's extension?"

"Yeah. I guess he tried to call, but I didn't answer."

"I'll be back in a minute."

Steven turned toward the nurses' station, where several nurses busied themselves. "Claudia, can I have room 236's discharge papers?" The oval-shaped counter held a series of charts, none he cared to look through himself. Going on sixteen hours, he'd wait and take a breather.

He needed to call George back. Hopefully it was about the meeting, not another fundraiser. Steven knew what he'd agreed to after accepting his offer. The newly-acquired stress tightened his muscles and left him with little time for much else but work. Exhaustion settled into every inch of his being. He leaned against the counter.

"Here you go, Dr. Moore." A nurse handed him the clipboard and a pen.

He took the papers, scribbled his name across them, and handed them back. "If you need me, I'll be at lunch. But if it's not important, please don't give me away." He smiled.

"Of course."

Mike appeared from behind the counter with his hand extended. "Here you go."

"Thanks." Steven slid his phone into his coat pocket.

"How are you, Claudia?"

"Doing well, Mike. Sabrina woke me up at three in the morning. I'm looking forward to going home soon to try to take a nap."

"She's a cutie for sure. I'm going to steal this guy for about forty minutes. Can you cover for him?"

Claudia laughed and glanced at Steven. "I'm sure I can. Have fun."

"Thanks." Steven turned into the hall and slipped his phone from his coat pocket. Two missed calls. He'd call George, and whoever else, after lunch.

Mike caught up with him. "You know what I think you should do?"

"I have no idea." Steven headed toward the cafeteria, but when Mike didn't answer, he met his friend's gaze. "What? Hold that thought. Whatever is behind that look, forget it, I'm not interested."

"You should ask Claudia out."

"No. I know what you're trying to do, but I'm not interested. I have a lot on my plate right now."

"You don't think she's attractive?"

They strolled into the dining area, and all he wanted on his plate at the moment was a side of beef. "Help me find the roast." Steven glanced from one food bar to the other.

Mike tapped him on the shoulder. "Over here." He pointed. "I'm getting a burger."

Steven headed to the line, plopped his food on a plate with a few greens, grabbed a drink, and searched for an empty seat. He found one in the corner. Any alone time, even with Mike, did him good as long as his friend stopped with the dating game. He wasn't playing.

"Here you are." Mike sat down. "I'll pray this time. God, we thank You for Your many blessings, and we thank You for this food. Amen."

Steven slipped his plastic silverware out of the wrapper. "I needed a bit of privacy. A huge palm tree next to the table should do the trick." He smiled.

Mike took a bite. "Now, what were we talking about?"

Steven shook his head. "I'm not going there, but I'll talk all day about the ketchup up your nose."

"It's been almost a year since her husband passed."

"Not interested. You, of all people, should understand. I've lost two women I loved. I'm not willing to do it again."

"Sorry, man. I know. I just want you to get past everything."

"Me too." Steven took a few bites of his meal. "I think after tomorrow I'm going to take a day off. I'll run it by George when we talk. Speaking of, I should probably give him a call." Steven reached into his pocket.

"Wait until you're done. George is an understanding guy. He knows how hard you've been working."

"Maybe you're right." He laid his phone on the table and stared at the missed call button. George was one, but who was the other? Taking another bite, he glanced at his phone again. He pushed recent calls and stared at the screen. He swallowed down the food knotting his throat.

Mike chuckled and angled his head. "What is it?"

Steven held his phone out.

His friend took it from him, and his smile faded. "Samantha? There's a voicemail."

"I saw that." Steven's pulse pounded in his head.

"Are you going to hear what she says?"

Steven scanned the dining area, eyes fixed on a couple who entered hand in hand. He pushed Elizabeth's image from his mind. "I want to, but what happens if I listen to the message and I find out I'm not the man I claim to be? That this entire time, all I've struggled to do to follow the Lord comes crashing down? You don't know how badly I want to know if Elizabeth is well, but I can't. It's not worth it."

Mike slid Steven's phone across the table.

Steven opened the screen to his messages and pushed the delete button. "I can't worry about her anymore. She didn't choose to be my wife. Now God led me here, so He will take care of her." He scowled. Would he ever truly be free? He grabbed his drink and washed down the salt entering his mouth.

"I'm sorry, Steven."

"I need to call George." Steven stood and swiped his phone from the table. He searched his contacts, found the number, and dialed.

"Hey, George. What can I do for you?"

"Steven, I called to remind you about the board meeting tomorrow."

"I'll be there. I wanted to let you know, I'm taking off the day after tomorrow. There's something I need to do."

"That's fine. See you tomorrow."

"Thanks." Steven hung up and squeezed his phone in the palm of his hand. He'd drive to Monticello and spend some time at his wife and son's graves. The only family he truly had. Well, once had. He returned to the table.

"What did he say?"

"Meeting." Steven clenched his tray. "Are you ready to go?"

"Yeah." He stood. They dumped their trash. Mike stopped him heading out of the cafeteria. "I'm here."

"I know, and I've never doubted that. I can use your prayers," he said, his voice above a whisper. "I hate to admit it, but I'm still hurt by the way she left. I thought seeing her that last time would be enough. It wasn't."

"How much longer do you have before you head home?"

"Two hours."

"You go get some sleep. Susan and I will be on shift when you come in tomorrow. How about after your meeting we'll get together to pray?"

Steven nodded.

The last two hours crept by, but when he finally made it home, he fell into an empty bed and stared at his phone.

Chris sat on the edge of the couch, fingers digging into the armrest. Using the ship's internet, Sam and Elizabeth booked a flight to and from Atlanta. Holding back what he wanted to say, he bit his tongue so hard he felt sure he pierced it. The ship arrived at the port of Miami at eight in the morning; her flight left the next morning at seven-thirty. They had less than one day to be home before she left.

"Do you want to sit on the balcony?" Phillip patted his shoulder.

"I think I'm ready to go, instead. We leave in the morning, and we haven't packed our things yet."

"Oh, you're right." Elizabeth rose and strolled to the door. Samantha and Phillip followed them. "Thanks, sis, for all your help." She hugged her neck.

"Anytime. I'll finish everything up for you."

"Can we pray before you leave?" Phillip clasped Samantha's hand. Chris took Elizabeth's and moved them forward into a circle. "Lord, please be with Chris and Elizabeth these next few days. They are going to need Your guidance, protection, love, and forgiveness—but most of all, they will need to trust in You…"

As Phillip continued to pray, Chris prayed. He couldn't stop the freight train from barreling through his life; he had no control. He had to rely on God, or he'd never make it through the days ahead.

"Amen."

Chapter Thirty-One

The white gold chain tickled as it shifted around Elizabeth's neck. She wasn't used to wearing jewelry to bed, but Chris had bought it for her last night. He'd never given her a diamond pendant before, and when he'd placed it against her skin and his fingers grazed her collarbone, tears had sprung to her eyes. How could she leave him? All she wanted was to be home in her husband's arms. To give herself to the man she loved—body, mind and soul. But she couldn't. Not yet.

Chris touched her lips with his finger. His eyes danced. "If you only knew how much I love you. How much I need you."

She wrapped her arms around him as tight as she could, wishing she never had to let go. *God, I'm hurting him. But I have to leave.*

Chris met her gaze, and there was no need for words; she felt the desire. He leaned in to caress her lips when his phone rang. He fell back into the bed and huffed. "Now what?" He reached over to the nightstand and grabbed his cell. "Hello?"

Her husband listened for a few seconds, glanced at her, then raised up. "Everything is packed. Might as well. Sure. Ten minutes." Chris threw his phone on the corner of the bed.

"Phillip?"

"Timothy." He slung the white sheet to his side and rose. He ambled over to the balcony window.

She went to him, sliding her hands around his chest, placing her head against his back. Closing her eyes, she inhaled the natural scent of his skin. "You're mine, and I am yours. As you said to me once, bone of my bone, flesh of my flesh. If you want my scars, I'll give them to you."

He turned around, holding her against his chest. "I want all of you."

"And that is why I need to go. I've been holding a part of myself from you and God, and I don't want to do that anymore. I want to be free from the past and be whole again. God is calling me to do this."

He moved her from his chest. "Then you need to go, because I want all of you. I want every passionate thought, kiss, or moment to be mine. I want your heart and trust."

"What about body?" She chuckled.

"You would have to remind me." He smiled and gave her a peck on the mouth. "All of you."

"Just wanted to make sure." She laughed as he grabbed her tight against him and nibbled on her ear. "You never did tell me what the call was about."

"Oh!" He released her. "We are supposed to meet everyone for breakfast."

"No time for a shower." She rushed to change.

Chris forced himself to think only of today as he readied, because this time tomorrow, she'd be gone.

Elizabeth pulled their luggage down through the terminal. Lindsey laughed riding on Chris's shoulders. They both giggled when he pretended to tickle her feet through her ballerina slippers. The picture before Elizabeth sent warmth to her depths. *Not much longer now.*

"What are you smiling about?" Samantha grabbed her arm.

Sarah grabbed her other one and looped hers through. "I want to know."

Elizabeth laughed. "I don't know what I would have done without you both. Thank you for everything."

Sarah stopped abruptly, pulling them to a stop. "I know this upcoming trip will be hard for you, but we will be praying and waiting for you until you come home."

"Thank you, Sarah." Elizabeth pulled back and wiped her cheek with her fingers.

"Are you ladies coming, or are you planning another trip by yourselves?" Timothy hollered, about to exit the terminal.

"That's a thought..." Sam giggled. "Come on before our husbands get lost without us."

"So true." Sarah laughed as they made their way outside the port.

Green and yellow taxis pulled in and out of lanes, while cars dropped off passengers or picked them up.

Chris slid Lindsey from his shoulders. "Timothy, I think Elizabeth and I will take a cab home."

Sarah glanced up. "Lindsey, say goodbye to Auntie. She's going."

Elizabeth nodded. Home. She knelt on the curb with wide arms. Her niece ran and clasped small hands around her neck.

"Can I come home with you, Auntie? You said next time, and you promised."

Elizabeth smiled. It wasn't what she'd meant, but who could say no to this child? Not her. Never. She kissed her cheek and set her at arm's length. "I'm getting ready to go somewhere, but when I get back, I'll call your mommy and we can plan a time for you to come over, okay?"

She turned to Sarah. "Can I, Mommy? Can I, Mommy?"

"Of course." Sarah smoothed down her hair. "Now we need to let Uncle Chris and Auntie go, all right?" She lifted her into her arms. "I'll miss you, Elizabeth. Call when you get back." Sarah kissed her cheek.

"I will." Elizabeth smiled. "Right, Lindsey?"

"Yes." Her niece nodded.

With a deep breath, Elizabeth turned into her sister's embrace. "Am I going to be able to do this?"

"I know you can."

"I've hidden so much from Chris. I hope he forgives me." She glanced over her sister's shoulder at him loading their luggage.

"I thought you were talking about Steven."

Elizabeth squeezed her sister and whispered. "I never had the surgery. I can have children." She couldn't see her face, but Sam's body trembled in her arms. Whimpers followed. She pulled her back. Tears streamed down Sam's face.

"I'm so happy for you, Elizabeth. One day I will be able to hold your child in my arms. I will be able to share in your joys, replacing the ones I was never a part of when we were younger. I missed out on so much, but God heals. Don't ever forget that." She laughed. "And don't think for one minute Chris will be upset."

"Don't say anything. When I get back, I want to tell him."

"I won't."

Phillip placed a gentle hand on his wife. "You're crying." But when she met his eyes, a smile spread across his features. "I can't wait to hear."

"Hear what?" Chris placed his arm around Sam, giving her a hug. "What did I miss, saying bye to Timothy and Sarah?"

Sam cleared her throat. "God is so good. What more can anyone say?"

"You've got me there." Chris winked at Elizabeth, and her stomach fluttered. In a few days, nothing would be hidden. God was bringing her out into the light, His light of freedom. But first, she needed to face her past.

After saying their final goodbyes, Chris whisked her into a cab. "Not much longer and we'll be home." He intertwined their fingers. "I wanted to tell you. Timothy needs help at the shelter, and I told him we would."

She leaned back from him. "Did you really?"

"What is that face for? I can help."

"You are a changed man, Mr. Chris Roberts. A man I'm proud to be married to."

He cradled her shoulder, bringing her against him. "Timothy's cook will be there for a few more days, so I thought I'd shadow him tomorrow while you're gone."

Glad to hear Chris had made plans, she smiled. "Then when I get back, you can tell me all about it. Cooking, huh? Is he teaching you how to cook, too?" Laughter bubbled from her chest.

"Hey, now. I can boil a mean hot dog. Don't forget."

"How can I? That was all you fixed me when I was on bed rest."

"And grilled cheese."

"How could I forget that?" She glanced out the window and lifted from his chest. "We're home, Chris."

The taxi pulled forward a bit to allow the security guard to see Chris and wave them though. Rounding the curve, their house came into view. The cab parked in the drive. She opened the door and slid out. Chris followed her and began speaking to the driver.

The ivy seemed to have grown since their trip, flourishing into a deep green, concealing the entire middle roof and left side of the house and protecting it from heat, storms, and winds.

"Let's go." He tugged two suitcases.

She took one from him and headed to the entrance way. As he unlocked the door, she gave his mouth a peck. "Thank you for this."

"I will always be waiting for you here."

A knot grew in her throat as he opened the door. Did he truly believe she wouldn't come back? Chris was her home.

Chris peered around the corner to their room and took a step back into the hallway. Elizabeth was looking through her bookshelf. Could she be searching for her yearbook? He'd given it to Samantha.

Elizabeth had been quiet at times throughout the night in deep thought. He wanted to ask but refrained, afraid of what she might say. If he knew, maybe his insecurities would lessen like they had this morning. The few hours they'd spent alone before breakfast reassured him of her love, though the temptation to claim her before she left never passed. Even now he battled with what he felt in his heart. God had given her to him and no one else.

He strolled into the bedroom. Elizabeth sat on the floor and packed a small bag. "Can I do anything for you?"

She smiled up at him. "No, but thank you. Will you sit with me?"

He sat next to a Bible and another book. "Are you taking these?" He lifted them in his hands.

"I am. They're Steven's."

Heat seeped up the back of his neck. He set them back down. Steven's—and they'd been here this entire time? He wanted to chuck them.

She grabbed the Bible from the floor and flipped to the first page. She leaned to him and pointed to the dedication line. "My mom bought this for Steven before her death."

He noticed the last name. "What is with the name Carrington? How can it be Moore now?"

Closing the Bible, she seemed to hesitate, avoiding his eyes. "Steven grew up in an orphanage. The last name they gave him was Carrington. He changed it."

"Why?"

She stuffed the books into the bag. "Growing up, Steven wished he had a family like everyone else, a family he could claim as his own. He changed his last name a few weeks before the wedding. It was to represent new beginnings, hope, and a future. He was so happy ... He chose it for us."

"Chris." She met his gaze. "I don't know what to do. How do I apologize?" Her lip quivered, yet she seemed strong. When had this happened? No tears. She didn't hug her middle, and she wasn't running. No longer fearful. She was facing this head-on. Was God healing her and making her whole? *Lord, please forgive me for standing in Your way.*

"Let me pray with you." Chris took her hands and led her to the couch. There they knelt. Steven no longer mattered. His wife mattered and, if he could be there to help her through this time, God would show him the way.

Chapter Thirty-Two

Elizabeth wrung her hands and scanned the plane as it touched down in Atlanta. When it slowed to a stop, she grabbed her bag from in front of her feet and eyed the Bible. Steven had always talked about having a family, reading to their children, and writing scriptures along the doorposts of their home.

"Would you like to go?"

She glanced up to find a woman standing in the aisle, holding back other passengers.

"Oh, yes, thank you." Elizabeth rushed out of her seat and headed out into the terminal. She glanced at her watch. Six hours until her flight departed back to Florida. First things first, she needed a taxi, or she wasn't going anywhere.

After finding her way through the terminal maze, she stepped outside and hailed a cab. "Atlanta Children's Hospital, please." She slid in and buckled her seat belt.

"Which one?"

"I don't know. How many do you have?"

"Three."

Great! "Where are they located?"

"In Atlanta. You choose, and I'll drive."

How was she supposed to know there were three? "Can we sit here for a few minutes?

The taxi driver glared into his rear view mirror. "Look lady, I get paid for driving around, not sittin' in one place. You got one minute before it's your money." The driver thumped his fingers on the steering wheel. The only other sound she heard was her pulse. She'd come all this way. She had to see Steven.

She grabbed her phone from her bag and searched the web for the hospital numbers, writing each one down. She glanced at the first number and dialed. "Does a Doctor Steven Moore work there?"

"Can you hold?" The operator asked.

Yes." She waited, tapping her pen against her chin.

"No. He resides at the Children's in Egleston."

"Thank you so much." She hung up and leaned forward. "Take me to Children's in Egleston." The car zoomed out of the parking lot, forcing her back into the seat. Maybe she should start praying more about making it to Steven than about what she would say.

They settled onto a major highway, judging by the speed of traffic. She closed her eyes. Dear God, please give me the words. Help me to know what to do once I see him. Steven never called back, so I assumed he doesn't want to see me, but I'm coming. Help me to be strong in You. I pray he will forgive me. Please be with Chris right now as I'm —" Her body jerked forward and her eyes flung open.

"I know a short cut. If it wasn't for my plans tonight, I'd make you pay for the longer route."

Elizabeth didn't know if she should thank him or tell him she'd walk the rest of the way. Where was she? They turned and a medical building came into view. The sign out front confirmed she was in the right place.

The driver stopped in front of the emergency room. "That will be twenty-five dollars."

Slipping her wallet from her red leather bag, she paid him and scurried out of the cab. She let out a breath and pushed herself through the doors where two nurses sat be-hind a horseshoe-shaped desk, one helping an older gen-tlemen, the other with her head down. "Hi. I'm looking for someone."

"What's your name, your child's name, and date of birth?" The nurse scribbled on a note pad.

"Uh…"

The nurse's head lifted. She squinted and looked around. "I guess you're not here for the obvious. No kiddos."

Elizabeth smiled, her pulse racing. "No. I'm here to see Dr. Moore."

"I'll tell you the easiest way to get there." The nurse leaned in and pointed. "Pass this desk, and the first station you see on your left, ask them. They'll tell you where to go from there."

"Thank you." Elizabeth clenched her bag's strap, dig-ging her nails into her skin as she turned. Her stomach dropped with each step into the hospital. Nausea swirled up her throat as she approached another nurse's station.

"Elizabeth?" A man in a white coat peered at her from a file he was holding. He dropped it on the counter and headed toward her.

She froze. He looked so familiar. "Mike?" His smile lit up the room. It had been too long. Her eyes watered. It wasn't only Steven she'd walked away from, but her friends and the life she knew. "Oh, Mike." She hugged him.

Another voiced asked, "Don't I get a hug?"

Elizabeth pulled back and saw her high school friend, college roommate, and the woman who should have been her maid-of-honor. "Nicole."

Nicole pushed Mike out of the way and held her in a tight squeeze. "I was your best friend," she whispered. "You should have told me goodbye."

"Please forgive me." Tears filled her eyes. "I was wrong."

Nicole's eyes moistened and smiled. "I forgive you."

Mike directed them to a corner. "Maybe we should take this over here. Nurses are gawking. We know how that is."

Nicole looked toward the station where some eyes lingered. "How long can you stay?"

"For a few hours before I need to catch my plane back to Florida. I wanted to see Steven."

That familiar voice she constantly recognized over these months came close.

Nicole and Mike turned and stepped back. Steven spoke to another doctor, then headed out the door.

"Steven," Mike called.

Steven smiled until his gaze found hers. He took a sharp turn toward the exit.

Elizabeth stared after him. "What do I do?"

"Go after him. I know you're not here to rekindle anything, but I think I know why you came. He needs this. Go." Nicole pushed her to move.

Elizabeth started down the hall when her friend called her to wait.

"I need a hug goodbye this time." Nicole ran to where she was and hugged her in a tight embrace.

Elizabeth sighed, releasing her dearest friend. "Did you marry?"

"John." She grinned. "Look me up under Nicole Scott."

"I knew you would. And I will." She hurried down the hall, stopped, and glanced around.

"Are you looking for me?" Steven walked toward her. "This is not a good time or place."

She straightened. "I came to see you."

"I'm getting ready to leave. I'll be back in about four hours." He walked off and out of the building.

"Wait!" She drew people's attention, but followed close behind and stopped at a sporty black car. "I have to leave soon. I can't wait until you get back to talk. I came all this way to see you."

Steven's brows furrowed. "Chris knows you're here?"

The sound of his name strengthened her resolve. "Yes."

He took several steps, looked around, then met her gaze. "Do you have time for a short trip?"

"I do."

Steven unlocked his vehicle and opened the door for her. She slid in and waited for him to get into the driver's seat. The car roared to life as he revved the engine, backed out of his parking spot, and headed for the road. Once on the freeway, buildings and cars flashed by them. She glanced at him a few times, but he never looked her way. Why had she come? He had never forgiven her and never would.

Chris arrived home exhausted from working at the shelter, but his mind never left Elizabeth. He searched their new downstairs bedroom for their clock and remembered he had never gotten it from the upstairs room. She would need it when she came home.

He jogged upstairs and yanked it off the wall, taking the nail with him. He glanced around as memories filled his heart. He stopped at Katherine's room and opened the door. A musty odor filled his nostrils. He sneezed as he entered. Big black letters spelling his daughter's name still hung against the pale pink room; brown and black circles blotted the walls. He walked to her crib, and with his free hand, ran it along her quilt. He tried to snuff out the desire to have another child, but the closer he and Elizabeth grew, the hotter it flamed. He wanted something he couldn't have. He touched the dresser as he was about to leave the room, picking up a framed picture of his wife and daughter.

"Elizabeth," he whispered. "Please, come home to me."

Elizabeth perked up when they arrived in a small town. Old four-column homes rose against the sun, snuggling between pecan trees. They came to a stoplight. She'd never seen a town square before, only in pictures. Nestled in the middle of nowhere, she couldn't pry her eyes from the town's beauty. They drove by the courthouse, and people waved at Steven as he passed a flower shop and then a church with a football field.

"Can you imagine having a Super Bowl party in there?" She smiled and turned to him. "Where are we?"

"Monticello, Georgia. This is where I used to live when Jess and Steven were alive." His chiseled features had never looked so hard.

He was married. His family was gone? Sadness nestled in the deepest part of her heart.

They turned left onto a narrow road and passed an old park before driving between two large stone posts. They arrived at a gravesite, and heat pricked her skin. This wasn't where she wanted to be. She scanned the whitewashed tombstones, stretching out in the distance of the treeless landscape.

Steven cut the engine, but hesitated before getting out. She wanted to say something, but hardly knew what. "I'll wait in the car."

He slid out and closed the door.

Elizabeth watched him walk down a row of markers. His shoulders slumped, and his steps slowed before kneeling to the ground. These were his family's graves. Not only did Steven know her, but he understood what she had gone through with Katherine. She looked down at her hands, inhaled, then glanced back at him.

Opening the car door, she got out and quietly pressed it closed. As she walked, she thought about Katherine, her husband, and the man who should have been. A solitary tear fell down her cheek. She shuddered standing in front of two headstones.

"Oh, Jess. I've missed you." His voice quivered. "This is so hard without you. Some days…" His head fell into his hands.

Elizabeth knelt and wrapped her arms around him.

He cleared his throat. "Why did you come?"

She sat back on her heels.

Steven turned to her with watery eyes.

"I had to come. Once everything came back to me … I need to ask for your forgiveness."

"You had it a long time ago. But when I saw you in the hospital room with Katherine, I realized the pain was still there." He twisted back around.

"Steven … I…"

"This is my wife, Jessica. I used to tell her she rescued me." He chuckled. "Can you believe she married me knowing my feelings were for you? I've never known a love so pure and open as hers. And this is our son, Steven Daniel Moore. Jess wanted to name him after me."

She placed a hand on his shaking shoulder. "Will you look at me?"

Moans sounded through his breath. "I can't right now."

She moved to squat down in front of him. Watermarks covered his shirt. She'd done this to him, to them. Her own tears raced to her chin. "I'm so sorry, Steven. Forgive me."

"I didn't know what happened. I couldn't find you. I searched. Days. Weeks. For two years I prayed. I didn't know if you were alive or dead."

"When my parents died, I was so lost I wanted to run, but I came to you. I needed you."

"But I took something from you, and you disappeared. That's why you left."

"No, Steven. I gave you my heart, and it scared me. Everyone I ever loved left, and I couldn't handle the thought of you leaving me."

"So *you* left."

"I was wrong. I broke my promises to you, and I've never been able to forgive myself. I've carried this with me all this time."

"Don't cry." He pulled her into his chest. "It's okay, Lizzy. We're okay. I'm so glad you came. But I have to know. What triggered your memory?"

She lifted her head and tucked a hair behind her ear. "We went on a cruise and I passed by a bar when something you said came to me. Do you remember the night you dragged me out of the club and said, 'I will drag you out of here every night if I have to'? I laughed when I thought of it, but then I realized God was healing me, because the temptation to drink was gone."

"I had been praying for you."

"Chris didn't take it so well. Oh, the drinking part, he couldn't have been happier, but remembering you, not so much. This is hard for him. That's why I've come for such a short time."

"I can understand how he feels. What time does your flight leave?"

She glanced at her watch. "Two hours."

"Then we need to go, but I would like to show you my property here. It wouldn't take long."

"I'd like that."

He helped her up and placed his hand on the small of her back, leading her to the car.

They headed out of the cemetery, and Elizabeth grabbed his free hand. "Did we just bury everything back there?"

He squeezed her palm and smiled. "We did."

They turned onto one road, then another before he slowed almost to a stop but continued down a gravel road. Trees covered both sides of the drive.

"We're coming up to the dam. Look on the driver's side."

The trees opened as the road narrowed even more. Just then, a lake appeared. A curtain of emerald trees stood in the backdrop. "This is beautiful."

"I love it here. Would you like to get out and walk for a minute? We won't have time to see the house."

"Sure."

"Then let's go." He stopped the vehicle and smiled as they got out of the car.

She met him by the side of the water and pointed. "Look at the trees' reflection in the lake. It's almost a perfect image."

"I planned to take Steven fishing here when he became older."

"Will you ever marry again?"

Steven glanced down at his hands. "No. I don't think so. But I still want children. God has been telling me to wait."

"I talked to Chris the other day about adoption. I still want a large family, but that was more our dream, wasn't it?"

"A lovely dream."

"One I'll never forget." They stood in silence, staring out at the water.

Steven touched her arm. "We should go if you plan to make your plane."

"Oh, yes. I can't miss my flight." They hurried back to the car. As they drove up the dam, they passed the house. "I would love to live in a place like this, secluded from everyone and everything, so different than Florida."

"Not even close." He turned the car around and backed out the way they came. "I'll take you to the airport."

She looked at the lake one last time. She could picture herself here with this man next to her and the family she'd always wanted.

When they reached the airport, Steven parked the car and walked her to the check-in. They were lining up the passengers to board.

Elizabeth touched his arm. "I have something of yours I've been keeping." She reached into her bag, took out the books, and handed them to him.

His brows furrowed before meeting her gaze. "What is this?"

"The bottom is your medical history, birth certificate, and a few others."

Steven opened the book and flipped through several pages. "I had been looking for this for some time. But a Bible?"

"My mom. She bought this for you." She flipped it opened in his hand to the first page and pointed below the dedication.

To Steven,

Though you never knew your mother, I'm so blessed you have become my son. Take care of Elizabeth. Read these words to her and to your children, always.

With much love,

Cynthia

Steven glanced around quickly with tears, and took a step to her, sliding his hand along her chin. "You will always have a place in my heart no one can fill."

She ached. "Steven…"

"It's okay. You've given me a precious gift. I can let you go now." He kissed her cheek. "Chris is waiting. Love him." He met her gaze and smiled. "Bye, Lizzy."

As his hand fell away, she wanted to stop him, but she couldn't. He was right. Chris was waiting and so was their future.

Chapter Thirty-Three

Elizabeth had one thing to do before going home. She parked outside her apartment, but entered through the bookstore entrance. As she locked the door behind her, the natural light barely shone through the dust hovering in the air. She flicked on the lights and set her bag on the counter before heading upstairs. Opening the door to her apartment, she knew God had led her to this moment.

In the middle of the living room, she knelt and bowed her head. Tears poured not only from the emotions of the day, but from her soul. "God, I'm ready now to give You my gift." With legs tucked beneath her, she leaned down on the floor and held her hands out. Empty. But to God, they were full. "I have nothing to bring that You would desire, except for one thing. I give myself to You. In my love, in the fears, and in the pain, I will trust You."

She rose from the floor and wiped the last tear. "I've finally found my happily-ever-after." A chuckle escaped through her lips. "It took me a while, but You were there the whole time."

With a deep breath, she glanced around the room. Soon the walls would be torn down, but the memory of this moment was seared onto her heart. No matter how far she ran, nothing separated her from God's love, not even herself.

With a hurried anticipation to see Chris, Elizabeth skipped down the stairs, slung her bag over her shoulder, and then clasped the handle to the bookstore. Without looking back, she prayed. "God, bless this new addition to our store. May it also bring new beginnings to others." She pulled the door closed and locked it behind her.

Minutes later, Elizabeth stood at the front door to her house, hand on the handle. All she had to do was walk in, but she couldn't. How would she tell him? Several sentences ran together in her mind, but they were too jumbled even for her to be able to repeat. *Maybe I should just come out and say it. "Chris, I can…"* No. How about, *"Do you remember when…?" Lord, I give it to You.* She pushed through the door to find Chris standing on the other side.

"I didn't know if you were going to come in." His brows wrinkled together, he stood a foot in front of her and made no attempt to move toward her.

"Why wouldn't I?"

Within that one step, he drew her in his arms and gently caressed her lips, tingling every nerve. Her knees grew weak.

"Chris." She breathed between kisses.

"Yes."

"There's something I need to tell you."

His lips slid down to her neck. "Yes."

"I … I can have children. Never had surgery."

His mouth lingered before he met her gaze. "We can have a baby?"

She bit her lip and nodded. "And I'd like to try now."

His eyes grew wide, and a smile stretched across his handsome face. Taking her into his arms, he began to carry her into their bedroom.

"Chris, wait! You forgot to close the door."

About the Author

Tanya Eavenson is an international bestselling and award-winning inspirational romance author. She enjoys spending time with her husband and their three children. Her favorite pastime is grabbing a cup of coffee, eating chocolate, and reading a good book. You can find her at her website www.tanyaeavenson.com.

Books by Tanya

Unending Love Series

Unconditional

Elizabeth wants to forget. Chris wants to save his marriage. Can they trust God with their future and find a love that's unconditional?

Restored

Unwilling to deal with his prognosis, Dr. Steven Moore retreats to a happier time in his past—to the woman who once stole his heart, never suspecting she might offer hope for his future.

Gaining Love Series

To Gain a Mommy

When Hope Michaels decides to face her past, she unknowingly purchases the house across the street from her former fiancé—the man her twin sister married, then widowed. Fire Captain Carl McGuire can put out any flame, except for the one Hope sparks within him—some things never change.

To Gain a Valentine

As Valentine's Day approaches, will Patrick and Amabelle miss out on the love they've always desired? Or will their love take flight under the stars on this very special night?

To Gain a Bodyguard

Undercover ICE agent Madi Reynolds has spent years infiltrating a human-trafficking ring, but when her life is threatened, she is forced to walk away and advised to leave the country. War Veteran and ICE agent Brice Johnson faces the biggest assignment of his life—protect the woman he loves.

All
Roads
PUBLISHING